Evil in the Land Without

A novel by
Colin Cotterill

Evil in the Land Without
Copyright © Colin Cotterill, 2003
First Published 2003

This 2014 edition published by
DCO Books
Proglen Trading Co., Ltd.
Bangkok Thailand
http://ebooks.dco.co.th

ISBN 978-1500994914

Dedicated to the minority groups in Burma.

The Karen live in Southeast Asia, mostly in the Irrawaddy Delta and on the Thai-Burmese border. Since 1942, they have been fighting for their traditional homeland, Kawthoolei, "The Land Without Evil."

1 - Kawthoolei, 1978

You are to leeve this place. If you are found here when we return in seven days, you will be considered enemys of the state and distroyed.

It was a simple note, written by hand and not carefully spelt. The paper had been torn from a pad of greying report sheets and fastened to the wall of the elder's hut with brown masking tape. It hung slightly askew like a loosened tooth and flapped in a breeze that warned of an incoming storm.

Sherri stood before it and wondered at the magic of the flimsy sheet that could wipe away her history. It was indeed a powerful paper. The village had been the whole of the six years of her life. She had seen her first daylight through the bamboo slats of her family hut. She had played in each of the nine homes and grown up with the assortment of naked babies and toddlers that ran amok through the world there. She had learned from a woman so old she was unable to walk unaided to the latrine, but who was so much of a genius she could make marks on paper that spoke to the children she taught.

This was the history that the grey note with its rudely spoken words was wiping away. Thanks to old No Ay Me, she could understand the words but not the scrawl at the bottom. She was told it was the signature of a great soldier. The great soldier wore the uniform of the government and he could kill a man, they said, just by clicking his tongue against his teeth. Since she'd heard that, Sherri had been afraid to let her tongue make any sounds in her mouth. Sitting at dinner had filled her with dread as she listened to the clumsy smacking of chops as people ate.

And as she stood alone in front of the drunken paper, she wondered how there could be any other home, any other life beyond this village. To a six-year-old, what you know is your world, and any event in your life is world altering. The complete removal of that world is tantamount to erasing a life.

Everybody else—the entire population of the village, less the old teacher—was assembled down by the pond. They sat under the swaying banyan trees silently waiting for hope to arrive on the breeze. For some it was inevitable that they wouldn't be excused the displacement. For the majority who had been able to shut out the thought, this was an unwelcome reality.

"We should fight them," came one comment out of the quiet. It's speaker received no more than raised eyebrows, much more than the statement deserved. The sons and grandsons of the village had fought them and had nothing to show for it. The Karen Army had been fighting them for 33 years and had nothing to show for it. What did the small ragged band of children, women, and elderly have to fight them with?

No, it was agreed they would pack together their few belongings and begin the 18-day march to the new development zone. They knew what to expect. There they would receive small patches of infertile land and inadequate building materials, and struggle to survive. Eventually they would be forced through starvation to offer themselves as porters to the Military Council of Burma, the *Tatmadaw*, and eventually die of exhaustion. Such was the fate they knew was awaiting them, but against which they had no remedy.

-o-

They were a week into the walk. Sherri had never seen death before, or at least she couldn't remember anyone being dead. But it seemed a lot like sleeping. No Ay Me lay beside the dirt track with a troubled look on her crinkly old face. It was a look of annoyance that she had been forced to leave the village. It had been on her face since they put her on the litter and started to drag her away from everything she loved. Sherri knew just how she felt.

But as for being dead. That didn't seem to trouble the old lady nearly as much as being dragged. No Ay Me had told Sherri once about how the spacemen fly away from the earth and the air gets thinner and thinner until eventually there isn't any. If they don't take bottles of air with them, they can't breath.

The further they dragged her away from her earth, the harder it became for No Ay Me to breath. Sherri walked behind and watched her chest rise and fall as she fought to catch her breath. But on the sixth day, her chest didn't rise any more. Nobody was sure how many kilometers they had dragged the corpse, but it could have been a whole day. Sherri hadn't been bold enough to tell anyone about her suspicions that the lady wasn't searching for air any more. As the sun played hide-and-seek behind the trees at the end of the day, they lay down the bamboo stretcher and announced that the teacher was gone.

Sherri was unsure about how to feel. Her teacher was still there after all. She knelt beside the body and looked at her. Her mother told her that No Ay Me had gone, but that wasn't true. She hadn't gone anywhere. She wasn't lost. She just wasn't breathing. That was all.

Sherri leaned over the old woman and whispered to her, "It's okay, Ah Ah, I can see you. You're still here. They're sorry they dragged you. You can start breathing again now."

She waited for several minutes, but there was no response except for the buzzing of flies. "Listen, Ah Ah, they're talking about what they should do with you. They say they haven't got any tools to put you under the ground, but they don't want the animals to get you. Somebody said they should set fire to you and say prayers. You're going to have to start breathing again really soon if you want me to help you."

It was the frustration of No Ay Me's reluctance to co-operate, and the loneliness away from the village that finally drew tears to Sherri's eyes. Death was still a concept too distant to grasp. But once she started to cry, she had no way of stopping the tears. From then on, death would always suggest frustration and loneliness.

There would be a cremation that evening. The elders had decided that the most appropriate end to No Ay Me would be to show her the respect she had earned while alive, in a private ceremony on the plot of dirt where she had expired. She would be burned on a pyre of bracken and distributed to the spirits of the earth.

The preparations had even begun. They cut a bed of twigs upon which No Ay Me was to lay, and had cleared away surrounding vegetation so as not to raze the whole countryside.

The elder had dispatched many a body to the beyond. Through eyes bunged up with tears, Sherri watched him prepare for the ceremony. He produced the prayer book from his cloth shoulder bag. He carefully unwrapped the white gown from his pack and hung it over a branch for the creases to drop out. And that was as far he got.

The soldiers approached in such a casual manner it seemed unlikely they had bad intent. The elder seemed unfazed also. He produced all the legal papers from his bag and summoned a smile to welcome the ranking officer of the bunch. There were eight, all silent and ragged in mismatched uniforms.

"Welcome sir," the elder greeted the young man in almost faultless Burmese, a language he only used for official duties. He knew the soldiers were unlikely to speak Karen. Most were from the central plain, sent to oppress a race they knew or cared very little about.

The officer was in his early twenties and his 'men' were barely post-pubescent themselves. He had a face so smooth and inanimate it could have been molded from river clay. He stopped a yard from the elder and focussed his yellowing eyes on the old man. Sherri had noticed the machete hanging from his hand. She watched it rise and slice through the elder's neck. In a fraction of a second it was back hanging at the soldier's side barely pink with blood. The elder's head wobbled slightly then toppled to the ground. His body, as if suddenly realizing it had no head, turned slowly in search of it, then crumpled to the dirt.

Sherri looked about her to see that the same fate had befallen the other four men in her group. There was a moment more of silence before the screams of the women brought on the screams of the children. Only the machetes of the young soldiers could quiet them. There was a flash of light inside Sherri's head that distanced her from the horror. She was numb. She was somewhere else. She looked at the scene without understanding what had happened or why. When the bloodletting was over, only five villagers remained alive; two younger women, Sherri, and another two girls her age. Each of them stood silently, hoping their silence would render them invisible to the boy soldiers and their boy officer.

2 - England, 2000

He recalled his penis.

"I recall my penis," he said to the small gathering before him. The other seven unattractive men chuckled like schoolboys into their wine glasses. The speaker continued:

"It was once such a magnificent creature, so proud and unashamed in its exuberance. I could barely restrain it when I was in school. Just the close proximity of a naked inner thigh, or the sight up a pair of baggy shorts, and it was up and away. And I can't begin to tell you of the trouble I had wrestling the beast down in the shower room."

The audience laughed loudly. They were in a stuffy suburban living room lit desperately by one desk lamp. Brownish oil paintings of dales and rustic fences adorned the papered walls. With the heavy curtains drawn, the lamp provided just enough light for the present speaker to see his script but not enough to draw the faces of the other men out of the shadows. A couple of them were quite drunk. Some had already taken advantage of the man sized tissue box on the coffee table and been to the bathroom to wank themselves off. Such was the tradition at gatherings like this.

It was a full Saturday afternoon programme, and one they had been looking forward to for several months. They didn't gather nearly as often as they should. To the neighbours, they looked like a bunch of chaps getting together to watch the rugby on ITV. They were all likeable enough fellows. There were two schoolteachers, one local councilor, a postman, two retirees, John, and a football referee. Two were married; two divorced.

Each of them had prepared a presentation. They had already seen two videos and one slide show, listened to a diary reading, and been given samples to take home from a photograph display. It was the function of the host—today a paunchy, red-faced man called John—to provide the equipment, drinks, and snacks, although John had actually laid on much more than the others realized. It was the host who traditionally provided the final show of the day and John, thirty but in a much older body, had prepared a finale they would never forget.

The speaker, stirred by the wine-stoked rapture of the audience, drew on his teacher storytelling voice to lead into his slide demonstration. "So you can imagine my distress, as the years passed, to see that the beast had not only become domesticated, but that there were days that I could barely find the little fella as it cowered quivering amid the pubic bush." He pretended to be calling a lost dog. "Here, here boy. Where are you my little lost dachshund?"

The men now roared with laughter as much from empathy as from amusement.

The thick curtain across the French windows kept out the Surrey autumn chill and made the single oil heater all the more influential in the carpeted room. The breaths of the unattractive men, the wine, the buzzing lamp of the old slide projector, all contributed to the uncomfortable warmth that smelled sweet and deliciously sordid.

The speaker clicked the remote lead and then he himself appeared on the wide screen, naked but for a pair of Y-fronts, spread-eagled on a bed pretending to be searching in his underwear for his fondly remembered organ. The speaker whose membership code name was 'Sir," was particularly popular at these get-togethers because he put so much work into his presentations. He was obviously a frustrated thespian, and there were so few outlets for works such as this.

"Naturally . . ." he went on, and to whistles from the audience, clicked the next slide. Here was a close-up of his hand holding his own insignificant penis. ". . . after the effort of searching for the animal, there was always the disappointment, the regrets, the memories. Would I never return to those dizzy heights of orgasmic greatness experienced in my school days? Would my Grecian javelin never fly again?"

One of the audience was so convulsed in laughter he almost choked himself on a cocktail sausage. A neighbour slapped him on the back, and the mood was lost for a moment as attention was diverted from the screen. But the next slide regained the rapt awe of everyone in the room.

"Only through the help of Anthony, my mathematics pupil, would I ever be sure." There were audible groans and sighs from around the room. On the screen was an angelic boy no older than nine. He was wearing a school uniform that was too small even for a child as young as he was.

"You dirty old bugger," came a voice.

"You lucky sod," came another. But there was complete attention to the screen and to the big-eyed blond boy who smiled from it, looking directly into the eyes of the eight men in the stuffy room.

To the unskilled novice watching the ensuing 24 slides, it may have appeared that young Anthony began by enjoying the play the old teacher and himself were acting out for the camera. But then there were expressions on the boy's face that suggested fear and eventually terror. But to most of the men in the room, there was no doubt that Anthony enjoyed every second of his time with Sir, and was a fine actor. There was a queue for the bathroom after that particular performance. For the postman it was already too late. He'd soiled himself where he sat, and apologized humbly to the host who grinned back at him.

The Boy Lovers of the United Kingdom Society— BLOUKS—had been arranging meetings such as this for the previous three years. It maintained a small membership because every application had to be checked thoroughly. There were far too many law enforcement agencies, too many tabloid newspapers, too many we-are-better-than-God child protection organizations trying to infiltrate these groups. To admit a new member, there had to be no doubt in the minds of the committee that he was to be trusted. Every potential member had to be recommended by a present member, and even then there were endless security checks. The committee had the resources to know more about applicants than they knew about themselves.

The society's website contained nothing that could be called pornography. It was an academic forum for the ill-informed to learn that BLOUKS was not a paedophile or pederast ring, but rather a club through which boys who desperately needed love and intimacy from older gentlemen could express themselves. For interested observers there were scientific readings on the desires of young people and the need for father figures in their lives. There were historical data from apparently more enlightened times when young boys had unrestricted access to older men without interference from the law. After a few hours at the site, one could not fail to be impressed by the good intentions and sincerity of BLOUKS and its small membership of unattractive men.

When the academic gentlemen were all nicely wanked off and washed down and back in the stuffy living room, there was a general feeling that the host would have to produce something pretty special to top Sir's little drama with angel-faced Anthony. John had only attended one previous meeting, and his contribution then had been rather lame: downloads from the internet that anyone could have found, and that most of the members had already seen.

But he was a new member and just starting out. He hadn't had time to put anything together that first time he said, but he promised that this next one would be special. He'd even volunteered to host it at his own home. Members usually had a lot of material at their own places.

John, sweating a little and ruddy from the wine, had put a video cassette into the player. He was obviously nervous, but they all had been at first. He creaked the old desk lamp up to reflect off the peeling white ceiling of his living room. It allowed him to see grey images of all the men gathered at his house. He looked at them one by one and smiled. Some smiled back while others felt a little uncomfortable at leaving the womb of the audience, even through eye contact. John was a man who read people's eyes.

"Gentlemen," he said, and took a large swig from his glass. "You're all under arrest."

There were titters of laughter from the drunks, but an embarrassed silence from the others. It would have been a poor joke in fact, if the French window hadn't slid open at that moment and ten police officers in flack jackets with truncheons in their hands not poured into the room.

John pressed 'play' on the video machine and the first of five full-length videos recorded from the fire alarm unit at the rear of the room began to play. Of course, they'd already seen the presentation from the first member in real life. But they didn't have time to see the recording because just five minutes into it, they were in the back of the wagon and on their way to New Malden Police Station.

-o-

John sat alone in the living room of the house that nobody actually owned, and poured himself another glass of wine. He still felt sick to the stomach from all the sausages, but it was the thickness of that stomach and the way it hung over his leather belt that made him ideal for the work he did. Nobody had ever suspected him of being a cop. With his one chewed ear, and his vertical red hair, he looked too much like a caricature of a pederast. Funnily, child abusers rarely adhered to the caricature. Most were invisible, normal looking people you would never suspect.

But it was more than the stomach that made John good for this work. It was his soul that put him ahead of others in the Surrey Child Protection Unit, the CPU. He didn't have one. Oh, he would have argued as a science graduate that nobody had one. He would have produced physiological evidence that there was no compartment provided in the human carcass for such mythology. But everyone who ever knew him, who ever worked with him, was amazed that he could be so cold to the obscenities he saw and heard in his work. John Jessel was an item of machinery. A very effective machine that could perform beautifully and knew no fear, but machinery nevertheless.

In reality, the afternoon's performance had disturbed him deep down as they always did. But he had been in control of his disgust for these troubled men. He saw no reason to call on his expression or his voice to describe how he felt. His feelings were nobody's business but his own.

Some argued that the years of work with the CPU team had taken their toll in other ways. He was a thirty-year-old who could look fifty on his bad days. The pleasant-looking young man who had joined the police academy had been replaced by an overweight cop with a shaving disorder and a serious drink problem. He didn't fuss at all with his ginger hair or care whether his clothes were wrinkled, even when he wasn't undercover. He had no close friends, no woman, and no life beyond the CPU. Kids were his investment. He hoped that by giving them all a chance now, they could help to sort out the world later. He hoped he could stop them growing up as unhappy as him.

The superintendent walked into the room through the open windows and turned off the oil heater. The sickly room had chilled considerably, but cold was one other thing that John didn't feel.

"Anyone for tennis?" said Yardly in her usual jolly style.

Emma Yardly was a strapping fifty-year-old woman who wore men's clothes so prettily, nobody would ever think her butch—and of course she wasn't. There was something manly about her face too, but even that she wore sweetly. She looked exactly like somebody's uncle pretending to be a raging queen at a party.

"I bet you've always wanted to do an entrance like that," said John, now without the Welsh accent. His own speaking voice was deceptively refined, like some historical BBC figure.

"I was in rep for four years. I've walked in through more French windows than you've had. . . ." She couldn't finish because she was sure John had had excesses of everything.

"How did we do this time, Em?" He really wanted the case and the evidence to be so convincing he wouldn't have to be slimy John again for a while. His first performance had been caught on micro-cam from the holdall that carried his collection of downloaded kiddy porn. At that show, only two of the ten members present had appeared on the films or slides themselves, and the police lawyer watching the monitor in the van outside had decided there wasn't enough to get a conviction on the others.

John had suspected as much and, as a first time member, when asked to make a speech at the end of the afternoon, he'd stood up and brazenly suggested they were all chicken. He said he thought this was more of a "hands on" organization—that got a laugh—and he was disappointed that the members weren't producing their own stuff. They protested that many of the photos and videos they had taken themselves, but John said he wouldn't be too "afraid" to appear in his own porn.

He had thrown this down as a challenge, and although he didn't get much of a response at the time from the slightly hung-over and spent group, he hoped there'd be a better showing this time. And there was. All but one of the members produced material in which they performed, and the public prosecutor in the ice-cream van at the end of the street was delighted. So was the super.

"You did us proud, John. We've got enough to stuff every one of 'em. We've got enough to search their homes, and I think we'll find evidence that will close these scum down forever."

Yardly wasn't one to keep her opinions to herself. "You know John, I sometimes wonder if I'm no less pathetic than the blokes we arrested today."

"What?"

"I sometimes feel that the pursuit of paedophiles is every bit as perverted as the paedophiles themselves. It's a fixation. I can't enjoy a meal in a restaurant if there's a man in there with a child. There's a 99 percent chance he's a caring parent or uncle, but I'm so fixated on his actions, the way he talks to the kid, I often give myself indigestion. I'm an anti-pervert pervert."

"You're right." John drained his glass and sidled across to the other end of the coffee table where a different flavour and colour of wine sat in a bottle barely touched. He poured a huge splash into his glass and looked up at his boss. "I think you should resign."

"I should what?

"Well, if it worries you that much, you should resign and buy a little needlework shop in the country."

"John, I think you've had enough to drink. I have to remind you, you're on duty."

He laughed. She did, too. But she wasn't joking. John's drinking gave her considerable concern. She ordered him to knock back the new glass and led him by the armpit to her car.

The uniformed driver laughed at the peculiar couple and didn't think once about opening the door and helping John or his boss inside. Once the door was shut, he crunched the gears and sped off to the station.

When they got there, John would drink several mugs of thick coffee. Once sober, he could begin the paperwork that would help put the BLOUKS in a place where they wouldn't be the most popular inmates.

None of them would notice the rented car in the station car park, or the zoom lens camera. And it would be several days before the CPU team realized just how much damage had actually been done on that chilly Surrey autumn afternoon.

3

A week later and John was two hours, 18 minutes late for the team meeting. The super had arranged it for the afternoon, just in case he was juxtaposed from his night out. But it hadn't made any difference. He arrived like a bag lady, shrouded in foul-smelling overcoats and disoriented to the point of walking into one of the empty chairs that blocked his path.

"All right, that's enough." Yardly shifted in her seat and pointed her knees at him. It was body language she'd learned at a staff management workshop. It didn't seem to threaten him. He popped open the cap of his cappuccino and swigged it back as if it were a cold drink. The super had decided to make a public stand next time this happened.

"I want you out of here now. You go home, clean up, sober up, and come back as a policeman. You've had 12 hours to get over last night, and this isn't what I call over it."

John finished his coffee and re-emerged from the Styrofoam with a bubble and chocolate moustache stuck to his own stubble. "I'm okay."

He looked anything but okay. Yardly was good at her job, and that alone commanded the respect of her team. It wasn't, however, enough to maintain discipline. Respect and discipline are different. She didn't have the traditional British police officer's authority to whip her troops into line. She relied on her personality, and there were times such as this when they recognized that she was soft.

The six people in the room knew that it was 3:15 p.m. and John was drunk. If it had been anyone else they would probably have been officially reprimanded, even laid off. But John was beyond regulations. He got away with stuff they couldn't, because his brilliance was recognized and they decided the rest was tolerable as long as they achieved the results they did. They wanted to help with his drink problem, but he saw drink as an answer to problems, not the problem itself.

He was a good officer. He would never have done anything to compromise or endanger the team. He knew he should have gone back to his untidy apartment and slept and woken refreshed and jogged and drunk fresh juice and eaten fucking muesli and put on clean underpants. They knew he knew all this. The only thing they didn't know was why he had stayed there on the street last night, even after the case was wrapped up.

He had done what none of them could do. He was acting as a vagrant, sitting with the drunks and derelicts on the pavement in front of the target. He could convince the winos that he was one of them. But when it came to the raid, he'd been together enough to tell the doorman that his pal outside had had a heart attack. It confused the man long enough for John to stumble past him. And once he'd eluded the bouncer, who else could have moved so fast up the staircase, crashed open the upstairs door, and grabbed the video from the camera before they could destroy it?

By the time the rest of the team arrived, no more than 11 seconds later, John Jessel had removed the young lass from the bed, wrapped her in the counterpane, and was talking to her like some happy uncle. He was the best.

So why had he refused the ride home and gone back to the drunks? It couldn't have just been for the half-finished vodka. The team in their unmarked cars looked through the rain-smeared windscreens as they drove the pornographers off, and saw Jessel hunch himself back down into the soggy shadows. History told them he wouldn't be in early the next day.

-o-

He wiped a palm over the stubble on his face and started to unwrap the stained greatcoat. Inside he was comparatively respectable in a grubby, bachelor kind of way. "Really. I'm okay."

He fumbled in the pocket of his jeans and pulled out a small slip of paper. He handed it to Yardley. "You should get the boys at registration to check out these two numbers. They're cars that stop by yesterday's MGM studio on a regular basis. You can see from the make, they're a wee bit out of place in that area."

Paddy Somersbee had been doing the surveillance on the property for a week. He was the only other man in their team. He took the paper from the super. "How come I didn't see these? You sure about your source?"

"If anyone knows anything about sauce. . . ." Maggy O'Leary was cut short by one of Jessel's evil stares.

"You didn't see 'em because you're a pratt."

Somersbee laughed defensively.

"These people aren't nearly as silly as you. They parked half a block away, went through the alley, and came in through the back. Can't imagine why you'd think of watching the back door."

"What do you want, Jessel? We have a one-man surveillance. You prefer me to park at the back and miss everything that goes through the front?"

"If I had a choice, yeah."

"Knock it off." The super was often refereeing the two men on her team of six officers. "Can we trust this info, John?"

"No, but it's worth following up."

Somersbee wasn't finished. "Which particular wino pal did you squeeze this out of, John? Did he force you to drink with him all night?

Jessel smiled. "This particular wino was 14, and he had some issues."

"And half a bottle of Gin."

"Somersbee."

"Yeah. We drank that and I bought another and we drank that, too."

"Jesus, Jessel. We're supposed to be helping these kids, not getting them plastered."

John was getting bored of sparring with Somersbee. He turned to the super and shook his head. "I don't know, Em. This kid has been through all the programmes. He's getting regular methadone to kick heroin. He's had his thirty minutes of counselling a day at the clinic. I'm not a psychiatrist, but it seemed to me he just wanted someone to kick his arse and tell him to sort himself out."

"Sound child psychology." Somersbee snorted.

"Somersbee." The whole team joined in this time.

"So what did you do?"

"Got him drunk. By four, he'd thrown up his life savings. I was expecting his internal organs to come out. When he was empty, I beat him up."

There were groans from around the group. Somersbee laughed and walked off to the water heater.

The super was less sympathetic. "Now tell me that was a joke."

"It was a joke."

"Thanks."

"I only had to hit him once and he was unconscious."

"John."

"It was a momentary decision." He slurred the word 'decision.'

"It was a momentary decision we didn't learn about on the street kids rehab course," one of the others put in.

"Look, I know. I know. I was so close. I'd spent, what . . . six hours with the kid. I got through the shitty language and the tough stuff and I saw this scared little bloke who just wanted to get a shake from someone to wake him out of his stupidity."

"You know it doesn't happen as fast as that."

"Usually you're right. But this was a fast-track rescue. He was at the give-up point. I got the feeling if I hadn't worked with him then, he'd be a stat today. He'd worked out how he was going to do it, Em. Up the fire escape at the back of the telephone exchange and head first onto the car park. He was describing it to me . . . how it felt going down; how all the sadness would go away once his face met the concrete. He wasn't bluffing."

The team members minus Somersbee were attentive now. They'd all had so many disappointments with street kids. They knew there was no one answer, no one treatment. Every kid was unique. Every story was more tragic than the last. But Joe Public didn't once look at them as victims. The kids absorbed the disgust they received from 'normal' mothers with their 'normal' unpolluted offspring who passed them on the street. Everyone saw them more as trouble than troubled.

Unorthodox situations often called for unorthodox remedies. John Jessel had the Southern England franchise on those

"Why did you knock him out?"

John shook his head. "Sometimes I forget just how strong I am."

That drew a laugh. None of them would describe Jessel as a fighter. He usually gave over the rough stuff to the ladies in the team. "In the films, you just have to punch a villain once and he's unconscious. I used to think that was a movie thing 'til I did it last night. It scared the nipples off me. I thought I'd killed him; he'd had a brain clot or something."

"But why did you hit him?" O'Leary asked.

Somersbee came back with his cup.

"He dared me." They looked on in disbelief. "Okay. Well, not so much dared as coerced. We'd come to some understanding on the suicide thing. It was less inevitable. But I suppose he wanted to see whether I was just talk. He asked me what I'd do if he said he was still going to jump. I told him I'd beat the idea out of him. Of course, I had no intention. . . .

"But the bugger tested me. He said I'd have to be a lot faster and tougher than I looked, 'cause he was off to do it, and I knew he really wanted me to stop him. So I went after him. I gave him this little tap and he went down like granny's drawers on granddad's birthday."

"Charming."

"I checked his vital signs, decided he wasn't dead, and took him home."

"How did you know where he lived?"

"I er . . ."

Marion King, the quiet thinker of the team, spoke for the first time: "He didn't. He means he took him back to *his* place."

Somersbee laughed again. "Bloody marvelous, Jessel. You spend the night with an under-aged boy, get him drunk, knock him out, kidnap him, and put him to bed in your flat. Front page of *The Star*. '*CHILD VICE COP BEDS UNDER-AGED STREET KID.*'"

John had to laugh. "It might be worse than that. I gave him your card with this address."

The team collectively slapped Jessel with their meeting agendas. John laughed again.

That was why. That was exactly why they didn't want to change Jessel. For whatever reason, all the chances, all the gambles John Jessel had taken over the years had paid off. The unit had a reputation better than any in the south. But you could never officially condone a Jessel action for fear that lesser officers would accept it as policy and screw it up. Only Jessel could do Jessel.

"Jessel. In my room, now." Yardley stood and walked away without looking at him. It was a ploy which didn't fool anyone. She had called John into her office a hundred times just to get him away from the others. He followed her like a *misérable* to the guillotine. Once there, she spoke to him as a friend and he respected her diplomacy.

He went into her office and closed the door.

But this time there was no artificial admonition and no smile. She flopped into her chair, opened the drawer, and frowned at what she saw inside. . . . "I think you should take a look at this John."

"I was expecting a bollocking."

"This is worse." She handed him a transparent plastic document folder.

John held it up to the light from the little window. It contained a picture postcard. On one side was a Kenya postmark. On the other was a photo of two young Masai girls smiling for the camera. They were about six or seven and naked but for tribal beads and earrings. It was a postcard that aunties sent home from holidays. The girls were exotic and lovely and would have elicited warm, parental feelings from the average tourist.

But this was the CPU, and mail like this raised hackles. They knew too well of the men who had winter residences in Arusha, Mombassa, or other seaside resorts on the East African coast. There they assembled stables of houseboys or girls only too grateful for a few shillings and a meal. If it were necessary to provide sexual services to the nasty foreigners . . . well, it was better than a slower death by starvation. Sometimes.

The customers were safely beyond the gravity of British law, and had the petty cash to keep the local police deaf and dumb. Interpol kept a list of temporary foreign residents in Kenya, mostly Germans, Italians, and British. Many were known but not convicted paedophiles. Extra-territorial laws were their allies rather than their foe. They fondled and fucked with impunity in their beachfront villas, then returned to overtly conservative lifestyles in Europe. So little funding was available to pursue offshore crime by even the most brazen offenders that those who understood the system were able to float effortlessly beyond its grasp.

John flipped over the postcard and read the text. He was expecting a 'wish you were here' message from one of the many sleazebuckets who had slipped out of the British prosecution process due to some ambiguous legal crap. But what he read disarmed him. To be true, it shocked him deep in a place he believed had become immune from feeling.

John Jessel,

It isn't you in control. You exist as long as I allow you to. How proud you must be of your round up of the pathetic BLOUKS. Your arrogance has made me angry, and it isn't wise to make somebody as powerful as me angry again. You will have to learn the hard way. You have caused unnecessary hardship to those you profess to protect.
This is the revenge of The Paw.
XXX

P. S. My regards to Eddo.

John looked up at Yardly. He hid the chaos with his clever eyes.

"Don't even think of telling me this is a crank, John.

"Well, isn't it?"

"Not our regular. How does he know your name? How does he know about the raid? And us? The CPU doesn't have a registered address." She held up the envelope to his face to emphasize that John's name and the CPU location —*"3rd floor, Securities Building"*—were clearly printed beside the message

"He's a crank," John repeated and stood and headed out of the office without waiting to be dismissed

"And who's Eddo?" She called after him

"No idea, boss." And he was gone.

She sat clenching her fists, wishing she were a male copper who could get his way just by having a deep voice. She wasn't and she couldn't.

He walked past the open door to the briefing room without bothering to stop in and say good-bye. As ever, Beth was on duty at the front desk. To people passing outside, this was just one more office belonging to one more company with a forgettable acronym. From outside the glass doors, Beth looked like a frazzled but otherwise boring receptionist. But boring or not, nobody got inside that office unless she wanted them there. She looked up at John, and before buzzing him out she asked, "How well do you get on with your neighbours?"

"What kind of question is that?"

"Present simple tense. Non-rhetorical."

"Well . . . okay I suppose. Is there a point?"

"We got a call from Sutton Central. There's been a complaint about you."

"Me? What have I done n—" He nodded his head as the possibility occurred to him. "The street kid?"

"Your neighbour at 17A reported there was a wino living opposite her who's molesting young boys."

"Boys? I'm only molesting one."

"You know how neighbours like to exaggerate."

John walked into the corridor and ran down the stairs to the rear door of the building. It was raining. Under the small porch he removed the mobile from his pocket. It was usually switched off. He prodded the numbers for his sister's house.

When John needed someone to answer the phone in a hurry, they never did. It rang so long he felt the battery would run out. He was just about to give up and go over there when Susan answered.

"Jesus, girl. Where've you bloody been?"

"I'm very well thanks, John. And you?"

"Hello, Chick. Sorry. Didn't mean to snap at you."

"You couldn't possibly have had a bad day already. It's only mid-afternoon and I know you don't start work 'til lunchtime."

"Bad night, Chick. I have my bad days at night. Listen . . . er . . . how's Eddo?"

"He's annoying. Can't you hear him?" John noticed for the first time the happy singsong that accompanied the background stereo music. Edward Fossel was possibly the happiest three-and-a-half-year-old John had ever met. Even his rare tantrums fizzled into laughter as if he realized himself how silly he was being. His granny accused her daughter of giving the boy mind-altering drugs and she of all people should know.

She inferred that Eddo was a passive inhaler of ganja. She argued that the boy would grow up to be some happy fool if his parents didn't learn to control their drug habit.

She had dropped by to annoy them all one winey Christmas. She didn't come by that often. She'd insisted John arrest the parents. She said she was prepared to sign the complaint. Susan and Bruce were unfit. John was cross-legged under the dining table at the time suckling a bottle of supermarket Scotch. But you couldn't blame dope for the way Eddo was. He was one of those naturally 'up' kids

"Chick."

"Yup?"

"Have you noticed anything . . . out of the ordinary at home?"

"You mean apart from Bruce?"

"I'm serious."

"Stop it. You're scaring me. Like what?"

"Anybody, I don't know . . . hanging around, watching you?"

"Oh bum. Now I really am going to have heart failure. What are you trying to tell me, Johno?"

"Have you, Chick? Have you noticed anyone?"

"No. Now tell me." The fact that there had never been a secret between them was occasionally difficult for John in his line of work. This was one of those occasions. But he had to tell her straight.

"One of our weirdos . . . er, mentioned Eddo."

"What? Oh, John."

"Look, I don't know how he knows Eddo, or how he knows me for that matter. But it's okay. He isn't in the country. He sent a postcard from Africa."

"They have planes you know."

"I know. I know. It scared the shit out of me, too."

"Well, what do we do? I don't want a siege here at the house."

"Me neither. I didn't tell the boss. She doesn't know Edward's nickname. She'd be obliged to have you watched 24 hours a day. I was thinking about Aunt Maud."

"You want us to run away?"

"I just want you out of harm's way for a while so I can keep my mind clear. Do some investigating."

"Well, you really know how to stuff up a girl's pregnancy leave. The first chance I get for some peace and quiet away from the caveman." Bruce was off in Berkshire completing a second doctorate in something as useless as the first. So, Susan, Eddo, and the fetus were sharing some quality time together. "But I suppose Aunt Maud's would be nice."

"Right. That's settled then. Don't open the door to anyone. I'll be there in forty minutes."

"Bloody hell. That soon. . . ? Okay. It's all quite exciting really. Bruce will love all the intrigue."

"That's the spirit."

She was a peculiar lass that Susan. But then again John wasn't exactly 'normal' himself. And their mother was nuttier than a box of almonds. But in situations such as this, insanity came in handy.

"We'll be ready." She turned to Eddo who was singing karaoke into an old Sunlight washing-up-liquid container.

"Okay, Eddo me boy, get your boots on. We're off to visit Auntie Maud."

John heard the cheer and he knew there wouldn't be any trouble. At least not from his family.

As he ran to his car through the cool autumn drizzle, he thought about 17A. He didn't feel at all resentful. In fact he intended to commend her for her community vigilance. What this country needed were more people with the balls to report their suspicions, and stuff the consequences. He often suspected 17A had balls. She certainly had a moustache. He'd buy her a bunch of flowers and a razor.

If he'd been less disturbed by the contents of the card, he may have noticed the rental car and the slightly open window that closed once he'd finished the phone call.

4

It was two weeks before he was able to get anything on the postcard threat, and then two leads arrived within an hour of one another. The first he went looking for.

This "Paw" character was obviously distressed about the BLOUK raid, so there had to be a connection. One of the seven men arrested that day had vanished but apparently not left the country. The others were on bail, pending trial. John spent the day visiting them at their homes or work places. Naturally, they weren't delighted to see him. It wasn't in his character to be embarrassed about interviewing men whose lives he was in the process of destroying. But it was also not his way to treat them with disrespect.

He personally believed they were bad eggs and that no amount of psychological rehabilitation would take the smell away. But they'd been caught and were being punished as the law saw fit. Being rude to them would serve no purpose. What he felt inside about them was his problem, not theirs.

Only one of the six afforded him what could be described as a conversation. The ex-teacher 'Sir,' lived in a fussy terraced house with lace chair covers and fresh cut flowers. It smelled of these and other strategically placed bowls of dried petals. That and the sweetness of his tea made John feel queasy.

Sir had a common teacher's disease. He enjoyed the sound of his own voice. He sat in an armchair and talked as if John were a neighbour dropping in for a chat.

"You fooled me, old boy, I tell you. I didn't even pick the phony accent. And I've been lied to by some of the best. You probably recall I'm something of a performer myself." He looked dreamily towards the lace curtains for a second. "What will happen to my slides?"

"They won't make it onto *Britain's Funniest Home Videos* if that's what you mean."

"Too bad. Such a lot of planning went into it. I'd hate to think of them being destroyed."

John looked into the watery eyes of the old man and saw no remorse whatsoever. "We'll probably hang on to them and use them at the training college to show recruits how pathetically compulsive child abusers can get."

"Ah, that's a relief. I would so hate to be forgotten."

John put his China teacup on the table beside his chair. "You will be careful with that, won't you. It's very old. It was my mother's."

"What does the name The Paw mean to you?"

Sir stared again at the curtain as if his lines were all written there.

"The Paw, The Paw .... Well, it could be a rather exciting secret name for a cat burglar, or a dog handler."

After years of interviewing, John had a keenly developed sense of observation. He was sure that the name had found a match somewhere in the teacher's mind. "What do you know about him?"

Sir smiled and looked from the curtain to John. "Well, personally I thought his performance lacked originality."

"You've seen him?"

"As have you, of course."

John's stomach churned. "You telling me he was at the BLOUK meeting?"

Sir's smile was beginning to annoy him but it confirmed that The Paw was one of the other six at the presentation. "Which one?"

"You're no Miss Marple are you, Officer. The chap who did the other slide show of course."

The members usually gave false names when they communicated but it was obviously difficult to keep your identity secret when you invite people to your home. The CPU had been able to collect data on all the men captured during the raid. They had been to their homes, confiscated evidence, and apparently knew everything there was to know about all of them. John had studied it all. He went through the charge sheet in his mind:

Marcus Aldy.

BLOUK Code name: "Dong."
37 years old. Born in Burgh Heath, Surrey.
Occupation: Self-employed.
Residence: Large flat in Colliers Wood.
Marital Status: Single (lives alone).

That was all he could recall offhand, except that Aldy was missing. He hadn't reported to his local station as stipulated under the bail agreement, and he hadn't gone back to his flat to collect his clothes. He'd just disappeared. Immigration had no record of him leaving the country, but there was any number of ways to slip out of England's green and pleasant land without leaving a trace.

"What makes you think he was The Paw?"

"Honestly. You're making me wonder whether I missed my true vocation in life all those years. I should have been a policeman."

"Just cut the fucking crap and answer the question."

Sir was deeply offended by the language. John's outburst had surprised both of them. It was out of character and it confirmed to John that this case was getting to him.

Sir was in a deep sulk. "Do you have a warrant? I imagine not. In that case, I think you should leave."

"No. I'm not ready yet. You have one more question to answer." John stood, picked up the delicate cup and saucer with its hardly-touched Earl Grey, and held it high over the cream filigreed lace tablecloth.

"Oh God, no don't."

John's hand began to shake. "I don't think I can hold it much longer."

"No, wait. You really are a beast. It was written in the tattoos."

John scanned his memory.

"Tattoos? There was nothing on the ID sheet about Aldy having tattoos."

Sir rushed across to rescue his teacup. "The tattoos on the boys, Miss Marple. On the boys."

5

John raced into the evidence room, not troubling with protocol. He ignored the requisition ledger and went straight to the rear shelf where the BLOUK evidence filled eight cardboard boxes. He found Aldy's slides and took them to the conference room. There he impatiently slotted them all in the slide carrousel and pulled down the screen. In his haste he confused the buttons on the remote.

It was midnight, so flicking off the overhead light left him drowned in eerie blackness. He struggled with the control to escape the darkness until at last a square of dazzling white appeared on the screen. He was annoyed at his brief panic. Darkness had always filled him with dread. It was a phobia he had mysteriously dragged around since before his father's death. At that moment it was the only thing he was afraid of, but it was soon to have an ally.

He displayed the first slide. Unlike the teacher, Aldy was apparently not one to build up the mood. He and the boy were already sitting naked, side by side on a mattress on the floor. John walked to the screen and looked at his adversary. Nothing about him prickled John's instincts. Nothing in the eyes spoke to him.

He was a plump man, not fat exactly, but with the build of a soft person who had never seen a need for exercise. His was the face of a million middle-aged white men. The hair was dyed black and there were indications that the eyebrows had been touched up. The lips were a little too red, the cheeks too pink. But beneath the stage make-up was an otherwise dull face.

The boy was small, perhaps eight or nine, of African origin, and sadly undernourished. The possible Kenya connection registered immediately. There was no sign of the tattoo Sir had spoken of. There was a series of six slides with this particular child, and none of the first five showed a tattoo. John had seen far too many such scenes, but he never failed to look into the children's eyes to remind himself of how much damage was being done to their souls. It was there to see if you knew how to look. The men who abused them never bothered to look at all.

It wasn't until the last shot—the act done, the boy alone, face down on the mattress—that John noticed the first tattoo. It was etched across his buttocks as if he were some branded calf. With dark letters on brown skin, you would have to be paying careful attention to notice. It was no wonder he hadn't spotted the tattoos at the club showing.

He never paid much attention to those shows once he was sure there was enough evidence to put the men away. He always focussed on a point to the right of the screen, the way you do when something gory happens in a film but you don't want the other people in the cinema to think you're squeamish. So Aldy was The Paw. Here was his calling card stamped on his victims.

He went back over the previous five slides, but there wasn't an angle to get a clear look. The next six followed the same pattern: one seated together, four action, and one face down on the mattress displaying the tattoo. But there was one slide where the child's backside was half-visible, and John could see no sign of letters. There were a total of six children, and each sported the tattoo only in the final shot. It was almost as if it were inflicted only after the assault. But these seemed to be clinical marks, like carefully scripted welts. There were traces of fresh blood. Time had been taken over them. Why had the boys lain patiently through what must have been a very painful ordeal?

John isolated the six slides which bore the The Paw brand, and displayed them over and over trying to understand what it was that troubled his subconscious. A person in a photograph, or at least the two dimensional representation of that person, gives clues as to what they were feeling at the time. Even a sleeping child, through the angle of his limbs, the mood on his face, can give hints as to what he's dreaming. When a photograph fails to give up those clues, it can mean only one thing.

John decided that the photos of the six boys gave up no suggestions of life, because life had been removed from them. He came to the conclusion that the boys were not resting. They were dead. And, with that in mind, when he looked again at The Paw's photographs, it was as clear as day that the boys had been branded after being murdered. How could he have missed it?

A familiar ache took hold of his heart. It was the grief he felt on all his cases, in all the instances when kids were hurt. But as he looked at these boys, an anger inflamed the grief. What type of person could kill in the pursuit of pleasure? What type of monster was Aldy to openly boast of what he'd done; to turn up at a showing of his crime?

John leaned against a desk, his blood pumping fast. He took his mind back to the day of the arrests. He walked through the scene at the house and paused whenever Aldy appeared. He replayed the man's expressions in the slide presentation. There was a certain arrogance, a pride that John had interpreted at the time as conceit. Now he could see it as bragging. Aldy, The Paw was laughing at him. And at that moment was born a hatred that would cloud John's judgement and lead to errors.

What was previously a paedophile inquiry had now become a homicide investigation.

6

"Yes. What can I do for you?"

"Is that Major Muthoga?"

"It certainly is."

"Your English is very good."

"So it should be, my dear sir. I've been using it for 56 years."

"I see."

"Inspector Jessel, I assume. . . . It has already taken you quite some time to get your call transferred to this office. I also assume you don't have an unlimited international phone budget."

"Or in other words, get to the point. Right. I have suspicions that an English paedophile has murdered at least one Kenyan child, perhaps more."

There were a few seconds of silence from the African end.

"That's a very serious allegation."

John knew what was coming next.

"Do you have any evidence to support it?"

"I've sent you copies of photos by international courier. They should be there this afternoon sometime." As he described his findings to the major, he realized the limitations of his evidence. He didn't know at all whether the children were Kenyan, or indeed if they were dead. Aldy's postcard could easily have been a spoiler, a trick to send him off on a wild goose chase halfway around the world. But he had no other leads to go on. Once he'd given Muthoga everything he had, there was that same pause from Nairobi. . . .

"Very well, Inspector Jessel. I appreciate you sharing your hunch with me. I look forward to seeing the photographs, or not, as the case may be. Leave me your number and I'll get back to you as soon as I can."

John fell back onto the bed and wondered how much of his salary he had just spent. He couldn't phone from the office, not without filing a full report and bringing in the murder squad and Scotland Yard and Interbloodypol and the UN peacekeeping forces and whoever-God-knows else. He'd discussed his theory with the CPU of course. They'd gone through those slides a thousand times.

Reactions had been mixed. They obviously couldn't be sure the boys were dead, and with no real leads there was nowhere to go with it. Homicide had told them there could be no murder inquiry without a victim. With Aldy missing, there was nothing official a Southern English police unit could do. It was left to John to find them connections . . . and bodies, on his own time.

He had one body of his own curled up on the couch in his little living room. For almost three weeks Mick had crashed at John's. 'Crash' was the optimum word for Mick's stay. It hadn't been an easy time for either of them. Of course, John knew he could expect chaos for a while. He'd worked in D and A for a spell and had been on many rocket rides with kids coming out of their respective addictions. But in those days he could leave his problems at the office. This one was waiting for him when he came home. John didn't know whether to expect a gourmet sandwich or a bloodied bread knife. It didn't help his nerves any.

But there, purring on the couch in his *Teletubbies* T-shirt, he was just another adolescent. If only there were a way to keep him unconscious 22 hours a day the relationship would improve no end.

When they talked, when Mick was down and clear, they talked as friends. He was a tender boy with feelings of concern for the world, for people, for other street children: "They just want to be heard, John. Like me. If someone had listened . . . if someone had been interested about what my stepdad was doing, I wouldn't have run out on Mum."

But when he was off his head, he was nasty: "You think I'm fucking stupid? You think I don't know why you got me here, you fat-arsed faggot."

John picked up the phone again and called Aunt Maud.

A gruff, permanently annoyed voice answered. "C. S. Maudling."

"'Lo, Maud. It's Jessel."

Aunt Maud was neither an aunt nor a Maud. But it had stuck as Chief Superintendent Maudling's codename while he was still in active service on the force; ever since he set up the CPU in the late eighties.

"Now what do you want, Jessel?"

"I was hoping to speak to my sister if it's no trouble."

"I'm afraid I have her spread-eagled and tied to the bed posts with her stockings right now. Could you call back a little later? This isn't a good time."

John clearly heard the sound of an open palm slap against a bald head, and Susan came to the phone.

"Sorry, Johno. He got me confused with his inflatable again."

"'Lo, Chick. How's it going?"

"Are we safe to come back to civilization yet? We're getting far too comfortable here."

Aunt Maud's large cottage was deep in the Cotswolds. It was a setting common on birthday cards that seventy-year-olds send one another. It was exquisitely thatched and surrounded by assorted greens of grasses and greys of pasty skies. It wasn't so much built as kneaded into a shape that best suited the scenery. For Eddo it was an environment of unlimited action adventure; of potential broken ankles, death by sheep goring, random lightning strikes, and abduction by passing village idiots. But Susan being the type of mother she was, let him at it, and trusted his Jessel common sense. There was little could restrain him anyway, so it was better to have faith in his judgement and avoid heart failure.

As his mother spoke, he was standing on the well wall heaving up the bucket by hand.

"How's Eddo?"

Susan watched her son through the window. "He's just about to fall down a forty-foot well."

"He can swim, can't he?"

"Yuh, but I haven't taught him to fly yet."

"It'll do him good. How's John?"

"I won't tell you again. We aren't calling my fetus 'John'."

"Not even if it's a boy?"

"And have all his school friends believe his mother has no imagination?"

"You always worried too much about what ten-year-old boys think about you. Is Maud treating you both all right?"

"Like royalty. Did we catch the baddy yet?"

John briefly considered making her feel better by lying to her. It passed. "No. I've got no more idea now than I did before you left."

"Do we stay here forever?"

"Perhaps. Is that a problem?"

"Johno, I know you wouldn't make me and Eddo go through this if you weren't afraid for us. I'll do whatever you say, of course. But if you don't catch this bloke. . . ."

"I know, Chick. I'm asking a lot. But I'm not going to send you home 'til I find out how this bugger knows about Eddo. And if I don't find out. . . ." He hesitated, not for effect but because the reality had just occurred to him. "You may have to move permanently."

"You know something you aren't telling me."

"Yeah. He kills kids. I don't have proof, but I'm certain of it. He kills cold-bloodedly." Now, John really had no idea what reaction he could expect. His sister was silent for a moment.

"Chick?"

"Wales sounds nice." There was a tremble in her voice.

"Eh?"

"Wales. I fancy a little terraced place in a disused mining village. Women in tall hats called Gwyneth. I mean the women are called Gwyneth, not the hats. Eleven and a half months of rain a year. I could make elderberry wine and be pickled by lunchtime."

"Chick, you're the tops. Really."

"I'm lucky to have a big brother who looks after me."

"If it weren't for me and my bloody job, you two wouldn't be in this mess at all."

"Oh, do shut up. You're starting to sound like mother. We're proud of what you do. I want to be part of your life. Eddo can write a bestseller about it when he grows up."

"You're really weird, sis, but I love you."

"I know you do, sweetie. Now leave me alone and go catch the bum. I have to phone my present husband and break the news to him that we're moving house again."

When she tried to hang up the phone, Susan's hand was shaking so badly she could barely find the cradle. Like John, she had developed the bad habit of hiding her true feelings. She used humour like a weapon to keep people away. She cracked jokes to deceive. She laughed when she should have cried.

The fear was building in her with every phone call, but she presented herself to those in her shrinking world like a court jester. It should have occurred to her that her unborn child was living inside her tension. It should have occurred to her that her four-year-old wasn't old enough to be fooled by words. Only Aunt Maud believed she was "a really strong girl." In fact she wasn't strong at all.

-o-

Two days later, John was in the middle of de-briefing a new team member when he was called to the phone. It took him a moment to realize who he was talking to. Major Muthoga was more animated than he had been during their previous conversation.

"Inspector Jessel, how have you been?

"Well thanks, Major. I take it you have something for me."

"Unfortunately I have a lot. Tell me. Do you have any vacation time coming up soon?"

7

The Ethiopian Airlines flight landed at Nairobi International Airport at 10:00 a.m. It was the cheapest ticket John could get at a day's notice, so he was foolish to be expecting legroom. The Economy-Class syndrome had made him irritable. The free booze had made him hung-over. He made the mistake of writing "*meeting*" on his entry form, and the large Immigration officer at tossed his passport back at him.

"Visa. Over there. Fifty dollars."

"But I'm British."

"So what?"

"Well, it clearly states here in my Lonely Planet guide that British citizens don't need a visa for Kenya."

"I don't work for Lonely Planet . . . sir. I work for the Kenyan Immigration Authority, and they say you need a visa if you're here for a meeting."

"What if I'm not here for a meeting?"

"But you are."

"Well, let's just imagine I'm not, for the next time."

A Scotsman way back in the queue was getting irritated. "What ye daein' up there? Get a move on will ye?"

The officer shot him a look that turned him to salt, but took it out on John.

"Look, mister. You aren't here as a tourist, so get over there to the Visa-on-Arrival counter, pay your fifty dollars, and let these other people go through. Right?"

"Yes, ma'm."

For no other reason than sheer bloody-mindedness, under the gaze of the officer and the Scot, he marched over to the Visa-on-Arrival desk and asked for another entry form. He filled it out, this time writing "*safari*," and tore up the old form. When he was sure the first officer wasn't paying attention, he joined a distant queue and got through for nothing.

"Have a good vacation, sir."

"Thank you."

So it was with a sense of victory that he arrived in the station-like arrivals lounge. The uniformed police delegation looked beyond him as he shuffled out with his cricket bag. He walked directly up to the ranking officer who was as tall as an NBA centre, but the man continued to look over John's head. He was probably expecting somebody more James Bond. When Inspector Jessel introduced himself, the man reluctantly looked down at the plump, unshaven specimen, took his bag, and walked off towards the car. The men on either side however, saluted, smiled, and made John feel most welcome. As it turned out, the fellow with all the badges was the driver.

It was about forty minutes to the police station. The country was surprisingly cool, and he'd left all his warm clothes at home. The grass verges were brown, and the long road into Nairobi was dusty. The people he saw all seemed somewhat depressed. At the traffic lights, street urchins came rushing up to all the cars but theirs, and worked their scams to get money for glue.

"They're annoying little bastards."

John looked at the sergeant who'd made the comment so nonchalantly.

"Whose annoying little bastards are they?"

"They're from the slums mostly. We're always running them to Juvenile Justice for this or that."

"Why aren't they in school?"

Both officers laughed. "That isn't so easy, sir. You'll notice we have one or two structural weaknesses in our country."

The driver came to life. He was obviously pissed off about the structural weaknesses. "The place has been run to the dogs. There aren't enough hospitals to look after the sick. There aren't enough police to catch the criminals. There aren't enough teachers or schools for the children." He ran over the toes of a group of people who'd thought they might cross the road, as the light was red. None of the policemen reacted.

The driver continued, still glaring at John in the rear mirror as if it were all his fault. "These kids are on the street because three million primary-school-age children can't get into school. We don't even start to count secondary level." He braked heavily to avoid running into a bus.

John was impressed by his fire, but could see why he hadn't made it beyond driver. "Three million? You fellows shouldn't be arresting the kids. You should be running in some of the criminals up in Parliament House."

The driver laughed for the first and last time. "You aren't wrong boss. You aren't wrong."

-o-

At the nondescript building they told him was Police HQ, they marched him up the steps like a suspect and deposited him in front of a large grey door. He knocked.

A familiar voice yelled out, "Yes. Come in."

Muthoga, an Idi Amin look-alike, had the same disappointed first impression look as the driver, but he quickly got over it. He rose from his desk and offered a hand. John shook it gladly.

"Inspector Jessel." The solidly built policeman gestured for him to take a seat. "I assume you do a fair bit of undercover work."

"I get the feeling I should've worn my tall and respectable disguise today."

"You're in a place where show is often more important than substance. But all that glitters is not gold."

"So I've heard."

"Tell me, Inspector. Are you here on holiday?"

"Yup."

"So, you're paying for this trip yourself?"

"We had a whip-round at the office."

"Your colleagues must have a lot of faith in your judgement. Do I also get the impression that you are personally involved?"

"I am, sir."

"Then we should waste no more time. Your hunch was correct. After looking at your unpleasant slides, I sent feelers out to the morgues. I also had our filing chappy go on a hunt."

Muthoga pushed one of the two glasses of milky tea on the desk towards John. He picked up the other himself, tasted it, added two heaped spoonfuls of sugar, tasted it again, and leaned back in his chair. The whole performance took a lot longer than John was prepared to wait.

"And. . . ?"

"Well, the first news came back very quickly. My lad at the Mombassa butchers shop recognized the brand straight away. There was only one victim at that stage: a boy found in the beach area. We compared the autopsy photos and there's a ninety percent chance he's one of yours."

"Only ninety percent?"

"The body was badly decomposed by the time it got to the morgue."

"Where did they find it?"

"It had been buried deep in the garden of a holiday home. If the owner hadn't decided to install a pool while the place was empty, we would probably never have found it at all."

"Do you know anything about the boy?"

"Not a thing. Mombassa has as many beachboys as we have street children in Nairobi. Mothers don't report them missing unless they rely on them for income. A lot of them have been out on their own since they were six or seven. They're lost and unwanted." Muthoga said it in such a way as to suggest he didn't want them either.

John picked up on something else the chief had said. "But since then, you've had another case. You said 'one victim at that stage.'"

"Ah, a real policeman." Muthoga smiled and sipped at his tea. It was a gesture that was as at home in the room as the slightly brown photographs and the cluttered bookshelves. John had seen them before, these in-built senior officers who'd been so long behind a desk their bodies took on the appearance and the hue of their environments. They longed to be back where the excitement was, but first promotion, then lethargy had stood in their way. Now, like Muthoga, they couldn't leave those offices if they wanted to.

Still looking at John, the major put down his cup where he knew there'd be an empty space, and reached into an open drawer. He handed a folder to John, who opened it to see a familiar scene in an unfamiliar photograph: a naked boy, face down with the words The Paw tattooed across his backside.

"My filing chappy had this on his desk even as my memo reached him."

The date on the photo was two days prior.

"How long had he been dead?"

"He was fresh: a few hours at the most."

The implication hit John like a bull. "That was one hell of a coincidence. That would put the time of death just after my call to you."

Muthoga smiled his affirmation. "It was just one of three devilish coincidences, Inspector Jessel."

"Tell me." John already had that increasingly familiar feeling of discomfort.

The Kenyan once again reached into the drawer without looking and pulled out a sheet of paper. He put it on the desk before John. "Beside the body there was a postcard. That is now evidence, and I'm afraid I can't show you the original. But this is a copy of the text. It strikes me as rather corny, but I assume we should take it seriously."

John felt his hand shake as he reached for it. The letters crawled from the paper onto his neck like insects.

Policeman Jessel,
(How did you lose your ear, by the way?)
As I warned, you are causing the deaths of those you pretend to help.
Here's another to your score. There will be more. First the boys. Then
the girls. You will be last as you are the easiest.
XXX
This is the revenge of The Paw.

And if the postcard itself weren't numbing enough, the postscript rendered him bloodless:

P. S. I trust Aunt Maud is taking good care of Eddo

8

It was 1:00 in the morning and John had run the poor room-service boy at the Court Hotel into the ground. The electricity was off as usual, so the lift wasn't a lot of use. Bar fridges hadn't made it to three-star Kenya, so every half-hour the boy had to run up to the sixth floor with two cold beers from the ice chest in the basement.

John hadn't been able to get a phone call out to England until 5.30 p.m. when the service came back on. To his relief, Aunt Maud had told him that Susan and Eddo were fine and had taken his car into town to do some shopping. But there were two anxious hours waiting for his sister to get back. When she finally arrived, their escape from Maud's had already been planned as only an ex chief-super could. It involved two changes of vehicle and an elaborate false trail. It was amazing how many ex-policemen there were in cottages in the Cotswolds.

So now, feeling only moderately more at ease, he sat by the phone and drank beer by candlelight. He knew that Maud could outwit even the canniest of criminals, but The Paw looked like a certifiable nutcase. You could never be sure with a nutcase.

On the glass-ringed coffee table, copies of the postcards flickered in the light of the flame. The handwriting was neat, compulsively neat, but it didn't give anything away as to the personality of the author. John had circled one word from the first message: "again."

It isn't wise to make somebody like me angry again.

"Again?" What had he done to upset The Paw before? Who was he? Nothing John had done could ever have warranted this. Surely not. He'd have to go back over ten years of records and mug shots.

When the phone beside him rang, his heart smashed against the inside of his ribcage. This case had hold of him and was destroying all his natural defenses. He was a nervous wreck.

"Yes?"

"Big brother?"

"Chick? How are you?"

"Fine."

"Where are you?"

"Can't tell you."

"Good. Yeah. Really good. Just say you aren't pissed off at me and hang up."

"Oh, John. Don't be silly. I know you're living this worse than us. I'm worried sick about you."

"I've survived worse. I'm a trained professional. Remember?"

"We'll have some stunning cocktail parties when this is all over. 'I tell you darling, while I was being stalked by this manic serial killer. . . .' It's exactly what a suburban vegetable like me needs. Anyway, I can't talk all night. I have to flee terror. Love you. Bye." And she was gone.

"Bye-bye, Chick." The receiver seemed to stick to John's hand. Something in his mind relaxed, but only slightly. One small corner of the disaster was out of harm's way. But the rest of it stretched out before him, beyond the papers on the coffee table, beyond the hotel and the dry brown countryside of rainless Kenya. It was so immense he'd never be able to float above it to take in its enormity or to see how he fitted into the landscape. The Paw was God, and was reminding John how insignificant he was. Every day there was a sign; a symbol of His omnipotence. His power even trickled down to the third coincidence.

Here sat John, sleepless and sober in the Court Hotel. It was where the police usually put up their guests. A floor below his was a room with police adhesive tape across the door. It was the room in which they'd found The Paw's last victim.

-o-

The following day, blotchy and bloated from beer and sleeplessness, John arrived on foot at police HQ with his moth-eaten cricket bag over his shoulder. He had found himself shooing off street urchins he should have been feeding; pushing them away with his half-empty bag; forgetting temporarily that they were a lot more than petty annoyances. He was too tired to be sympathetic. He'd been searching through the crime scene at the hotel when he should have been sleeping, but had found nothing.

He was booked on a flight to Mombassa, and intended to get this courtesy call to Muthoga over with as soon as possible. But the major had one more surprise for him. . . .

They were sitting in the untidy office waiting for tea. The major seemed unable to begin any point without a cup in front of him. But on this occasion the tradition lost out. He took a folder from the shelf behind him and placed it in front of John.

"It arrived this morning."

Inside was the same postcard of the Masai girls, but on the back Her Majesty's silhouette lay eyeless on the pillow of the stamp. It was stickered *EMS, Express*. John squinted to read the smudged postmark. He prayed silently that it wasn't from the Cotswolds where Susan and Eddo hid. It wasn't. But it was almost as bad. He could read the "*on*" quite clearly, and a vague "*Tham . . .*" and it was quite obvious that The Paw had stood at a postbox in John's own postal district of Kingston upon Thames, not four days before. He knew the bastard had smiled as he pushed the card into the gaping mouth of the red pillar-box.

John looked into the sympathetic face of the major, who seemed to instinctively understand yet had no charity to offer. It was just the helplessness of it. It was the pathetic, useless lack of intelligence. Why couldn't they live in a world where scum like this couldn't get away with terrorist games they'd learned from airport novels? Why hadn't they tagged him with a nuclear implant after they arrested him so they could blow him up if they found DNA traces on a postcard like this?

Instead he was laughing at them. He was dragging John around the world by the scrotum and enjoying the power. It annoyed the hell out of him, but scared him at the same time. He read the words aloud, although he knew Muthoga had already been over the card:

Jessel,
I do hope you enjoyed your welcome-to-Nairobi present. I didn't leave many clues, did I. You aren't as quick witted as him. What irony. There you are, away on holiday, while I'm here looking after your loved ones. Idle, idle youth. Forever sleep.
XXX
This is the revenge of The Paw

The chief must have felt John's despair. "I'm so sorry you are having to go through this."

John nodded. The Kenyan handed him a photocopy of the card and stood. John rose, also. Muthoga held out his hand, but the resulting shake was more like the desperate clutching at a drowning shipmate. The major saw John sinking but was in no position to save him.

"My captain will take you to the airport," he said finally. "You will have the full co-operation of my colleagues in Mombassa."

John, drained of ideas and hope, turned and obediently followed the captain out of the office.

It was more than an hour before his senses returned to him. The small twin turbo-prop was clattering its way over thirsty terrain and brittle vegetation. John stared through the smudged porthole not seeing the scenery. The huge, soft man beside him had long given up on conversation and was now sleeping, semi-inflated like a failed hot-air balloon.

John had overcome the fear and was feeling guilty. His work had spilled over into his private life, and he was responsible. His sister and nephew were in danger and their lives were chaotic, and he was responsible. Two children, probably more, had been killed, and he was responsible. What in heaven and hell had he done to The Paw to provoke such a compulsive quest for revenge?

He looked again at the photocopy. It didn't give him any answers, only more questions.

"You aren't as quick-witted as him."

Who?

Perhaps it was meaningless. Perhaps it was part of the torment. He didn't know what to do to turn off this machine that was processing him. The only evidence, the only clues he had were supplied by the enemy. John had learned nothing by himself. He was always one pace behind. But now there were bodies. If he could connect Aldy to the crime scene, he'd be on the attack at last.

9

The house was the usual whitewashed holiday villa near the ocean. A local detective sergeant called Moses showed him around the place. In the garden he pointed out the groove where they'd dug the child out of the dry wall of the swimming pool excavations. John learned nothing that wasn't in the report.

The renter had paid the advance in cash under a false name. Nothing unusual. John would go to see the agent later. If the owner hadn't decided to put in the pool, they would never have found the body. Perhaps The Paw had made his first mistake here. John just wasn't sure whether he'd recognize it.

The detective was friendly but obviously busy with other matters, so John thanked him and said he'd like to stick around for a while if it was okay with him. The Kenyan didn't care one way or the other.

When he was alone, John slowly walked through the house once more, trying to picture the events that led up to the assault of the boys. The mattress lay in the bare back bedroom as it had appeared on the slides. He could only imagine what horror took place in this house. He needed the walls to tell him what they'd seen.

"You want somptin', mista?"

John turned around to see a small, dark figure in the doorway. "What you got?" He walked towards a boy who remained a silhouette even when he was in focus. He was about nine or ten. His clothes and skin were dusty like the roads, but his smile was polished bright. He shone it at the puffy white *moosoongoo* in front of him.

"You goin' to live here?"

"You never know."

"I be you boy. All right, sir?"

"What can you do?"

"Everythin'."

"A rare talent indeed." John moved close enough to see there was some intoxication in the boy's eyes, probably from glue fumes or some local weed. He leaned against the inside of the door-frame and slid himself down to the floor. The boy lowered himself against the other jamb so they were both sitting looking into the spacious living room.

"You ever been somebody else's boy?"

"Yes, sir. Lots." He smiled his confident calculated smile again. It was the only really attractive thing about him, so he used it liberally.

It worried John that the boy was so openly touting for business. "What about the man who lived here a few months ago?"

"Him? No, sir. You know him?"

"Yeah. He was a friend of mine. You saw him here?"

"Yes, sir."

"I've got a picture of him here I think." John clawed through his bag for the blow-up print of Marcus Aldy, alias The Paw. "Aha. Here it is." He put it down on the floor between them as if it wasn't particularly important whether the boy looked at it or not.

He glanced at it briefly. "Nah." He shook his head.

"No what?"

"Nah is not him."

John was jolted. "You haven't seen my friend here? He said this was the address."

"You goin' to live here or what?"

"I don't know. I want to talk to the man who was here before. See what it's like to live here."

"He was a Chinaman."

That came as such a surprise that John instinctively assumed he was being spun a yarn. "Yeah. And I'm Ugandan."

"I never been there. Is nice?"

"I don't . . . was he really a Chinaman?"

"Little eyes, you know?"

"I know. Did you speak to him?"

"Yes, sir. I have the interview, too."

"What interview?"

"He was interview boys. He say he pay for study in . . . someplace. I don' remember name. My friend, he pass the interview. Now he study engineer in big university." His glazed eyes could see that big university and that big life he'd missed out on.

John took the photos of the faces of The Paw's victims from his bag and spread them out on the floor.

"You know these boys?" The daylight glinted off the six confused expressions of soon-to-be-dead beachboys.

"These two." He poked them with his toe. "I don' know."

"So the others you do know."

The boy nodded.

"And did they have interviews?"

"They must ha' passed. One day they come for interview, next day they gone. You interviewing, too? I do better this time."

"What did the Chinaman ask you?"

"Usual stuff. Name? How old? What I do before? Family. . . ."

"Have you got a family?"

"My ma live here in Mombassa."

"Do you live with her?"

"Sometime."

John thought about it. That was probably why this boy had failed the interview. Connections. Aldy and the Chinaman wanted boys that wouldn't be missed. This was a co-ordinated effort. There was nothing spontaneous about it. He should have realized there was someone else involved. The photos had been taken from various angles. It would have been difficult for Aldy to run around re-positioning the camera and performing at the same time. Whether Aldy hired some kiddyporn Chinaman to take the pictures or whether they were working together made little difference. Either way, John decided they were both sick bastards.

Things were starting to fit together. He told the boy he was hiring him as an assistant for one or two days, and it had nothing to do with sex. They agreed on a salary and John gave him a day in advance.

"Listen," he said after handing it over. "There are two conditions attached to this."

The boy didn't respond and probably didn't understand.

"One, you give half of this to your ma. Two, before you buy your glue this time, you buy food and have a good meal."

The boy feigned indignation. "Why you think I want glue, sir? I not like that."

"Three. No bullshit. I know too much for you to get away with that. Got it?"

The young fellow smiled to himself. "All right."

They made an appointment for that evening. John knew that in his short stay he wouldn't get this or any other street kid off a glue habit. But he could improve his physical and social conditions a bit, and increase the boy's self respect. He couldn't save him, but perhaps the boy could start the process of saving himself. And there was some angel on his team already who had kindly failed the interview for him.

Before he left, John asked him his name.

"Jackie, sir."

"Was that the name you were born with?"

"Nah. Is my street name."

"What's your real name?"

"I don' remember."

"Then the first thing we'll do is give you an off-street name. How about—"

"You don' like my name?"

"Not much. How about 'Tiger'?"

"My name Jackie, like Jackie Chan."

"Well, I'm changing it. To me you'll be Tiger, like Tiger Woods. Greatest almost-black golfer the world's ever seen. So, see you this evening, Tiger."

The boy was confused, but he'd met a lot of peculiar *moosoongoos* in his brief but miserable life. This one was paying, so he could call him anything he liked. He followed his smile out into the sunshine.

John always found some way of changing the street names of the kids he worked with. The name was a large part of the identity they hid behind. It was the tough-guy image that supported the drug and sex habits. It was the image that repossessed the ten-year-old child and turned him into a pretend adult, ill prepared to understand the messed-up world.

John walked back into the garden to look at the pool pit. Back home, when a body was found, the police tended to look around, just in case another one turned up. He'd asked the Mombassa sergeant why they hadn't dug up the whole garden.

"It's hot, sir," he'd said, "and this is a very large garden. If such an operation were necessary, I fear I would have to do it all myself, as we are extremely short staffed." And something in his tone added: "And this was only a street bum. And the perpetrator was a foreigner and has long since left the country, so why bother?"

John knew there had to be more bodies in that garden. He knew somebody would be digging it up, and he hoped to God it wouldn't be him.

He made two stops that afternoon. The first was to the real-estate agent who had rented out the villa. The lady confirmed that the person in the picture had been to the office four months earlier. He had paid the whole six months' rent in advance and pointed out that there was no reason to be disturbed during his stay. It was the direct connection between Aldy and the murders John had been looking for. It fortified his confidence and justified the journey.

His new mood made him aware of how attractive the real-estate agent was. He asked her questions the report didn't cover, and the handsome woman answered them patiently.

"Did you mention the pool to him by any chance?"

"The pool?"

"Yes, the pool. Did he know the owner was planning to put in a swimming pool?"

She looked through her files. "Yes. They'd already started the foundations. He had the option of the pool being installed immediately. But he said he didn't want workers running in and out. They could do it when he left. He didn't need a pool."

"Thank you."

So, The Paw knew there would be excavation. He knew the body would be discovered. He wasn't seriously trying to cover his tracks. He was leaving enough exposed to keep John struggling a few steps behind. Again he had the feeling that Aldy wanted his identity known, and was in some way co-ordinating the investigation for him.

-o-

Back at the hotel he spoke to Muthoga in Nairobi. He explained his theory and what he expected to find in the garden. The inspector was openly embarrassed that there hadn't been a more extensive search, and promised to get on to Mombassa straight away.

In the evening, Tiger came by the hotel an hour late. John docked him ten dollars from his salary. "You work for me and you come when I tell you, not when you feel like it."

The boy looked shell-shocked.

"Did you eat?"

"Yes, sir."

John knew there wasn't much point in asking him what he did with the rest of the down payment, and he probably didn't want to know anyway.

"All right. In a few minutes an artist is coming to make a sketch . . . a picture of your Chinaman." He didn't mention that the artist was attached to the local police. There was no love lost between the beachboys and the authorities. The kids were often beaten by the police. Some had complained that they'd been abused by them. But who could they go to when that happened?

"When that's done, you'll have all night and half of tomorrow to find me any kids who knew the Englishman and the Chinaman; anyone else who had an interview, or anyone who did jobs for him."

"Fucking?"

"Anything."

"All right, sir."

"And Tiger."

"Sir?"

"I think you're a smart kid. You've got a great future in front of you."

"Me?" He somehow looked in front of himself for it.

"Uh huh."

-o-

The next morning at 7:00, John wasn't the most popular person in Mombassa. Five police uniform shirts were hanging from the washing hoist. Their owners, already perspiring heavily after only ten minutes of hard labour, were reluctantly shoveling earth.

As he had no jurisdiction there, John sat on the rear doorstep with a cool beer and smiled at them. He didn't speak Kiswahili, but if this were South London, and he were a nosey Kenyan copper, he knew what the local lads would have been saying. So he smiled again and raised his bottle.

It took only another six minutes to find the second body, no more than five metres from where they'd found the first. It had long since given up its pretence of being a human being. It was gnarled and lumpy like a charred ginseng root. The earth had already blotted away its smell. It had once been an eight-year-old boy.

The discovery re-activated a case that hadn't been particularly active in the first place. Sergeant Moses was called back and the search took on a more optimistic-cum-pessimistic air. When the press arrived, the digging officers proudly displayed their sweat for the photographs, and expressed their deepest concern over the situation. If it had been John's investigation, the hacks wouldn't have been there stuffing up the crime scene at all.

But it wasn't, so he returned to the cool of the sunless kitchen, took another beer from the fridge, and awaited the inevitable body count. There was no question in his mind now that the boys he'd seen on the slide screen in their last minutes of life were now carcasses in the back yard. Apart from one very serious error, his hunches played out. They would find all five of the other boys before lunchtime. But the next body uncovered was that of an adult. John had told the major they'd probably find one.

Given The Paw's track record, it was inevitable that the Chinaman, having outlived his photographic usefulness, would have been planted out there alongside his models. When the officer came in to report the find, John was feeling smug. Always a mistake for a policeman.

"You want a job in Mombassa?"

"You found the man?"

"Yes, but I think you'd better come and take a look at this."

John followed him outside and over to the heap that had just been excavated. It was peculiar how the dry earth had shrunk and mummified the bodies over a relatively short period. In England they would have been moist, putrid, and crawling with maggots for many more months yet.

John sank to his haunches to stare the Chinaman in the face and look for any leftover secrets on his mind. But when that face stared black-browed and hollow-eyed back at him, he tumbled back into the legs of a cameraman. The air suddenly became oppressive to the point where he struggled to catch his breath. The press corps attempted to help him to his feet, but he shrugged them off. He wasn't confident to stand on his own legs as long as the meatless face and empty eye-sockets of Marcus Aldy stared back at him.

10

John sat in a dark corner of the hotel coffee shop waiting for Tiger. He craved alcohol, but knew this was the worst time to get into it. Even sober he was no match for whichever demon was orchestrating his chaos. But he wasn't leading in his waltz with drink either, so he let it have its way.

Even a fourth whiskey drowned in Pepsi hadn't been able to sweeten the memory of Aldy's bitter smile, or remove the taste of his own victimization. This evening, on a day when six bodies had been removed from the earth, John considered himself more of a victim than any of them

The recent postcards had been sent after Aldy's death. So, was the Chinaman The Paw, or was he one more token? And Tiger? Was that all set up, too? Had The Paw arranged for him to be there at the house? He really didn't know what or who to believe.

Ten minutes early, while John was still hating him, the boy appeared at the table. He wore a smile that was uncharacteristically real.

"I do very well, sir."

"Sit down, Tiger."

"And I early. Do you back me ten dollar from time before?"

"Depends." John looked deep into his intoxicated eyes and could see no obvious treason. He took out the artist's pad and flipped to the sketch Tiger had described the previous day. It was now a thousand times more important than it had been then. It showed a man with bad, dark skin and cropped white hair. The prominent feature was a large pair of sunglasses

"Couldn't you do any better than this?"

"How?"

"Well, couldn't you perhaps describe him when he wasn't wearing the glasses?"

"He always wearing."

"Night time, too?"

The boy was losing his smile and his temper. "I never see him at night. Only day."

"If you didn't see his eyes, how do you know he was Chinese?"

Tiger was offended by both the ridiculous question and the tone of the interrogation. He stood and leaned over the table like someone twice his age. "You put Raybans on me, you stop knowin' I African?" He turned to walk away. "And my name Jackie."

John stood and called to him. "Tiger, wait. I'm sorry. Please come back."

The boy walked a few more paces before turning back to look at John. It was the first time an adult had ever apologized to him, and he liked it.

"What you say?"

"I said I'm sorry."

Tiger raised an eyebrow in contempt, smiled at the other customers, but returned to the table and sat down.

"Did you find me any boys?"

"I find four," he replied in a sulky voice.

"Four? That's great. Good man."

Tiger held in his smile.

"Where are they?"

"Outside. I bargain them down to twenty dollar each."

"Twenty dollars?" John smiled so as not to show that the remains of his last day's budget had just been appropriated. "Good deal. How well did they know him . . . the Chinaman?"

"Same me."

"Just the interview?"

"Yes, sir. I think the Chinaman don't touch no boys."

"Not one?"

"No. Only the *moosoongoo* with lipstick do fucking. He come back from last year. I were his boy one time last year."

"You? You said you didn't know him."

"I say I don' know him this year. Not really lying, right? This year he come with the Chinaman. I don' see him this time, but these boy say he drunk a lot." He looked down at John's half bottle.

"Tiger. Have you heard what happened in that house?"

"Yes, sir. I hear. Everybody hear." He unleashed his smile. "I guess I'm lucky I fuck up the interview, right?" The tough guy was doing all the talking, but the nine-year-old inside couldn't prevent a tear from welling up.

"I'm sorry, mate. I guess some of them were your friends."

"No place for friends in this world, sir. More you love, more you hurt." That single tear freed itself from his eye and crawled down his cheek. He slapped at it as if it were an annoying insect.

"Okay, Tiger. Let's go and meet the lucky ones." He stood and held out his hand. The boy could have shaken it like they did on the street. But instead he took it and held on to it tightly. They walked out of the restaurant hand-in-hand, and all the other customers thought they knew what they were going to do, but preferred to say nothing. As always.

11

As John was boarding the Kenyan Airlines flight to Gatwick, a meeting was taking place on the other side of the world. In a small wooden office in Chiang Mai in the north of Thailand, an attractive young Asian woman sat before three men. Despite their age, not one of them could wrestle down the fluttering in their old hearts. Her hair was cut short and she wore no make-up, but she was lovely.

The three represented the ethnic minorities in conflict with the Burmese junta. One was Mon, one Karen, and one Karenni. They asked their questions in English. She answered in a perfect Boston accent, even though she hadn't begun to speak English until she was nine. She was remarkable in many other ways, also.

But to the three members of the National Health Committee, it was her medical certificate and her willingness to work for next to nothing that were her most powerful attributes. The dedicated and often brilliant floating board members of the NHC represented health workers all along the Burmese border and deep into Mon territory. They had limited funds and no guarantees of safety. Some of these men and women in exile who worked tirelessly for their homelands would have received awards and prizes had they been born anywhere else. Here, playing hide and seek with the Burmese military, they were just happy to receive regular meals and a modicum of respect.

The Thais tolerated their presence on Siamese soil, ostensibly because the world was monitoring their levels of humanitarian concern over their minority neighbours. Some argued that the Thai military also needed to keep the border keepers happy so as not to disrupt unofficial border trade. But whatever the reason, those living and working at the NHC headquarters were registered and legal temporary residents in Chiang Mai. The Thai undercover officer in the garage opposite had photographs of everyone who entered the bland, unmarked suburban house. His latest catch was a real babe. They'd love her back at Fifth Army HQ Intelligence.

The three men on the committee had little doubt from the moment she'd sat down that she would be the new medical officer. The fact that she spoke Karen was a considerable plus. She would be spending a good deal of time traveling through Karen areas between the refugee camps at Mae Hong Son, Mae Sariang, and Mae Sot. These camps alone were home to some 80,000 refugees displaced by the junta.

They had been forced from their homelands for political reasons they weren't able to understand. Many arrived on the Thai side with physical and mental ailments the volunteer medical personnel on the border couldn't begin to cope with. Any qualified help they could afford was more than welcome. They congratulated the woman on her appointment.

She told them her name was Shirley, but not that it used to be Sherri. There were other things they didn't know about her. There was information she had withheld that may have influenced them against her. She hadn't mentioned for example that she spoke the language of their enemies as well as she spoke English. She had also neglected to mention that her main reason for returning to the area was not to cure, but to kill.

12

When Emma Yardly was there to meet him at Gatwick, John knew there had to be bad news. He immediately feared for his sister.

"Susan and—"

"No, John. I haven't heard from them. There's something else. We'll talk in the car." But John didn't want to talk in the damned car. He wanted to know immediately. The walk to Short-Stay took an age, and finding her Mazda took another. When they were at last seated, he reached across to stop her turning over the engine.

"What is it?"

Emma looked through the windscreen at the concrete wall she'd embarrassed with her headlights. "It's Mick."

"Oh shit. What's he done now?"

She looked across at him. "He's dead, John."

"Oh, Jesus." He shook his head but showed little surprise. "Stupid kid. How?"

"It was nothing he did. He was at your place. The autopsy said he was clean. No dope. No booze. He was clean as a whistle. His. . . ." She coughed unnecessarily and looked John in the eye for the first time. "His throat was slit."

"What?"

"Your place is a mess."

"A break in?"

"John, it was The Paw."

John slammed his fist into the glove box. The flap dropped open on one hinge. Emma chose to say nothing. That name. That damn name again. Why? What could he have done to the man that was so terrible? Of course he would go for Mick. Why hadn't he realized when he got the card from Kingston? The 'idle youth' crack should have told him.

"What have I done to him, Em? What do I have to do to release myself?" And to the absolute shock of his super—for Mick, and for himself—John Jessel burst into tears. It was so unexpected and so un-Jessel, she was forced to turn away. She had never seen the man inside the man, and there were no appropriate condolences. She waited him out, instinctively feeling that was the best way. It was a long wait.

Once he had purged himself of the despair, his mind returned to the car and he smiled at his boss. Her puffy eyes smiled back.

"They don't make glove boxes like they used to." He flicked the dangling flap, and they both laughed as it swung back and forth on its last screw like a hanged man in a strong wind.

They went directly from the airport to the apartment. Emma had brought copies of the crime-scene report, the autopsy, and the witness interviews. John went through them in the car. The killing had taken place just two days earlier. They hadn't been able to contact him in Mombassa because the phones were out.

The murder squad had pieced together what had happened. The perpetrator must have come to the door and slashed a blade across the boy's throat as he answered the bell. There was a great deal of blood on the wall beside the door. As the knife had shredded the boy's larynx, there would have been no audible cry. The boy must have staggered back and collapsed on the couch. That was now crusted brown from several liters of blood that had drained from Mick together with his life.

From there, he was stripped, dragged to the carpet, and tattooed. It was carefully done and would have taken some time. There was no evidence of sexual assault. The place hadn't been ransacked, and nothing of value appeared to be missing. And through all this, the Paw had neither left prints nor alerted the neighbours. Not even 17A.

The time of death was put at 2:00 p.m., yet nobody recalled seeing a stranger in the building at that time nor hearing a commotion. He had floated in and out like a nightmare.

John called Aunt Maud on the car phone and got an assurance that Susan and Eddo were safe and well, and he felt temporarily relieved. This news was not only balm for his conscience, it was also the only tangible evidence he had that The Paw was not all-powerful. Or, at least it left him with some hope that he wasn't. It was vital at this point to believe that the devil was not invincible.

-o-

The ailing Victorian building had no lift, so they walked up the creaking steps to John's fifth-floor flat. When he unlocked the door, the stench of congealed blood rushed into their faces and forced them two paces back. Emma put her handkerchief to her nose and went in first to open the window. John followed her and stared dispassionately at the bloodstains on the sofa as if they may offer up their secrets to him.

"What are you going to do with this place, John?"

He answered as if he'd already decided. "Re-decorate."

"You aren't going to stay here?"

"Why not?"

"John, he knows you're here. He could come back anytime. He's already killed one person here."

"So the answer is I keep running? I quit my job? Because he knows about that too, you know. I keep my family hidden away forever? No. That wouldn't work, Em. He could have killed me anytime, but he wants me around for some reason. He doesn't want me dead yet. I'm last . . . 'after the girls.' He quoted the postcard. He wants me tormented. So I'm staying put. I'll go and see my sister and my nephew for a day or so though, if that's okay with you. Before I start work."

"Work. . . ? John, you're the target of a murderer. How could you concentrate on other cases?"

"'Cause I'm a professional. And because I have an interior decorator to feed. It'll be nice to fix this dump up."

Emma was once again amazed by the man. The outburst in the car was out of his system. Now, John was treating this like any other case. She watched him walk around the flat as if he was on the job. It could have been anybody else's place, anybody else's friend laid out on a slab. There was no more sadness for the boy he had come to like very much. He methodically went through his things to see whether anything was missing, but there was nothing out of place.

"Okay, boss. All done here. What say we go look for the detective who's handling this case and ask him a couple of questions?"

"You're a most peculiar person, John Jessel," she said, half to herself, and followed him out of the flat.

13

"I'm starting to feel like Salman Rushdie."

Susan was sitting in the living room of the beautiful Elizabethan cottage in the grounds of Mendleton House. John and their mother sat on the plastic-coated settee opposite her.

"You're starting to look like him, too," their mother put in without any pretence at humour. "A little grooming wouldn't come amiss, dear. Being a refugee is no excuse for letting yourself go."

John snorted and Susan feigned to chuck a scatter cushion at the old girl. They were on their second bottle of red, and Susan was just starting to get over the shock of John turning up with their mother of all people. It wasn't a decision John had been able to make for himself. He certainly didn't want her there. But she was just as likely a target as any of them, and he wanted her out of harm's way. He and Aunt Maud had arranged a place for her in the country. To nobody's surprise, she had refused point-blank.

"If I can survive the war against the communists, I'm certainly not afraid of some psychopath. Let him come for me. See what he gets."

They knew she'd been nowhere near a war in her life. The toughest thing about the old lady was her tongue. Her armour was counterfeit. She could have been vanquished by a stiff breeze. But her pig-headedness was unyielding. John knew there was no point in trying to change her mind.

Colleta was an elegantly wrinkled woman in her sixties. When she first seduced her selected husband, she had been a fragile Hungarian ballerina. It appears she wasn't a good enough ballerina to get out of the country on her talent. She needed a foreign husband. The groom she ended up with was a heavy, unremarkable insurance assessor representing a large British firm. His passport and his compliant nature were more important to her than his looks.

She'd originally intended to ditch him once she'd made her way in England. But he was away on business so often, and her lifestyle was so comfortable, that she didn't get around to it. One of the groom's trips home produced John Jessel, and one more left them with Susan. Then, before the children were old enough to remember him as more than just a curious visitor, he stopped coming home.

He was listed as the corporate version of 'missing in action,' and it was believed he had died of some tropical disease in Southeast Asia. His body was never recovered. Colleta received a very generous company pension to make up for her inconsiderable loss, and she went on to bring up her two children with style but very little motherly affection with the help of a parade of nannies. They all loved the children, but could stand very little of their obnoxious mother.

Despite a very expensive residential education, the children had turned out to be disappointments to Colleta. One was an overweight policeman of all things. The other had given up a promising career in the arts to marry an old hippy. She barely mentioned them to her social peers, and when she did, they were referred to as "the youngsters." They, in turn, hated her.

That afternoon in her apartment, John had made the mistake of telling the old girl he was on his way to see Susan and Eddo. She told him to wait a few minutes, and before he could make a run for the door, she was there in her hat and coat with her permanently packed overnight bag on her arm. He began to tell her how difficult the trip was going to be; the changes of vehicles, the false trails, but she looked right through him as she always had.

The tension of the journey was magnified a hundred-fold with the woman there complaining and giving out with her endless yacking. She blamed him of course for this mess they were all in. She blamed him for his mindless career decision. She even found ways to blame him for the dullness of her own life. As she droned away in the background, he recited the lyrics to himself of every Creedence Clearwater Revival song he could remember, and wondered how he could get her address to The Paw.

As a copper he remained focussed on the trip. He was confident that if anyone had begun to follow them, they certainly wouldn't be there now at this lovely place. The estate was everything tourists expected of an English country home. The lawns were cropped and emerald green. The flowers in their beds were lined up and spaced out like a legion of brightly plumed Roman soldiers. But the main house was being renovated in a way that would render it more Elizabethan than when it was built. The company empowered with the security during the closure was headed by an ex-CID man who owed Aunt Maud one or two favours. That's how Susan and Eddo got themselves into the gamekeeper's cottage off the main lawn.

Eddo was out on the grass, playing cricket with the gardeners. So it was just the three of them in the Glad-wrapped room: one comically bitter old lady and her two under-achieving offspring. Their rare family gatherings invariably ended in acrimony. But things seemed to be going well. Perhaps it was the tension of their enforced victimization, or the buzz from the wine. But there was something softer than usual in their mother's tone that encouraged the youngsters to be naughtier than they would normally dare.

One of the few things they had in common was their mysterious father, although Colleta was rarely in the mood to talk about him. When they were growing up, John and Susan would make up stories about him. In their pre-sleep world, he would have families like theirs all over the globe. He was a pirate and a spy. He was an international arms dealer, and a secret astronaut. They liked their make-believe father much more than the dull stocky man in the photos: the man who had rudely died before they had a chance to love him.

"Come on, Colleta, he must have had some redeeming qualities." John had his stockinged feet up on a circa-1572 mahogany table. His mother slipped a copy of *Horse and Hound* under them and grumbled about his lack of respect for history. The ambience in the room suited her.

"He was completely without personality." Her blunt reply surprised them both. She was lisping slightly from the wine. It was no doubt causing chemical reactions with the vat of pills inside her. "He would come home unexpectedly after a four-month absence, have nothing to say of his journey, and retire to his room to recover from ever lengthening bouts of jetlag."

"You'd think he'd be feeling horny after being away from his bit of skirt for so long wouldn't you?" Susan suggested, winking at John.

"How did you ever get so crude, girl? I do not know where you get it from. Certainly not me. Your father, I must tell you, was not an emotionally active man."

"Well he must have activated a bit of emotion to produce us," John offered.

"He rarely wandered into my garden of delights."

She had said it so straight-laced that despite themselves, the youngsters fell into fits of laughter. Such a comment was totally out of place from this woman who had never talked to them as equals. Colleta allowed herself a coquettish smile and sipped at her wine.

"Perhaps the garden gate was locked," said John.

"Or the gardener was already in there pottering around," Susan added.

Colleta blew wine out through her nose and the three of them laughed till they cried. Eddo came running in to see what he'd missed, but none of them could contain themselves. He left again in a Jessel huff, which just made them laugh more.

It had been a surprisingly good meeting. It was the best Susan and John could remember.

It would be their last.

-o-

As John and Colleta were leaving the next day, there was very nearly a group hug. Colleta managed to pull out just in time. Instead, she air-kissed the offspring and allowed Eddo to briefly put his arms around her neck. John and his sister held on to each other for the longest time. She squeezed his hand tightly through the car window. There were a lot of things they didn't need to say. They had grown up parenting one-another and had an inborn, ant-to-ant understanding.

When finally, after an endless journey home, they pulled up in front of the tall terrace in Knightsbridge where he'd grown up, all John wanted to do was drop the old girl off. She insisted he come up. It was a pain because it took him half an hour to find somewhere to park and walk back.

"This had better be good, Colleta," he grumbled as he walked into the stylish apartment.

Nothing had changed, not even the exact position of the door key on the dresser in the hall. It was hard to imagine that this museum had once been disturbed by two children growing up. There was certainly no evidence of it .

"Come here, boy," she called. She was in the bedroom on her hands and knees, attempting to pull an old leather suitcase from beneath the bed.

He knelt down to help. "Going somewhere?"

"Not anymore. This old chap was the one I first brought with me from Budapest."

"Ooh. An antique."

"Don't be insolent. You aren't too old for a smacked bottom you know. Policeman or no policeman."

John giggled and put the suitcase on the bed. He went to open it but she put her hand over the catch.

"No, not now. Take it with you."

"What do I want with it?"

"You'll see. Now go away and let me have some rest. Your driving's given me a headache."

With the suitcase in his hands, he couldn't strangle her.

14

The smell of fresh paint was quite strong but it was too cold to open the window. John liked the way his place looked now. Even the old furniture seemed more welcoming. The bloodstained couch had gone to the dump and been replaced by a second-hand, peach-coloured sofa. It had influence. It made things in the room that had previously just been old and mismatched, look chic. Even the mouldy cupboards blended in. He felt chic himself, arty.

He grabbed a beer and wrestled with the rusty locks on the old suitcase until they sprang open. Inside was full of old stuff. An old-stuff smell drifted up into the room and did combat with the paint fumes: a duel of old and new.

As soon as John realised what was contained in that old case, it became treasure. The scent was one of anticipation. But he felt guilty to be rummaging through the case without his sister beside him. That crazy old lady had kept mementos of their father—though she'd never seen a need to share them with her children.

There was the wedding photo in faded shades of brown with its two unsmiling, unloving principle players. There were a dozen or so square snaps of events from their early life surrounded by a lot of people who appeared happier than them. Mother always had that 32-teeth cocktail smile. Father always looked like he'd just woken up in a strange bed. He looked exceedingly dull. The thought of having a boring father worried John more than having a dead one.

He went through the few personal documents and legal papers the man had left behind. There were picture postcards from India, Singapore, Vietnam, and Thailand, all asking her to give his love to John and Susan and signing off with an unconvincing, "*love, Jim.*" It was all trivial stuff. None of them actually said what he was doing or when he would be back. He must have been a frustrating man to be married to. The couple deserved each other.

There were one or two letters from the company he'd worked for. They talked about superannuation and increments and long service bonuses, but they didn't mention his father, the person.

It was 2:00 a.m. by the time he'd gone through everything. He still didn't know what his father did for a living. He had to be at work by 7:00, but there was something to be done before he could sleep.

He felt the Imperial Insurance Company owed him more than the brief letter of condolence they'd included with the cheque. They owed him an identity. They had an obligation to fill in the missing pieces of the memory of his father. So he wrote to them and claimed his inheritance.

15

Under the flickering flame of an oil lamp, Shirley signed her name to the letter. Tears had streamed from her eyes from the first stroke of her pen. Grief came with every word, with each memory. From behind the flimsy rattan wall, the troubled groaning of malaria victims was apt music to accompany her confession.

She had always believed her final therapist would be a lover or an understanding colleague. But she had been too entangled in her studies to respond to any of the offers from men. There had been no lovers, and she doubted now there could ever be.

This letter to a woman she didn't know would have to be her salvation. Those dreadful years had been held inside, trapped like a bear in a bamboo cage. It strained to get loose, growing bigger until there was no more room to move. Until tonight, the bear had been wearing its cage painfully like a girdle.

I was too shocked to move: too stunned to scream . . .

. . . it began. And on she wrote. And with the writing came a slow release. It oozed from her like puss from a sore and was absorbed by the blackness outside her lamplight. Words she had never spoken, never thought aloud, were seeping out of her and onto the flimsy paper. It surprised her how it was able to bear the weight of them. She wrote all of it. All the details and the feelings. She wrote until it was all out and the bear stretched its knotted limbs and she stopped crying. The bunched bandages in her hand were sodden from tears.

She thought at first she would read over what she had written. But her words were only words. It was like reading someone else's sorry story. It was a poor, two-dimensional version of the reality. But it would do.

A patient called to her from the ward. She folded the pile of airmail sheets and put them back into her medical satchel. She locked it and slipped the key into the pocket of her shorts. The first part of her home-made therapy was over with.

16

The Paw case had gone nowhere. It was stalled. The murder of Mick had led to the involvement of Scotland Yard. Four detectives had interviewed John and taken copies of his evidence. They all promised to keep him up to speed on their findings, and he promised to pass on anything that came in.

But it had been a month and he'd heard nothing from them or from The Paw. Far from being a relief, it was a time of tension. Anticipation can be more terrible than terror itself. Susan and Eddo were still in hiding. Every doorbell ring, every letter delivery, every phone call threatened. Every day without aggression built up the tension in him to a peak of horrible expectation. He knew that when it came, it would make the previous horrors seem trivial. All his non-working hours were spent hiding behind a barricade of drink.

His normal duties filled his days, although he could find little of his old enthusiasm. He deliberately held back from making friends with the kids in case he was being watched. He handed sensitive cases over to the others for fear of breaching security, and everyone was being so damned sensitive and understanding to him. They all bowed to his demands at staff meetings and backed down in arguments. It was like being an invalid.

He was further insulted by the bloody Imperial Insurance Company. They sent another form letter stating that Mr. James Jessel had been in the employ of the IIC for 18 years, from 1963 to 1981. He had been a reliable employee, and—in case we'd forgotten—the total sum of 102,000 pounds of accumulated increments plus insurance premiums had already been paid to his widow, etcetera.

It shat him totally that they could be so cold about it. He'd been a loyal member of the company for all those years. Surely someone there could have added a personal note. All right the man wasn't Mr. Personality, but somebody must have liked him; remembered him at least. Finding that person became a quest.

-o-

They wrapped up a case early one afternoon. The known paedophile they were supposed to run a three-man surveillance on for a week, decided to stop off at a primary school and drag a bemused child into a toilet. John and Somersbee were on him like hogs on a truffle.

They had photos, two expert police witnesses, and a tearful confession. The paperwork was all done in a couple of hours. So John decided to take a ride into town. The Imperial Insurance Company occupied an elegant terrace with a view of the grounds of the Natural History Museum. The brass plaque attached to the front railing said 'money,' but the door didn't say 'come in.' It was locked. He pressed the bell beside an ancient speaker, and there was a long and annoying silence before a bored metallic voice said, "Yes?"

John looked down at the letter in his hand. "I've come to see Mrs. Wise."

"Mrs. Wise is away at our Singapore branch." He should have added, "Can I help you?" But he didn't bother.

"Well, Mrs. Wise suggested I stop by and talk to someone."

"That isn't very likely."

"It isn't? You mean there isn't anyone I can talk to?"

"Not really. There isn't anyone here at the moment."

"No. . . ? What about you? Or are you speaking from your Hong Kong branch?"

"I suggest you put your request in writing and—"

"My request is to come in." He contemplated affixing the words 'dick brain.'

"That isn't possible I'm afraid."

"Isn't. . . . What type of insurance company are you that doesn't talk to people?"

"Not that kind. Now if you'll excuse me."

Before John had a chance to excuse him or anything else, there was a thud from the speaker and it was dead.

It wasn't exactly what he'd expected. He thought he'd be sitting down with old Jenkins from the shipping department and hearing all the stories about good old dad over a cup of tea.

Through the grubby uncurtained windows, it appeared the ground floor was empty. In fact there were no curtains until the third and fourth floors. He could have just made that with a small brick. What exactly did "not that kind of insurance company" mean? What kind of insurance company didn't need people?

He pressed the buzzer again, but nobody answered. He pressed again, then leaned on the button. Nothing.

IIC was in the centre of the terrace. Getting in the back way would have meant climbing over 17 back-yard walls. Even if he'd been in shape, which he certainly wasn't, it would have still taken most of the evening. In his present condition it was 16 too many. But there was hope. Two houses down, there was a very upmarket travel agency. He flashed his badge at a girl whose hair was skewered to the top of her head with a chopstick, and walked through to the back. She rolled her eyes as if it happened all the time.

The yard was full of bottles, and the wall was eight feet high. He needed all three of the wine crates to get himself over. The old mattress in the next yard was mildewed and stank to heaven and back, but it looked soft.

It barely broke his fall. But it did come in handy to throw over the broken glass and barbed wire that topped the wall to the IIC. They certainly weren't *that* kind of insurance company. He arrived unwanted and breathless in their yard at about the same moment the testosterone wore off. He really wished he wasn't there.

He sat on a rustic rockery to catch his breath and a whiff of common sense. He didn't have a warrant, and they could already do him for breaking and entering. There was an alarm over the back door and both the windows were wired. What he should do now, he decided, was run through to the front of the building and away. But he didn't have time to think about all that.

He caught sight of the micro-surveillance camera just as the door flew open. Young men in shirtsleeves and ties stampeded down the steps towards him. He wasn't about to fight them, but he could tell they weren't there to negotiate. Two of them grabbed his arms. He felt a pinprick in his thigh.

17

Mr. Jessel. Mr. Jessel, can you hear me?"

John squinted at the woman leaning over his bed. She had some kind of sauce on the lapel of her white coat.

"You a doctor?"

"Yup."

"Did I do something silly?"

"You got drunk and fell on your head."

"I don't remember."

"With a bump that size, I'm surprised you remember what a doctor is."

But he really didn't remember. Anything. Oh, The Paw was in there of course, and the dead African boys. But details . . . he was missing details. When the doctor left him alone, he tried; he really tried to put some pieces together. It was March 12th. The last date he could put facts to was the 8th. Even then he had to concentrate . . . squeeze the memories out. What in hell's name had he been drinking, and why?

Emma came by in the afternoon, acting more than ever like an agony aunt. She held his hand and spoke in whispers. He felt like a corpse. She reminded him about the primary-school toilet arrest the previous day. She told him how they'd finished the paperwork early, and he'd announced that he had some business to take care of. It was all news to John.

"The police picked you up at three a.m. in Soho. You were slumped in an alley, bleeding from the head, and drunk as Lord Glenlivet. Incredibly, given the locale, you still had your wallet on you with twenty pounds in it. Your driving license was gone, but you could have left that in some bar."

He detected contempt beneath the caring. "Really, Em, I have no recollection at all of the last few days."

"All the drink catches up on you eventually."

"It's never been like this. I've been known to forget the night itself, but never the whole week leading up to it. What could have sent me on such a bender?"

"You've been under a lot of strain. Something had to give eventually, John. This Paw thing would have got to any of us."

He wanted to slap her. Instead he let her review the previous four days before leaving him alone to his confusion.

It was a blank, and it remained so, even after the sloppy doctor told him he was okay and could go home. The Soho coppers didn't push the drunk and disorderly charge, and Emma gave him a week of sick leave to get himself together. But how do you begin to get yourself together when you don't know where you left the pieces?

A drunk, a slob, a bum he may have been, but above all he was a policeman. And even on leave, professional policemen don't stop asking questions. Questions like: How do you get blind drunk in Soho and still have twenty quid in your wallet? He never carried much more than that. Not even on payday. Where was he going that was so urgent he'd leave work in the middle of the afternoon? What volume and strength of booze would it take for someone of his capacity to lose most of a week? And where was his bloody car?

He found himself rattling around his flat like a loose screw in a gearbox. The drink cupboard was stocked. There were cold lagers in the fridge. He had powerful cravings to get stuck into them. But instead he brewed tea . . . and thought.

He thought about his father and wondered why those bastards at the insurance company hadn't replied to his letter. But most of all he thought about The Paw and wondered whether this was all his doing. What if he'd met him? What if it was The Paw he'd been going to meet that afternoon? Where the hell was his memory?

With so much time on his hands, he was able to get really bogged down in thought, and wondering, and tea. The cravings stopped being just mental, and started to hurt him. The apartment with its smelly paint wasn't helping.

Emma wouldn't let him go to work, but she couldn't stop him following up on investigations of his own. The insurance company was somewhere up town. He could go and see them, have tea with old Jenkins in shipping and hear stories about his good old dad. All he needed was the address.

He went to the wardrobe and stood on the chair. His balance wasn't functioning properly. It took him three attempts to stand upright. His mother's small brown suitcase wasn't up there among the junk. He must have put it somewhere else. But in a two-room apartment there aren't so many elses. He looked in the few likely places, then the totally unlikely ones. But it wasn't there. He knew he'd brought it home from his mother's. He had written to the IIC. So where was it now?

He sat on his peach-coloured sofa and raked through his scattered memories. Was that the important business? Had he taken the suitcase somewhere? Back to his mother? He called the old girl, who informed him he was a disgrace and quite mad. He called Aunt Maud, who warned him that the direction his life was heading was one of destruction. He told him quite frankly that he owed it to his sister to lay off the drink and tackle the situation with a clear head. John surprised himself by agreeing and meaning it.

He walked to the mirror. At the point where his hair was shaved there were five stitches curving over a bump, like an insect sunbathing on a stone. It was a neat straight line. It was nothing like conflict with a broken bottle or a kerb. Just a nice straight line and a bump, as if he'd run headfirst into a metal ruler.

"Come on, copper," he urged himself. "Give me some answers." But he had to wait several days for them.

18

Those were hard days and sleepless nights when the booze he'd been through in his life let him know that it had symbiotic interests in him. It had moved into his body and now possessed great chunks of it. It wasn't about to be evicted or deprived of the companionship of those other bottles over the sink.

He sweated and wrestled with it and it nipped at his nerve endings. He rattled and twitched and shook without control. The cravings were more powerful than any he'd felt before, and it took all of his discipline to stand before the bottles and tell them they wouldn't be able to humiliate him anymore.

"Just one last taste," they begged. "Just one final, delicious swig to sign off." It was close. So many times he was ready to listen to them. His hand would reach for them as if it weren't connected to his mind.

He awoke from some twenty minutes of sleep on the afternoon of his third day of abstinence. The doorbell was so much louder without the alcohol fuzz in his ears. With the memory of Mick clear in his mind, he took up the iron bar from the end of his bed and crept silently to the door. After one deep breath he threw it open and jabbed the weapon towards the figure in the doorway.

Emma Yardly staggered backwards into the balcony. John dropped the metal and ran forward to catch her arm and stop her toppling backwards down the stairwell. She had an expression of horror on her face.

"Holy Mother, John. I don't know whether I should call for a psychiatrist or an exorcist. What's happened to you?"

"What do you mean, Em?" His voice was hoarse. It was the first time he'd spoken for 72 hours. He invited her inside and she entered reluctantly. He could see fear or sadness or something in her eyes.

"John, have you looked at yourself recently?"

He hadn't. During the combat he had taped the *News of the World* over the bathroom mirror. He didn't want to see that face of his. At some stage the image had joined forces with the demons to talk him out of his foolishness. The man in the mirror wanted him to drink.

He went into the bathroom, tore off the newspaper, and looked in amazement at the corpse that stared back at him. He could see that as they were leaving, the ghosts of Johnnie and Gordon and Stella and Captain Morgan and all the rest had taken with them the characteristics they'd let him use, and left him with the frame.

The hair and stubble on his head were clinging to a hollow grey skull. The puffiness hung down like folds of pastry dough, and his eyeballs were shot with blood from lack of sleep. He was scary looking: almost frightened himself. He probably didn't smell too good either. No wonder the super had opted to stay by the door.

He walked from the bathroom with a broad smile, and to her amazement he started to laugh.

She reached for the door handle. "John. I'll come back some other—"

"Hang on, Em. I know how this looks." He went and sat down. His skin had acquired a bronze stain from the unknown gallons of tea he'd consumed. He was colour co-ordinated with the peach couch. "This is good."

"It is?"

"Yes. This is what I look like without drink."

"Jesus! We should get you down the pub right away. How are you feeling?" She came to join him on the couch. She saw his hands shaking, and an involuntary tic at the corner of his eye, and understood what he was going through.

"I never felt this awful while I was drinking. Now I know what the kids have to go through at detox. I've a new-found respect for the ones that got through it."

"Are you through it, John?"

"No. But I think I know the way to the end."

"You need some help."

John knew it wasn't just words. She really would go through it with him. He could have talked her out of it, but if the truth were to be told, he needed someone there with him. He went to kiss her cheek, but she got to her feet in a hurry.

"Don't even think about getting any closer till you've had a shower, Jessel. You stink."

"Right. So this isn't the caring and sharing rehab programme you're offering then?"

"It's the 'burn that bloody T-shirt and put the kettle on' approach."

She stayed for the rest of the afternoon; called in sick for only the second time in her career. It was surprisingly good to have her there. They talked about things that were important to each of them. Sometimes they just sat. She read. He twitched. The shower, the meal she cooked, the company, it all felt right, and when the sun slid down the grimy window-pane and she walked to the door, she had a feeling he would actually be able to sleep. Wrapped in his blanket, clean and combed, he looked like a newborn animal. He met a new Emma, one he should have trusted with the safety of his sister.

"Don't see me out," she said as she opened the door and stepped into the hall. "Oh, by the way. The people at the Royal Albert Hall would like you to go and pick up your car from their car park." When she quietly clicked the door shut, 17A was standing in her own doorway.

"You with the social services?" she asked Emma.

"Sort of. Why?"

"I could tell you some of the filth that one gets up to in there."

Emma smiled. "Oh, you don't have to tell me. I'm having an affair with him. He's a real beast." She snarled at the busy woman with her moustache of grey fuzz and skipped off down the stairs.

19

He had only slept in fits. When the sun rose, John watched the shadows crawl down his kitchen wall. He felt awful. He felt that if he ever moved from that room, all his organs and body parts would head off in different directions. But he had to go out.

He had been thinking or dreaming about the news of his car and it was important he should go to find it. Like a man of 148, he walked carefully to the station and took the train up town.

They were renovating the Albert Hall, and needed to put up scaffolding. Someone from security had called the police to ask whether the officer who parked there could move his car. A trace of the number produced John. When he arrived at the mews behind the Hall, the guard on duty recognized him immediately.

"I thought you was never comin' back. You bin sick or somethin'? You look bloody 'orrible."

"Remember me, do you?"

"Never forget a face, me. 'Specially the law. I'm an ex copper meself, you know?"

John knew that was either a lie or a confession. Police don't become car park attendants unless they've been incompetent, or very naughty. "Really? Well, let's see if you still have your touch, shall we? Tell me everything you remember about that day I brought the car here."

"You serious?" The man's eyes sparkled at the challenge. He grinned and held his chin as all good detectives do when they think. "All right. Let's see. . . . It was about 'alf three, right?"

"You tell me."

"Eh? Oh, right. It was definitely 'alf three. You flashed your badge and asked me where you could park that wouldn't get bricks and debris falling on your motor. You was moanin' about the bastards at the Natural 'Istory who wouldn't let you park there even if you was the bloody prime minister. Right?"

"Did I tell you where I was going?"

"You said you'd 'ave to walk all the way back, was all."

"Ah. You haven't lost it, Officer." John saluted like a starship commander.

The guard returned the salute, stood to attention, and clicked his heels. John wiped the brick dust from his windscreen, climbed into the car, and drove past him trying his best not to laugh.

For an hour he cruised the area looking for anything that would spark a memory. But nothing came. The bastards at the Natural History were still bastards and they didn't recognize him or allow him to park inside. Instead he parked on a double yellow behind the tube station and set off on foot. His fight with the bottles had left him weak, so he ambled along slowly and stopped periodically to look around.

It was completely by chance that he should find what he was looking for. The sun jumped out from behind a cloud and bounced some rays off a small brass plaque across the street. He stood for some while looking at the plaque and the building, but it wasn't until he crossed the street and read the name of the Imperial Insurance Company that he knew this was where he had come that day.

He tried the huge, oft-painted door, but it didn't yield. He pressed the buzzer, but it gave no sound. It occurred to him that being a Saturday, the staff probably wouldn't be at work anyway. But then a small surveillance camera above the door budged ever so slightly and he knew he was being watched.

Back at the car, he turned on the windscreen wiper to swish away the parking ticket. He was convinced that the IIC had been his destination four days earlier, and that something bad had happened there. Something so bad he had run over to Soho without his car and got totally rat-faced without spending any money. It must have been something serious.

The terraced building that housed the IIC had parking spaces in front, and parking meters. But such spots were so rare that most cars never left. The wealthy owners hired boys to feed the metres all day. So, John double parked, allowing one very narrow gap for traffic. His horn was shrill and very annoying, and brought everyone in the street to their widows to see who was leaning on it. Except for the IIC.

With a rubber band and a half packet of Halls cough drops, he found a way to put the horn on automatic, and left his car to be annoying by itself. He went to the door of the IIC office and tried the buzzer one more time. On this occasion, not only did it sound, it also produced a response.

"Inspector Jessel. We've been expecting you. If you'd be kind enough to disarm your hooter, I'll unlock the door for you."

By the time John had moved and quietened his car, the IIC door was ajar and he walked inside. But as soon as he closed the door behind him and started up the uncarpeted staircase, he was already wondering whether he really wanted to be there. Again he had told nobody where he was going, so he could vanish quite easily without any hope of rescue.

He walked up to the third floor, where a grey man in a grey suit with a grey tie was waiting for him. He held out a firm, dry hand for John to shake. There was something government about that hand and its owner.

"Please come in."

John followed the man into a windowless room but which had superlative taste to make up for the absence of daylight. In his physical state, John was pleased to be shown to an armchair and given time to catch his breath. The man interlocked his fingers and danced them up and down, apparently to give himself something to look at other than John.

At last he got his wind back. "Why do I get the feeling you're about to say things to me that can't go beyond this room?"

The man smiled at his dancing fingers. "There are far too many secret-service novels on the market. We've been plundered of every original statement we've ever made. Every time we open our mouths it's a cliché."

It was John's turn to smile.

The man had a broad Yorkshire accent and wouldn't have won a part in any spy film John had ever seen. "I knew we'd blown it when we couldn't find your car. The obvious place was the museum."

"They wouldn't let me park there."

"We hoped you'd left it at some tube station in the suburbs and come in by train. Then you wouldn't have made the connection. Where was it?"

"Royal Albert Hall."

"Damn. All right. What have you worked out so far?"

What John had worked out, he had done so between the ground and third floors of the IIC. Until then he'd been completely clueless.

"My dad was a spook."

"We prefer the term 'Secret Service operative.'"

Whatever it was called, once confirmed, John felt a sudden rush of pride and relief that his father wasn't boring. He went on: "IIC is your cover. Although I'm a bit confused as to why you'd put your address on the letters."

"Actually, we don't use this building very often. There's usually only someone here to divert inquiries. I came over just now when the secretary saw you. We assumed you'd be back. It seems you invaded us on a bad day this week. We were short of space so we used this office for an operatives meeting. Normally you wouldn't have found anyone here. I suppose you could say some of the lads overreacted a tad."

"The bump?"

"No. That we gave you after. Hope it doesn't hurt too badly. If I'd been here, I would merely have called the police and had you arrested for breaking and entry. But with all the terrorist scares at the moment, they decided to use you for homework."

"What do you mean?"

"What's the last thing you can remember?"

John was impressed. "Don't tell me the Secret Service can erase memory."

"You'd be surprised how easy it is with short-term memory. The skill is in judging the amount you're supposed to forget. It's a relatively new drug, and we aren't too sure what the long-term effects will be."

"Nice."

"Eventually I believe it will be possible to remove certain days or events. Sorry you had to lose a whole week."

"You couldn't wipe out the past five years could you?"

"Yes, quite. We've been following you pretty closely since you wrote. It must be a tricky period for you."

Tricky wasn't the word John would have used to describe it. "He's killing me bit by bit."

"And *he* is?"

"I thought you've been following this. The Paw. He's got the better of me."

"Ah. The Paw. But you see, The Paw isn't a *he*."

"Eh?"

"It's a place."

"A place. . . ? Where?"

"It's in the northeast of Burma, or Myanmar as the junta would have us call it."

John was speechless. The man reached down beside his chair and picked up a large, folded map. To John's surprise, he then got on his knees and started to unfold it on the rug between them. "It's here exactly. Thirty miles from Pa-an, just about there."

John joined him on the floor.

"This is a terrible transliteration. Very confusing. You pronounce it 'Tay'—rhymes with May—Pao. Karen language. It's not too far from the border of Thailand, see?"

To John, these were just marks on a map of an area he knew nothing about.

"It's also highly significant as far as you're concerned, as it's the last place we heard of your father being alive."

"My father?"

That was an unexpected connection. The man who had been tormenting his life and was now nameless, and his unknown father. They had suddenly united in a bizarre turn of events. This was already more than enough to take in, but the man hadn't finished.

"We were shocked when we found the reference to The Paw in your files. You understand of course, we had to run a check on you after your silly stunt the other day. You seem to have done very well in Kenya."

John didn't feel a need to say thank you.

"You've also done a very fine job of hiding your sister and her child. I trust they're safe."

That was a feather in Maud's cap: outsmarting the spooks.

"They're safe. What happened to my father?"

"He died. As to the events leading up to his death, we have no idea."

"What did he die of?"

"Cyanide."

"He was poisoned?"

"We assume he administered it himself."

"What?"

"It was standard issue at the time. Particularly for agents in hostile territory. If our people can't see any other way out of a mess, they can end it."

"What was he working on?"

"Can't really give you any details I'm afraid. Except to say that he was on the side of the minority groups who were then, and are still, fighting the Burmese military government. The world doesn't appear to have come alive to the atrocities the Burmese have been committing for the past thirty years. We tend to notice only the atrocities that suit us."

John looked down at the map as if he were mentally flying over the countryside. "So. This was a covert operation in a hostile country. I assume Her Majesty would have denied all knowledge of him if he'd been caught."

"Absolutely." He left the map where it was and climbed back into the leather chair. "All of our people know the risks."

"Did you know him?"

"Not well. I worked with him on a couple of missions. We were on pretty much the same rung of the ladder."

John looked into the grey eyes. "Did you like him?"

The man looked for his dancing fingers but couldn't find them. At last he said, "I won't pretend he was a loveable character. He was immensely efficient and dedicated, but he didn't let himself really like anyone. You couldn't get close to him. That said, there wasn't a man or woman in the service who didn't trust him with their lives completely. He was the ultimate professional, married to the job."

"So why did the Service leave his body to rot in Burma?"

"Pardon?"

"You knew he'd died of cyanide poisoning, so there had to have been an autopsy. To do an autopsy properly, you need a body. Mother was told he was missing in action somewhere in Asia. If you had a body, why the hell didn't you fly it home and allow the poor bugger his plot in Berkshire?"

The man looked embarrassed by the question. He nodded his head to show that he understood it, then shook it in such a way as to show that it was impossible. "The widow . . . your mother, would have had the legal right to view the body. We couldn't take that chance."

"Why? What was wrong with it?"

"Let's just say that it wasn't in a state an insurance man would expect to be found in." There was a pause that John brought to an end with his stare. "It was quite horribly mutilated."

Every new fact blew holes in John's perceptions of his father. "Are you quite sure it happened—"

"After the suicide. . . ? Yes. No question about it. Whoever left the body in that condition, did so long after the poison had taken effect. Cyanide is quite instantaneous. So, in fact, it was an act of gratuitous vandalism. Which may bring us back around to your Paw. . . Te Pao chap."

"You think he's getting back at me for something my dad did?" It was a bizarre idea, but at last it was an answer of sorts where before there had been none.

"It's quite possible. The person haunting you right now is obsessive. He's quite mad, but frighteningly clever. That's a combination we could do without."

John levered himself to his feet, walked around to the back of the seat, and leaned on it. "And you really have no idea who he is."

"None whatsoever."

"So. What do we do now?"

"We?"

"I assume you've been sharing this all with me so I can help you with the case."

The man chuckled slightly but checked himself. "So you can help. . . ? Mr. Jessel, there is no case. The Service's connection to this matter ended with the demise of your father in Thailand. When this meeting finishes, there will be no further dialogue."

"Oh no. You lot aren't getting out of it as easily as that. You're the cause of all this."

"Technically not, young fellow. Whatever happened to Jim Jessel had nothing to do with the Service. We could find no connection between his work and his death."

"You mean he just stumbled into a life-threatening situation on his day off?"

"Pretty much, yes."

John looked deep into the grey eyes and saw no hope of co-operation.

"I suppose you've considered that I could go to the newspapers with this and blow the story wide open?"

"Yes."

"What's to stop me?"

"Firstly, the press aren't going to be terribly interested in a twenty-year-old spy story that can't be verified. Espionage takes a distant back seat to boy bands in today's media. And, secondly. . . ." The man reached into his inside pocket and pulled out a folded document, which he held out to John. . . .

"This."

John walked over to the man's chair and took the paper from him. He unfolded it, read the title, and laughed. "You aren't serious. The Official bloody Secrets Act? You've already told me all the secrets. You're supposed to make me sign it *first*. Why on earth would I do so now?"

The man seemed to be searching desperately for a non-clichéd response. "Because it's the least barbaric way of guaranteeing your co-operation." He was obviously sorry to have had to say it, but there were no indications that it was merely a threat.

John had already experienced Service 'hospitality.'

He dropped back into his armchair, put his hands behind his head, and closed his eyes.

The man waited patiently.

When John's eyes opened at last, he had made a decision. "What's your name. . . ? 'M' or 'Q' or 'C' or something like that?"

"Commander Doyle."

"That's original. Well, here's the deal—"

"The deal? I don't—"

"I realize you may think I have nothing to deal with. But I know from experience what it takes to get blood out of a carpet, especially a beautiful Persian like this one. So I'm sure you'd prefer to end it all with a pen rather than a bullet. I know you'd rather we were civilized about it all. I'll sign your document and make it all neat, if you give me a contact from my old man's last mission."

"It's all still classified."

"I'm about to sign the Official Secrets Act, aren't I? Surely we can add a couple of other little secrets to the deal. Make it worth my while."

"How far do you intend to take this investigation, Mr. Jessel?"

"You seem to forget, Commander Doyle. This isn't an investigation. This is a fight for survival. It's life and death. My family can't live a normal life until I remove The Paw . . . Te Pao from it."

"And what resources do you have at your disposal?"

John laughed and fell back into the leather. "Resources? That's a good one. Well, let's see. I don't have the Surrey police force because Burma's slightly beyond their jurisdiction. I don't have the Secret Service because the case has passed its use-by date. I suppose all I have is two months' accrued leave and chronic cravings for alcohol. Do you think that'll be enough?"

The man indicated to the paper. "Sign it."

He did, and handed it back. "There. Now what's your name?"

The commander smiled. "Woods."

"How do you do, Commander Woods? I bet the men call you 'Woody,' right?"

-o-

On the pavement outside, John looked back up at the brick terrace. He considered it something of an achievement to have made it out the door alive and with a memory. He gazed up at the third floor and wondered how there managed to be windows outside but none inside. But then a lot of wondrous things had taken place inside the IIC. His world had expanded there. His father had been re-born there. And a reason for his affair with the devil had been established there. It was a truly magical place. But nobody passing there in the damp street knew how special it was.

And he couldn't tell anyone.

When John arrived back at his flat, still dizzy from Kensington and the day's exertions, his phone was ringing. He didn't hurry to open the front door or get inside to answer it because he was sure it would stop just as he picked it up. But it didn't.

"Mr. Jessel?"

"Yup."

"Mr. John Jessel?"

"Right. I know. I get one more question correct and I win a year's supply of Viagra."

"Mr. Jessel. I'm afraid I have some bad news for you. My name is WPC Helen Thompstone and I'm calling from WC1 Police Station. I'm terribly sorry, but I have to tell you that your mother passed away this afternoon."

20

If the truth were to be told, the old lady hadn't passed at all. She'd been sent: dispatched without mercy or respect. She'd had her throat cut. She had opened the door to her apartment to a stranger, but the reason for that had accompanied her to the morgue. The assailant had swiped a naked blade across her throat with such accuracy that her vocal cords had been severed but the bone was untouched.

John considered the situation. It would have taken her some time to die, and she had carefully chosen to bleed to death on the hall rug. Despite the apparent concern for the furnishings, she had been unable to prevent the blood from spilling over onto the parquet. That would now have to be replaced, and it was so expensive to get an exact match for the original.

He felt no guilt at parodying Coletta. These were the irreverent thoughts that passed through his mind as he stood outside the front door, cordoned out of things by the police tape.

He had been interviewed but wasn't yet allowed inside. That was still a place for only the actors of the forensic theatre in their baggy pajamas and smog masks. He watched their anal pottering through his mother's things.

With this second murder, The Paw—or Te Pao—phenomenon would now become a serious investigation. An inquiry team would be set up, on to which—given his involvement—they would draft John. The irony was that the most pertinent piece of evidence, his father's role, he was not at liberty to disclose to the investigators.

He wasn't a murder detective, but in the past four months John had been involved in ten murder cases. Two of those involved people he had known; one that he liked. It was a fact: he had no love for his mother, and she had refused protection outright, so he'd resigned himself to the fact that she was a very likely candidate for what she got. Stubborn old witch.

But seen from the doorway, the apartment seemed to be missing its mistress. The place had housed her since the marriage to his father. She'd rather grown into it, like a tree root that grows into the wall of a cottage. He knew he should have felt more deeply about her death, but the recent events had exhausted his already limited supply of emotions. All he could muster was guilt, but even that, he could now shift on to his father's shoulders. He could see himself now as a victim of something that happened when he was too young to do anything about it.

One of the detectives came over to him and handed him his mobile phone. "Jessel, it's for you."

"For me? Who'd. . .?" He took hold of the plastic handset. It was an annoyingly small thing that didn't reach from his ear to his mouth. He held it gingerly. "Jessel." He was shocked by the strength of the signal that came back at him.

"Inspector Jessel? Hold on please. I have a call for you."

John walked away into the carpeted hallway and stood by the large window. Commander Wood's voice surprised him.

"John. I really am very sorry." He spoke softly.

"Thank you. It's nice to know you're still keeping an eye out for me. Is this a reminder of that bit of paper in your office?"

"Partly, yes."

"You'll have to start trusting me eventually."

"I will, John, but traumatic events often cause us to do irrational things."

John felt even more guilty that he wasn't traumatized.

"I was hoping you could come and see me when you're feeling better."

"Feeling better. Right. I could come tomorrow."

"So soon? Are you sure you'll be up to it?"

"Yes. It will help me, er . . . forget. You know?"

"I understand completely. I'll see you tomorrow then. About eleven?"

"Fine. Oh wait. You don't suppose I could get my mother's suitcase back then, do you?"

"Her suitcase?"

"Yes. Your boys lifted it from my place while I was in the hospital."

"No. I don't believe they did."

"What?"

"We didn't actually remove anything. There was no suitcase."

"Are you sure?"

"I was there."

"Shit."

The phone buzzed and fell silent, and he felt ridiculous holding it. The ominous presence of Te Pao returned to occupy his mind. If the Secret Service hadn't removed the case, he was sure it had to be him. He had been in John's place while he was away. It seemed he could come and go as he pleased. John found him easier to hate now. Te Pao was no longer an enigma to be feared. He was a man, probably Burmese, and he was driven by revenge. Such motivation often led to mistakes.

He delayed going straight back to his place, but he knew eventually he'd have to. It was 1:00 a.m. when he silently turned the key in his lock. He checked the two rooms and the closet, then night-bolted the door. For safe measure he wedged a chair under the handle, even though he knew it would have no effect on a determined housebreaker. He stood for several minutes with his arms around the bottles on the fridge. It was a scrum with old friends, but they didn't want to be hugged. They wanted to be drunk, and he wanted to oblige.

"One more night," he said. "One more night."

He lay on the bed fully dressed in the darkness. It wasn't particularly cold, so when he started to tremble he knew it was from something inside him. A vague image forced its way into his mind. It was dull and fuzzy, like a photo taken with an old box camera. It was the image of two small children playing in the sand on Brighton Beach. In the background, a slim ballerina swathed in pinks and purples hid under an enormous umbrella. She wore sunglasses that made her look glamorous, and high-heeled shoes that she'd refused to remove before her walk across the sand to the deckchairs.

"Smile, and don't fidget. These photograph people charge the earth as it is."

It was the only holiday they had taken together. The old lady had complained bitterly the whole time about the weather and the prices and the musty bed-and-breakfast place they stayed at. She had smacked the children more often than usual in her frustration. But to John and Susan it had been a marvelous excursion that even the bruises couldn't spoil.

As he thought about it, the shivering turned to spasms and he wept himself to sleep for the dead woman who had spared the time to give him birth, but not a life.

21

It took John two hours to get to Kensington. It normally took one, but he had to assume he was being followed. His route was convoluted and he was especially vigilant. His physical condition made every move, every thought hurt. The troupe had finished their search for clues at his mother's, so he stopped off there first to look around. He had a spare key.

Forensics had got a lot neater since he first started in the force. Apart from the massive stain on the floor, they'd left the place looking very tidy. Perhaps the old lady's ghost had been bullying them. He walked around shaking his head at the apartment's fussiness. She'd always insisted on them calling it an apartment, never a flat. He looked into the room that had once been a nursery, then a den, then a vacation room for when the youngsters came home from boarding school.

It was now a sewing and withdrawing room, the way she'd always wanted it. It had become overgrown by her knick-knackery, like some small hut repossessed by the jungle. There was no evidence in there of himself or Susan.

He went to his mother's room. The dressing table was a pharmacy of pills and creams and ointments to combat aging. Unfortunately there was nothing there to stop death. When he had last been in that room, she was on her hands and knees rummaging under the bed. He wondered what other treasures she hid there. What he found was the last thing he expected. The small leather suitcase was back in its hiding place. She had said nothing about it when he phoned her.

Although he was sure the murder team had already dusted it for prints, John used a handkerchief to drag it out by the handle. Perhaps they hadn't bothered with the inside. He used a nail file to click open the catch and lift the lid. The contents looked largely as he remembered them, although there was something—something different. He couldn't quite put a name to what it was. And what was it doing back here? He found a large bin bag in the kitchen and put the suitcase into it. Perhaps Secret Service could do him one small favour.

Before he could leave the shrine, there was one last unpleasant duty he had to perform. He had contacted Aunt Maud the previous day and arranged for Susan to call him here. He unscrewed the larger parts of the phone and checked for listening devices. As far as he could tell, there were none. He lay back on the satin counterpane and waited. At exactly 10:00 she called.

"Okay, big bro. What's so urgent?"

He paused for a second.

"Mum."

Susan didn't respond to the word straight away. The woman had always been referred to as "mother" or worse. She knew there had to be a problem. "She got herself killed."

"Right."

"Bitch. Silly bitch. Pig-headed to the. . . ." A lump climbed her throat. The past few months had brought her to the edge. There had been too much pretending; too much holding down her feelings. She started to cry despite herself.

John heard Edward's little voice: "What mummy? What did he say? Let me talk to him." Then the boy's voice was loud in the earpiece: "Uncle John. You made my mummy cry. You're very bad. I don't like you anymore."

"I'm sorry, Eddo. She got some sad news that's all. I want you to look after your mummy for me till she feels better. Okay. . . ? Promise. . . ?"

"Okay."

"Can I talk to her again now?"

"Yes."

"Chick?"

She blew her nose loudly into the receiver.

"Ouch."

Susan giggled and was able to gain enough composure to tell her brother to carry on. They both knew it wasn't the loss of the old lady that she cried over, rather the accumulation of everything.

John told her all he could without giving away government secrets. The temptation to tell her about their spy dad was overwhelming. He was sure he would eventually, but not over the phone.

When he finally hung up, he fell back exhausted onto the bed. He was still surprised by both their reactions to the death of Coletta: a woman they didn't particularly like. They were mourning the mother who had denied them the love they'd been due. They had found affection from some of the nannies, but it was their love for one another that had pulled them through childhood and adolescence. They had made each other well adjusted in a perverted kind of way. But emotionally they were still both peculiar.

Susan was given to excesses. She had fallen hopelessly into passion with every man that passed through her life. She'd had an uncountable number of affairs, all with totally inappropriate men. It was a miracle she'd only been pregnant once, although John had speculated that none of the relationships had lasted long enough for the men to ejaculate.

She was a surprise package. Before they unwrapped her, none of them ever suspected just how delicious she was. She didn't dress to show off her fine figure or make up her normal face to make it abnormal. Her blonde hair was usually bunched into something ugly. But on a beach or at a pool she would be the sexiest creature there.

Bruce had been different from the regular suitors. While Susan was studying classical music and out-performing her tutors, she met a man who reminded her of a malnourished, dark-haired Santa Claus. He was jolly and giving and quite balmy. He had a comical red nose whatever the temperature, and teeth that kept a polite distance from one-another.

When she found she was bearing Eddo, she naturally split up with the freak who had impregnated her, before he had a chance to desert her. There was never any question she would keep the child. She dropped out of college and went to work in a Wimpy burger bar. The manager of her branch had a political soft spot for unmarried mothers, so he allowed her to let out the uniform month by month until labour pains started.

But Bruce wasn't one's average freak. He hadn't been told of his fatherhood, or been informed of the separation. He just turned up to see her one Friday and she'd gone. A distraught professor told him she'd resigned from the course, and a classmate told him she was pregnant. So Bruce, two months from graduation, dropped out also, and set off in search of his woman. Three months later he found her scraping grease from a hot plate in Wimbledon High Street.

Their reunion was so Barbara Cartland, Wimpy diners had a hard time keeping their burgers down. Bruce swept her off into a marriage of squats and student grants and his undying devotion.

John, on the other hand, had found the nearest thing to undying devotion in bottles. They turned supermarket cashiers getting drunk after work into Swiss nuns, and if one of those nuns had been foolish enough to follow him home —"Really? You're a policeman? Can I see your truncheon?"—he hadn't the will to stop them. Brief relationships had landed on him like pigeon droppings. He hadn't wanted them there, and after a while they just dried up and crumbled away. In Susan he had all the feminine warmth he really needed. He had to keep her alive because she was his missing soul.

22

Shirley was in Chiang Mai buying overpriced medical supplies for her clinic. After months in the camps, she appreciated hot water and electricity much more than she ever had in the USA. Boston had softened her, and she needed now to be hard. It was her last afternoon before returning to the border. If things went well at the meeting later, it could be her last afternoon in Thailand.

She sat at the large wooden table at the post office by Lamyai Market where all the tradespeople came to send money orders here and there. Northern country folk with assorted accents yelled in the long distance phone booths. Old people pushed to the front of queues. Dogs sprawled on the concrete floor out of the sunshine.

She watched the chaos for a while, then pulled the plump padded envelope from her satchel. At last she had an address to write on it. It hadn't come cheaply, but no reliable information from Burma was free.

She copied the words from her scrap of paper—"*Khin Tan Aye, 321 Myo Myint Avenue, Tamwe, Yangon, Myanmar*"— and put on the stamps. There was no duplicate. If this became one of the 2.8 million items of mail the Thai postal service lost every year, so be it. She couldn't afford to be found with a copy. That it was out of her and on the paper was the important thing. If it failed on the mission of intrigue she had planned for it, there were other contingencies. She had drawn up so many.

She marveled at how much terror and misery could be squeezed into a three-dollar padded parcel. That, she supposed, was progress. She watched it stickered and franked and tossed into a canvas bag to begin its journey to another era. She sighed deeply, put on her dark glasses, and walked out into the sticky Chiang Mai afternoon.

23

John sat in the leather armchair at the IIC reading the photocopy Commander Woods had given him. It was from a news article dated 1981 from the *Bangkok Post*. The headline read, *"ENGLISHMAN'S REMAINS RETURNED."* He found the impersonal style of the article annoying:

Authorities at Khun Yuam district in Mae Hong Son province yesterday accepted the body of 41-year-old English insurance agent James Desmond from Burmese Tatmadaw military officers at the Thai-Burmese border. The Burmese military unit handed over the Englishman's remains and passport to District Chief Sombat Choangulia at 2:00 p.m.

According to a statement from the Burmese, Desmond had "Ignored signs posted at the border and had trekked illegally into hostile territory." Sombat told the Post reporter that the Burmese blamed him for the death. "They said it was clearly my responsibility to keep tourists away from the border."

The Burmese statement went on: "The Karen rebels in this area are violent and cannibalistic. Let this be a lesson to you." (The body had been mutilated)

A British Embassy spokesman in Bangkok said that the family of Mr. Desmond would be notified and the body shipped back to the United Kingdom.

Of course, the embassy had never contacted them. They had been too slow to block the *Post* article but were able to prevent the news getting back to England. He tried to imagine the situation. If his father had been working with the Karen, they certainly wouldn't have killed him. But it would have been to the Burmese military's advantage to make the world believe that's what happened.

John was alone in the room. Commander Woods had welcomed him by making it quite clear he shared his grief. John did all he could to look grieving. Sympathy, he thought, could get him somewhere with the Service people. It had already earned him a cup of coffee and a bun, which now balanced precariously on the chair's arm. Woods had given him the article and left him alone to read it. On cue he re-entered the room:

"It doesn't say much, does it? You've probably worked out that Desmond was his cover. That's all I could find that was relevant to the death."

"You don't have any files?" John took a bite of his bun. It was stale.

"John, I really do understand what you're going through. We aren't totally heartless here. I want to help you as much as I can, but the project is closed and we can't expend any resources on re-opening it."

"My father's a project now?"

The man looked down at his own cup. . . . "There is something. . . . The Southeast Asian liaison agent is retired now. But he lives in Thailand. I've talked to him. He's a very colourful character, and he was quite close to your father. . . ."

"I'm glad somebody was."

"He would be prepared to talk to you and help in any way."

"But he lives in. . . ."

The commander reached inside his jacket pocket and produced a small folder. He stood and handed it to John. It was a British Airways pouch containing an Executive-Class open return ticket to Bangkok with an ongoing connection to Chiang Mai.

"Wow. Did you win the Pools?"

"We have a small contingency fund. Of course it's entirely up to you whether you decide to go or not. But I'd appreciate it if you let me know what you find."

"Well, thank you, but . . . I'm really in no condition to travel."

"The ticket's open. You can use it whenever you like. And you do realize this is absolutely unofficial."

"And you'll deny all knowledge of me, like you did my dad."

"Yes."

The telephone by the door chirped and the commander seemed relieved to have the distraction. John noted that he was a little too sensitive for this type of work, sending men and women off to their deaths. Or perhaps John had an inappropriate idea of what spies actually got up to.

The call was one sided. Woods did all the listening, said "All right," and hung up. . . .

"Well. We have results from the fingerprints on your suitcase."

"That was fast."

"We're the government." He said it as if he believed "the government" could achieve the impossible. John began to understand the qualities one needed in order to represent the flag. He doubted whether he possessed any of them. His father certainly had. But in the cynical new millennium where would they ever be able to recruit enough people to defend the crown?

"And besides, the crime-scene boys had been over it already. There were two sets of readable prints. Of course, it doesn't discount someone with gloves handling the suitcase, but the prints do tell a story."

John waited for it as Woods organized it in his mind.

"There are, of course, your own prints on top of your mother's, presumably from when you took the case to your flat. But then again, there are also your mother's prints on top of yours. Which would suggest—"

"That the old girl took back her own suitcase."

"It would seem so. There were no other smudges or marks."

John considered this for a while. Coletta had had a spare key to his place since he moved in. But as far as he knew, she had never used it. Why would she suddenly go to his place to retrieve a suitcase she'd given him not long before?

"I don't understand it."

"Mothers are mysterious creatures," the commander offered.

"You don't need to tell me that."

-o-

Emma sat on the peach sofa with a big grin on her face. "I just can't imagine you on a beach with a coconut and a novel, that's all."

"I need a break, Em."

"I'm not doubting that." She was delighted John was cleaning himself up, and she didn't really want him around while he was doing it. She didn't need him and his baggage and his baggage handler jeopardizing her other cases. But she wasn't just going to kick him out. The holiday idea was perfect for all of them, but she didn't believe a word of it.

"So what's the problem?"

"You're John Jessel is the problem. You and your family are in danger. There's no way on this earth you'd go off and take a holiday now. Do you think I'm stupid?"

"That's a tough one."

She glared.

"So you aren't going to sign my leave slip?"

"I didn't say that. Of course I'll sign it. What I'm saying is, you're not the superhero you think you are. Physically you're a mess. Whatever great adventure it is you've got planned in Thailand, you're going to need help. I'll do whatever I can for you here, but over there you're on your own. Do you think you're up to it?"

"I really hope I am, Em."

24

"It's not safe," the smiling Karen told her. The smile was merely a temporary clasp to keep his breaking face together. The young woman, barely out of school, had openly argued with the aging doctor in front of his peers. She had not only discounted his strong advice, she had countered his warnings one by one so eloquently that he had emerged from the encounter sounding like an over-protective old fool.

She knew what she was doing to him and felt ashamed. He was a good man who had done marvelous work for his people, and she had infinite respect for him. But this was bigger than face. She had to go inside, and she needed the support of the Karen National Union to do so. They would only co-operate if they had the green light from the NHC and the Karen Refugee Committee.

"Doctor," she said finally. "I understand your concern at sending a young woman into a war-torn area. But you must agree the needs inside are far greater than here. In Thailand you have access to Medecins Sans Frontieres and a hundred other medical teams. Inside you have interns with a few months of training and no supplies. People are dying who shouldn't, because there are no qualified doctors."

The old man made one last attempt, although he knew he was fighting a losing battle. From his experiences over the last sixty years, he knew only too well what that felt like. "People are dying. They have been dying in the same way for decades, and they will continue to die. One inexperienced doctor isn't going to make any difference to that situation. Except, of course, we stand to lose an inexperienced doctor. Have you any idea what the SLORC would do to you if you were captured?" He used the acronym for the military, popular with those who hated them.

She knew what he meant better than anyone in the room. The Burmese junta gave her daily reminders of their methodology.

"I work with women every day who were used by the military, who have lost mothers or daughters to STDs or internal ruptures. I know the risk well, Doctor. I also know that I swore an oath on the day I received my qualification. I swore to do my utmost to use the skills I'd learned to the greatest good. Inside is where I can use my skills to the fullest."

The old physician slid back his chair noisily and stood. His knuckles rested on the table. He looked beside the insolent young girl to the Karenni nurse who raised her eyebrows in reply to his scowl.

"Then, if she wishes to kill herself, let her go. We can always find other less-foolhardy doctors for the camps, I suppose. But get somebody else to sign her obituary notice when it arrives here."

He took a cheroot from the communal pack on the table and walked outside with it. They had a no-smoking policy inside. So they all smoked in the yard.

"So I go?" she asked the others.

"You've worn down the old soldier, so I'm sure you would eventually batter all of us into submission," the nurse confessed over her notepad. There were no disagreements.

Shirley sighed her relief. "Thank you all. You won't regret this decision."

"Let's hope you don't," the Mon added.

They broke for coffee and chatted amicably about who she should meet and exactly what needed to be done inside. Once she had breached their defenses, her value as a qualified doctor on the Burmese side became apparent. She felt a surge of excitement and pride, and then shame.

Before she left, she walked into the yard where the old doctor sat in the slight shade of a papaya tree. He was still puffing angrily at the cheroot. He grunted and averted his gaze when she approached him.

"Doctor. I had no intention of insulting you. I want you to know that."

He laughed to himself. "When I was your age, I was a mule-headed fool, too. I needed someone to talk sense into me. I also believed that nobody could see through me."

She smiled.

He paused from working at his cigar and stared at her for the first time. His eyes were deep historical worlds. She was surprised at how many lives she could see in them. She compared them to her own. She imagined that when he stared back at her, he would see emptiness and silence. But she was wrong. He could see truths.

"You aren't here for us," he said, still glaring at her confessing eyes. "You have other reasons for being here. Not for the stricken soldiers or the violated daughters. You're here for you. And whatever it is you've come to do will cause more suffering."

Shirley felt her legs buckle.

"You aren't pure, girl. You aren't holy. You have evil in you, and you haven't fooled me."

Shocked and embarrassed, she couldn't look any longer at his cruel face with its fathomless eyes. She didn't even want to be in the yard with him. She turned away and half ran into the street. He had seen through her disguise, one she had selected and nurtured over ten painful years. After all the work, that this old man could strip her of it so completely was devastating.

Her heart pounded in time with her head as she walked weakly along the ash-dry street. She had left something behind. Her courage was still beside the old man under the papaya tree. She should have gone back for it, argued her innocence. The brilliant medical student who graduated a year before her classmates certainly would have done. But not now. That woman was lost. All that remained was Sherri, a seven-year-old, heading off into battle.

25

Three days later, the Thai Airways 747 carrying John and all his problems, touched down at Chiang Mai International Airport. He still hadn't slept for over a week. His dependency hated him for what he was doing to it. He'd shorn off his hair and hacked off his beard, but he'd have had to lop off the whole head to look and feel better than he did.

The last couple of days had wracked his already frazzled nerves. The bends had convinced him that Te Pao was around every corner, behind every door. He was sure his time had come. *"First the boys. Then the girls, then you will be last."* The girl had gone. His mother was dead. Was it his turn? Boarding the flight at Heathrow had been more like an escape than a departure.

He stumbled through Immigration and stood in the crowded terminal waiting for someone to recognize him. Several drivers of illegal taxis homed in on his solitude, but he scared them off with his crimson eyes.

It occurred to him that he had no idea what to do if his contact didn't turn up. He had no address for him, no phone number. He didn't even know his real name. He could hardly walk around the city asking if anyone knew Norbert.

He knew nothing about this place. Thailand was so . . . far; so un-English, so bloody hot. But he'd been expecting more squalor. He was disappointed by the air-conditioned terminal and the gaudy Dairy Queen and Pizza Hut. He was surprised that everyone dressed in fashions he could have found in New Malden. He was strangely excited by the trim, dark-eyed women who avoided his stares, and baffled by the words he heard.

A character with a Thai face, a grey cartoon handlebar moustache, and a black leather waistcoat over a Grateful Dead T-shirt pushed through the crowd towards him. . . .

"So. You're the son of the bitch," he growled in a *faux*-Yank accent.

John held out his hand but the man ignored it. He went straight into a bear hug that was so packed in muscle John felt like a tube of glue being squeezed of its remains. The man was getting on in years but was deceptively strong. "I told them I'd know you. No son of Jim could get past me, I said. Not 'less you was adopted or somethin'."

John found himself hugging back in a non-committal, English kind of way. "I assume you're Norbert," he huffed. "I wasn't really expecting you to be Thai."

"You assume on, bro. They sure haven't loosened you Limeys up none in the last generation. I'm a kind of Asian cocktail. My passport's Thai but my blood don't got no borders." He released John's body but held tightly to his hand as he led him through the concourse and out into the steaming car park. John had a strong feeling that Norbert was welcoming his father back.

They arrived at an old black Willy's jeep without doors, and climbed in.

"Where did you pick up that unfortunate accent?" John asked.

The man laughed a huge appreciative laugh that caused him to shake so much he couldn't get the key into the ignition. "You Limeys. . . . Throw your bag in the back there, but—"

John tossed his cricket bag over the seat. There was a dull thud and a loud, painful howl. He looked behind him to see what appeared to be an old brown blanket bunched up on the floor.

"I was gonna say, 'Be careful of old Bruiser there.'"

"What is it?"

"Broo ain't as frisky as he was."

The blanket was apparently a bloodhound—old, fat, and layered like a stack of inner tubes. He grudgingly got to its feet, waddled to the seat, and gave John a sticky lick of forgiveness. An excited tail was the only remnant of his boisterous youth. Duty done, old Bruiser went back to his warm spot and collapsed in a heap.

"Jim named him."

"Did he name you, too?"

"No, sir. This is the name my mama gave me. No idea where she got it from."

John felt a strange nostalgia. The affection shown by this stranger and his dog made him feel happy to be the son of his father.

They drove through the wide streets from the airport and on to the ring road. Again, John was disappointed. There wasn't much exotic about the exotic East; no elephants or golden domes, just 7-elevens, concrete, and Japanese cars. But it was all just a front. The further they drove from the city, the more different it became.

They started along the winding Chiang Dao Road and, despite Norbert's constant monologue, John began to feel that he was in a new world. Monks sitting smoking in front of their temples. Ladies in sarongs carrying enormous bundles of sticks on their heads. Dusty children engrossed in a game of flip-flop skimming. Every small village had its whitewashed temple compound, the sun highlighting the mosaics of glass on the chofa, the eave-like adornments on their roofs

It was probably a combination of jet lag and alcohol withdrawal, but forty minutes later, when the jeep pulled off the main road, John wasn't aware of anything his companion had said the whole journey. They drove through a narrow lane of trees up to a tall, wooden gate that opened immediately as if someone had been waiting for their arrival. They chugged through an orchard of strange fruit and parked in front of a beautiful, teak house on a riverbank. On the far side, trees smothered a hillside as far as the eye could see. Not a neighbour in sight.

"God. You live here?"

"Yeah. It's rustic ain't it."

"It's bloody beautiful."

Norbert led him away from the main house to a small guest bungalow in the trees. It had its own shower, and the large bed overlooked the stream.

The Thai surprised him by saying, "You're still pretty messed up, boy. Get yourself clean and catch up on some sleep. Whenever you're ready, come on up to the house. Okay? It's good to see you." He put his arm around John's neck and kissed him on the cheek. It was a gesture that was oddly appropriate. John accepted it on behalf of his father but kept it for himself.

When he was alone, he stood in the centre of the teak room and breathed in the sounds of the river and the birds, the clear air, and the sensation of freedom from an atmosphere polluted by The Paw. He showered in icy-cold water that must have been diverted from the stream; picked at the tray of food beside the bed; and rested briefly. The last thing he remembered was the shivering of the leaves on the far bank and the curious stare of a wall lizard reciting reptile poetry above his head.

-o-

He awoke 14 hours later, confused at first as it was still light out. He felt like a million dollars, or about 43 million Thai baht, and couldn't understand how a brief nap could make him feel so good. His watch didn't help. It was still on GMT and he hadn't thought to ask about the time difference.

He went wobbly to the main house. As there was no front door, he walked straight in, announcing his arrival with a hello. Norbert and a slim, narrow-eyed woman were sitting close together at a large table. The balcony it was on overlooked the stream. The couple obviously hadn't heard him. They appeared to be fooling around.

He coughed and they looked up.

"Hey. Son of Frankenstein back from the dead." Norbert rose from the table as he spoke, jogged over to John, and threw a familiar arm around his shoulders. "I snuck into your room during the night and checked your pulse. You looked like crap yesterday. I thought you might croak in the night.

"The night? Have I been asleep that long?"

"This doll here is my good lady wife, Kruamart."

John walked towards her to shake her hand, but she ignored his hand and prayed towards him instead. He prayed back in an ungainly way.

"Cuts down on the exchange of germs," Norbert said returning to his seat and gesturing for John to join them. "Hell of a lot more bacteria under your fingernails than there are up your ass. You know that?"

"Perhaps we should rub arses when we meet, then."

Norbert roared with laughter and then translated for his wife. She blushed but couldn't hold back. The more she laughed, the more beautiful she became.

"Isn't he a bit old for you?" John asked Kruamart.

"She prefers men with a few miles under their belts. And I didn't teach her English yet." He reached out to her, and she put her hand in his. It was a totally natural gesture. There was a lot of love between them, and John felt a pang of envy. He sat opposite and looked at the feast laid out under its city of mesh domes that kept off the flies.

"Are you expecting a party for breakfast?"

"Man who sleeps that long wakes up with a hell of a hunger. Besides, while you're eating I can tell you a few stories."

It was a fact. John was so ravenous he could have eaten the banquet and the table it was on. He'd pecked at food like an ailing bird for the previous month. Although he didn't know what he was eating, he went at it with vigor. Kruamart left them to their business and the Thai began to tell him about his involvement with his father.

"Didn't much like him at first. He was sarcastic like you. I wasn't used to it then. I am now."

"I'm glad."

"He messed with my accent, too. I told you this yesterday, but I didn't get the idea you was listening. I spent eight years in the States. Trained with the air force then Special Forces. Worked with a lot of CIA guys over here. You Limeys ain't very accepting of foreign accents, particularly American. First off, I thought your dad had something against me. I was his contact here for a mission in Burma. The CIA put him in touch with me. I had no contact with Limeys before, so I didn't realize how . . . un-American you guys was. Stateside they either hate the sight of you cause you're a chink or a gook, or they love you to death cause you're different.

"Old Jim, I could never work out what he was thinking. He sure didn't love me. I knew that. But . . . well, I guess I ain't allowed to tell you about the missions we ended up running together. We went over the border six times. I can blend in over there. My mama was from Mandalay. Shit. That would be one hell of a name for a pop song."

John almost choked on his papaya. Through the laughter he improvised, "Mama was from Mandalay . . ." to the melody of "Papa was a Rolling Stone."

Without a break, Norbert sang on: "Wherever there was a man she got laid."

John felt disrespectful to be laughing at the man's probably long departed mother. But as Norbert was in hysterics, he joined him.

"Anyways," Norbert said at last, wiping his eyes on a napkin. "You get to know someone real well over there. We knew each other over three years. When he died, I couldn't have been sadder if it had been my own kin. Man, I loved that dry bastard. He saved my sad ass more than once.

"You know, like I was saying, over there I can blend in pretty much. But he was always going to be a big, orange-haired guy. He couldn't afford to relax for a second. But he was focussed, man. He made me feel like an amateur. You knew he could speak Burmese, Karen, and Thai real good. . . ?"

John put down his full fork. "No. I didn't know. I really didn't know much at all before this Te Pao stuff started. I thought he was a boring insurance man."

Norbert smiled. "Yeah. And you would have gone to your grave thinking that . . . if you hadn't been so pushy. Still, like father like son. Ain't that what they say?"

"That's starting to sound like a compliment."

"Oh it is, boy. It is."

"And you've heard all about Te Pao I suppose."

"They sent me a brief. It's the shits."

"Got any theories?"

"Nothing concrete. But I guess we can piece it together. Whoever this guy is, he didn't expect you to get this far."

"I'm not sure what you mean. He advertised the name of the place they killed my dad, didn't he?"

"Yeah. But he couldn't of expected you to make that connection. It was secret. You only got here by chance. Maybe he don't even know who your dad was with."

"Then why give me the name?"

"I been thinking about that. I came to the conclusion he's nuts."

"I hope I'm not paying you a consultation fee."

"No. I don't mean just slash-slash nuts. I mean I get the feeling this guy's obsessed with something. This is all part of some ritual he's put together in his mind. I bet my life your dad did something real bad to this guy. I bet it was so bad, he wanted to kill old Jim. And I bet old Jim beat him to it with the cyanide, so he didn't get the chance. He didn't get his revenge. Know what I mean?"

"So he's going after the relatives one by one? That's a bit much even for an obsessed psychopath, don't you think?"

"I don't know, boy. He traveled halfway round the goddamned world to find you."

"Right. And that's another thing. How did he find me? How did he make the connection? If this was all so secret, how did he get to me?"

Norbert looked up at the sky for a moment, then stared at his guest.

"Fucked if I know."

"And why Kenya of all places?"

"Fucked if I know that, too."

"Well you're a fat lot of good, aren't you."

They both laughed. John stood and went over to the balcony railing. "Seriously. How do you think my being here is going to get answers to these questions, Norbert?"

"Listen, boy." Norbert joined him. "I can tell you all I know about that last mission. It got screwed up right from the start. Me and your old man got separated after some Karen intelligence turned out to be not so damned intelligent. I hardly made it back here with my balls.

"But we was nowhere near Te Pao, and nothing we'd planned would have got him all cut up like that. It was so quick. If he'd just gotten captured, SLORC or whatever they was called then, would have tortured him for a month. And I'm sure as hell they wouldn't have brought his body back.

"Whatever it was must have been somethin' private . . . somethin' he didn't tell me about. Or somethin' he stumbled on by accident like. I been wonderin' what that might have been, man. There ain't a day goes by I don't wonder what that crazy son of a gun did to get himself all sliced up like that. If you'll excuse the expression."

"Is there any way to find out?"

"Only one."

"What's that?"

"I go back inside."

"I thought you'd retired."

"How can I retire in peace with this thing naggin' at me? And now I got a good reason. I can help stop this guy wiping out Jim's kids. By the way, I was real sorry to hear about your mother."

"Thanks. Did dad ever talk about her?"

"Oh man. He loved that woman."

"What?"

"Absolutely, boy. Hell. He knew she didn't love him back none, but he had a thing for that woman bigger than Buddha." Norbert could see the confusion on John's face. "He always carried her picture, and yours and Susan's. But at night he'd take out the ballerina and talk to her real sweet. There were times, John boy. There were times when we wasn't sure we'd be around another day, and he'd tell me. He'd tell me how happy he was to have this love feeling inside him."

"Do you think he ever told mother?"

"At first he did. I guess she laughed at him one time too many. Seemed to me she treated him bad. Excuse me for saying, but I reckon he could have put his love into something better than that. But it's a funny old thing. love. One minute you're a human being; the next you got the jingly-jangly.

"He told me, when he met her there in Hungary, she just filled him up. That was it. If she told him to jump under a train, he'd be runnin' off to the station as fast as his legs would take him. She bewitched that big dumb Limey, and she knew he was under the spell.

"She knew what she was doin'. She rode his love. She climbed in the saddle and rode it all the way to England. She rode away from a life and a system she hated. And he knew. He knew he was being used. He knew she had other guys."

"She did?"

"Sure, man. Hungarian wife of a British Secret Service agent don't fart without it being on a tape somewhere in

Whitehall. They checked out all her fancy men, and told him about them."

The weight of it all was getting too much for John. He sat down at the table and poured a strong coffee for himself. "They figured he'd dump her eventually and make all their lives easier. But that big soft gorilla couldn't bear the thought of her not being there at the end of an assignment. He knew it all, boy. But he let her ride."

John shook his head. He could recall no affection between them; no touching, civil words. He'd grown up believing that mothers and fathers were separate things floating like planets in their own orbits. He was nine years old the last time he saw his dad, but it was all so fuzzy. There were no clear memories of that last time or of his parents' interaction.

He looked at Norbert, who smiled apologetically. He had to be in his sixties. The grey of his moustache and the balding crown gave it away. But he was a man who would always have the energy and honesty of youth. John thought about the Bible passage, something about having walked in the valley of death and not fearing evil. Norbert and Jim Jessel had walked in that valley. When you've been so close to death you no longer needed to be afraid of it. And you lived every day of the subsequent life with gratitude and joy. John had a strong urge to stroll in the valley.

"I doubt you'll let me come with you?"

"You can come so far. There's a lot of folks who want to meet you."

"Me?"

"Your old man had a lot of friends inside. They'd like to meet 'son of Jim.' They didn't have a chance to say good-bye to the original."

"You've already talked to them?"

"Soon as I heard. Trip's all planned. We leave tomorrow."

"Wow! What does your wife have to say about all this?"

"Well, there were two ways I could of handled it. I could tell her I'm going back inside, that I have a fifty-fifty chance of being blown away, that she and her three bambinos won't ever see sweet Norbert again."

"Whereas, what you actually told her was. . . ."

"I'm taking you on a tour of Thailand's historical north."

"And she believed you?"

"I ain't ever lied to her before, boy. So we better be back here with a suitcase full of Buddha images and a camera full of temples in a week or I'm screwed."

"Norbert." John looked into the grinning face of his father's friend. "I appreciate what you're doing. Really."

Norbert folded his arms and swung back on his chair.

"Yeah. I know."

26

They left early the next morning for the border. It took a little longer to get there than usual because they stopped at a dozen temples, took three rolls of film, and bought a few kilos of assorted artifacts. "Just in case we're riddled with bullets and can't do it on the way back," was Norbert's justification for it.

"How do we explain the bullet holes to Kruamart?" John slurped at a Coke, his feet on the dashboard.

"We'll tell her they're mosquito bites."

The scenery became greener and hillier, and John thought about where they were heading. "Give me a brief history of these . . . what do you call them? SLOCK. The Burmese junta."

"SLORC. . . . What do you know about Burma?"

"Not a great deal. They got drafted into the Empire late nineteenth century. There was some mix up with the Japanese invasion in the war, wasn't there?"

"Only a mix-up about whose side who was on. These smart young Burmese revolutionaries went over to Japan to train how to kick your British asses out of Burma. When the Nips invaded, these thirty kids came back as heroes and fought with them. The Karen stuck with you, but the Japs were hot stuff and they beat your sorry butts.

"The Imperial Army put the kids in charge of army units all over the place. Aung San—Suu Kyi's old papa—he was the top kid, and he soon figured out being a lacky of the Nips wasn't a lot better than being a lacky of the Brits."

"At least we cook our fish."

"You payin' attention?"

"Yes, sir."

"Right. So, Aung San swaps sides and fights with you guys against the Nips. This time you beat the crap out of them. But now the Burmans are back where they started. So they take advantage of the fact that you guys are flat broke after the war, and put in for independence. In 1948, they get it. But the minority groups don't like the way the Burmese have divided up the country and given themselves everything. The Karen are most pissed of all, and they start a full-on war. That was 1948 and the war ain't over.

"The Burmese Army—the *Tatmadaw*—pretended to be servants of the government for a while, but they couldn't stand watchin' politicians robbin' the place, so in '62 they just took over. Since then they been robbin' it for themselves. Any uprisings, they squash 'em. Any strong political opposition, they squash that, too. And the Karen? They didn't squash so easy, but bit by bit the Burmese, they been eatin' away at 'em. Fifty years of war can make you pretty damn tired."

"That's the truth."

"And the Burmese, they figure if they do somethin' shitty, all they got to do is change their name and the world will think someone else did it. In '88 they were the SLORC, State Law and Order something. Then they shot a few thousand people after they lost the election in '90 and violated a few human rights, so now they're the SPDC . . . some Peace and Daisy shit. It's like decorating. But most people still call them SLORC. It kinda suits 'em better."

"You don't like them much do you?"

"Not much." He smiled and drove his jeep on over the mountains to Mae Sariang and the Burmese border.

27

Aunt Maud sat in his favourite chair, reading a novel he'd read many times before. It was one of the pleasures of retirement in the country, to have time to re-read old friends and see characteristics in them you hadn't had time to notice before. His fine bones that had once supported an athlete were now virtually all that remained of him. Age had reclaimed his looks, his hair, and his teeth, but he still had the energy to work all day in his beloved garden.

He dozed often and re-awoke to the same silence and the same lawn stretched out beyond his conservatory. He thought, just for a second, he had seen some movement in the bushes. But he knew that by the time he'd removed his reading glasses and replaced them with his outdoor spectacles, whatever fox, or squirrel, or migrating goose had been trespassing, would be long gone.

It was such a curse, replacing all the worn down parts: glasses for eyes that didn't see, aids for ears that didn't hear, catheters for organs that didn't piss when you expected them to. If he didn't die soon, he thought, there'd be very little of the original left. Any more excitement like Susan's, and sooner or later they'd have to replace his heart.

He laughed at the thought, but there was that damn movement again. It was nearer the garden shed now, and too large to be a bird. He wondered if the neighbour's dog had got into his yard. He fumbled for his other glasses and eased himself painfully out of the chair. He walked to the glass doors that let in the rare spring sunshine but kept out the gales that blew down from the moors.

For a while he stood there looking into his neat garden, and seeing nothing out of the ordinary. It was a shame there was no aid, no artificial pump to replace a policeman's instincts that no longer sensed danger.

Just for a split second he saw the man, segmented by the arm of his spectacles. He had been concealed in the ivy. The scythe he didn't see at all. The intruder's aim was precise and deadly. The sharp point of the tool smashed through the glass pane directly in front of Maud's heart, passed through the centre of the organ, and exited just below his shoulder blade.

There he stood, pinned to the door, dead.

Bohmu Din stood back and admired his work before pulling open the french door and its carcass, and stepping inside the conservatory. He lowered himself into Aunt Maud's favourite chair and tossed the novel onto the floor. He had an excellent view of the garden and the corpse.

Ex-DSI Maudling's blood flowed down his body and in between the cracks of the crazy-paving. The effect was rather artistic. He'd seen worse at the National Gallery in his student days. He watched until the flow turned to a gooey drip and the body was as pale as bread.

It was a pleasure to see him dead. He had caused the Burman so much inconvenience. Bohmu Din had wasted far too much time searching the files for a real aunt. In the police car park they'd heard the fat boy telling his sister she'd be going to Aunt Maud's. It would have been easy to trace a relative. But they had been unlucky. Months had passed before the real connection was made; months that should have seen the end of his task. By now he should have been freed.

His people had been through the family trees, hospital records, old letters they'd stolen from Susan's, but finally Aunt Maud turned up by accident in the police gazette archive: "*Aunt Maud Hangs Up His Cuffs.*"

The grinning fool, holding his plaque, shaking hands with his successor in the photograph. Grinning at Bohmu Din for his stupidity.

"Not grinning now, Aunt Maud. Not grinning. Not breathing. A real retirement. So, now my dead aunt, it is time for you to tell me where you are keeping my angel."

28

Very few letters from outside Burma make it to addresses inside the country unopened. Packages are particularly tempting for the officers at the Communications Centre off Merchant Street. The parcels are checked against a list of people who are allowed to receive their mail untampered. This list includes selected diplomats, all in-favour senior army personnel, advisors, big investors, and influential underground figures. Mail to anyone else may be opened and confiscated at the discretion of the screening department. Edibles and re-saleables sent by relatives overseas stand no chance of making it past their strict surveillance.

Packages of hand-written notes such as that which arrived this morning from Thailand went straight upstairs. There were people upstairs who did nothing but read. Often a paragraph would be enough to decide whether it was a threat to national security or a love letter. Both made particularly interesting reading. But the confessions and allegations of Dr. Shirley kept the army sergeant enthralled for the greater part of the morning. He enjoyed the chance to practice his English, and found something oddly erotic in its brazen style. He wrote a brief summary of the contents, as was his directive, and sent it further upstairs to Director U Thay Winn.

Major Winn was one of the old guard. He had served a long apprenticeship at the Karen and Shan fronts before they were secured. Yet he lacked the ambition to join colleagues of equal seniority in parliament. He was however unquestionably loyal. The name he read in the summary— that of Bohmu Din—was well known to him. He had been a living legend to SLORC troops at the front, even a cult figure. He had quickly become a favourite of the Council. Winn knew that the information contained in these notes, if it were true, could be damaging to his career. There were no contact details for Bohmu Din, and telephone inquiries all came to very abrupt dead-ends. So, he had no choice.

He dispatched the memo, the original hand-written notes, and his official cover letter to the Security Council Office, to the man responsible for matters of ethnic insurgents. The letter spent a week there while research was done, and the following confidential memo was wired to Bohmu Din:

To the Honorable Bohmu Din,

The Office of Ethnic Control has intercepted a parcel addressed to a woman in Tamwe who passed away last year. It was apparently written by a Karen doctor who is active on the border and has connections with the KNU. Her name now is Shirley Heigh, although she was originally known as Sherri Ya Hei.

The document makes certain allegations about you personally, which I shall not enter into in this correspondence. More importantly, the writer appears to have had access to data that we had considered secret. The fact that she has returned to the region and is in contact with the enemy, makes this a very serious matter, as I'm sure you would agree.

Would you kindly confirm that this female was actually in your employ during the above period, and whether it is possible she had access to military installations or sensitive documentation.

We have amassed all security data collected from the Thai border over the past two months, and are presently analyzing it. We will await your response before launching a full investigation.

In confidence.
Lt. Major Mhin Thein

When it arrived encoded on Bohmu Din's desk, it wasn't read because he wasn't there. In fact, nobody at the office knew exactly where he was. He had been taking a lot of time off recently and not even his aides had been included in his plans. They weren't even sure he was in the country.

29

Bohmu Din had searched and trashed every room in Aunt Maud's house. There was nothing. There was no indication in any of the old detective's paperwork as to where they may have hidden the daughter. He could have tortured Maud, should have. But it wasn't to his taste anymore. He had people to do that. He sat back in the comfortable chair. There was a wind stirring outside and it flagged Maud back and forth on his door.

"Where did you send them, sir?" Bohmu Din asked.

There was a box of toys in the corner, so he was sure they had spent some time there with the little Eddo brat. He went across, sat cross-legged in front of the box, and upended it. The toys were all plastic rubbish: animals, cars, guns. At the base of the box were the boy's paintings. There were people and houses. And there was one with a sun, and what could have been tents. And copied at the bottom were the words "let's go to Les Sables."

He remembered a name-card on the pile on Maud's desk. It was the name of a campsite in Les Sables-d'Olonne, France. He sat where he was and considered this coincidence. The picture combined with the card had told him where to look for them. It was a momentous clue . . . and a false one.

"So, Maud. You were expecting me, I see. Such a suspicious mind you have." Taking a small wooden train engine, he stepped out into the yard to confront Maud's swaying body. He steadied it, and stared into his open eyes through the glass. "But you obviously spent most of your career dealing with a very low class of criminal. Did you really believe I'd be so gullible? You insult me.

"Are you saying that these toys were important enough to bring from their house, but not important enough to carry with them to their next hideout? I wonder whose they are.

And if, after all the trouble you've gone to to hide them thus far, why would you leave me two such clumsy clues?

"But you see, Auntie, in drawing me on to the false trail, you have inadvertently given me an idea. You see this. . . ?" He held up the train to where Maud could have seen it if he hadn't been dead. "Can you read it? Oh. No. I see you aren't wearing your glasses. Here. Allow me. It says, 'With love from mummy and daddy.' Isn't that sweet? 'From mummy.'" He smiled. "'And daddy.'"

30

Refusing alcohol was difficult and could have been taken as an insult. But John and Norbert had conjured up a credible liver disease as a result of hepatitis. Most of the jungle-based fighters around them could relate to that. They'd all had their share of tropical diseases. How John had managed to pick it up in New Malden was another question, fortunately one they didn't ask.

So he sipped tea while the five old soldiers threw back shots of cloudy rice whisky and grew slowly rowdier. He sat cross-legged and stiff on the grass mat and listened enthralled to their tales. These were senior Karen who had spent their adult lives fighting the Burmese. They weren't the saloon-bar soldiers from back home who made up battles to entertain the boozers. They were crusty warriors who had done it all and survived.

That's why the tea-sipper delighted so much in the stories they proudly told about Jim Jessel. He doubted the officials at IIC would have appreciated them as much. It appeared that much of what his father did was unofficial, non-commissioned, and illegal. As far as MI6 was concerned, he was there, on the Thai side, as an observer, a gatherer of intelligence. There were obviously some guilty consciences in the British government that regretted their predecessors' sell-out of their old Karen allies. In order to tidy up their mess and get on the boat home as quickly as they could, the Brits had struck a deal on a hastily-patched-together Union of Burma.

If joining a union meant giving up all they'd fought to defend, they could live without it. So began the war that the old Karen around John had watched gradually slip away from them, together with their hope.

If the truth were to be told, there was little nostalgia in Whitehall's decision to assist the minorities. Nobody could ever accuse British governments of sentimentality, particularly in Thatcher's seventies and eighties. There were business opportunities in Burma that Britain couldn't exploit as long as the junta was in power. The only way they could see to weaken, and ultimately break it, was to keep it at war. Thus had Jim Jessel been assigned as Karen liaison officer, and taken it upon himself to right history. From the stories he heard that evening, John came away believing his father had achieved more on his own in a few years than his entire government in a century.

Although officially based in Chiang Mai, Jessel had loved his missions inside. He had felt a purpose in his work by eating and sleeping beside these proud people. He would never have received permission to accompany the fighters on raids, or to the front, so he hadn't asked. If they'd known that he'd actually planned and led missions, he would have been on a plane and working behind a tea urn faster than you could say 'Iron Maiden.'

That night, a million miles away from belching car exhausts and blaring TVs, John lay under the mesh net and listened to the sounds of the jungle. But his head was full of his father. He felt more like an heir than a son. He felt that he should have inherited this greatness, but hadn't discovered it inside himself. Jim Jessel would have known how to cope with Te Pao, how to protect his own family.

How John would have liked, how he would have benefited from long talks with dad while he was growing up. There was something from his youth, from his father's later visits home, that churned around in his subconscious like a current beneath the surface of a lake. He had been there with his father but could remember nothing from their time together. Why was that, when so much else of his childhood was clear in his mind?

If he had been able to feel this pride when he was young, he was sure it would have made up for anything else that was missing. He took hold of his father's courage and wrapped it around himself. The night was blacker than any he had known, but the knowledge of his father's courage protected him from it. He was no longer afraid of the dark.

-o-

At 6:00 a.m., all the sounds of a busy new day reminded John that life began obscenely early in the jungle. He had slept like a felled tree. Norbert was long gone. His bed was rolled into a corner, and was probably cold already.

John bounced across the springy bamboo platform to the steps. He sat on the top one and looked around. Few Karen bases were permanent, particularly in those days. The SLORC had overrun most of their headquarters and turned the Karen army into the new gypsies of the epoch. In the dry season they split into small units so as not to give the Burmese time to set up an offensive. But now, in the long rainy season, SLORC could do nothing but sit in their Chinese nylon tents and plot the next season's indignities. The Karen could group and live briefly normal lives.

John and Norbert had arrived the previous night at Encampment G. It was a relatively stable place and had developed something of a community feel to it. Toddlers looked up from their mud paddling pool and laughed at the large but rapidly shrinking Englishman on the top step.

Soldiers with damp cheroots in their mouths carried leather rice pouches over one shoulder and automatic weapons on the other. Pretty ladies hid behind powder masks and greeted him with their eyebrows.

He walked around. There was a hut for schooling the children, and a large medical tent. There was a spacious area with a roof but no walls—for meetings he assumed, as there were already a number of people gathered there. The expanse of huts had adopted some of the trappings of permanence: plants in improvised pots; vegetables in polite rows; even, heaven knows where they'd come from, housecats asleep on humble front porches. But it was a deceptive calm. The camp could never get too large or too comfortable. When the rains stopped, it would be gone.

He wondered whether he could be useful somehow. He wandered under the canopied area and immediately interrupted the meeting. He could tell from the turned heads that he had disturbed something strategic. Even the subsequent warm smiles and hellos didn't amount to an invitation to stay.

For an hour he found himself as an impromptu English teacher at the school. He used the language on a daily basis, but it wasn't until that lesson he realized he knew nothing of its mechanics. It would have been easier to explain the process of dreaming. But the children, starving for education and culture and stability, gobbled up whatever they could get. They actually appreciated the value of learning and life, in a way the little buggers disfiguring walls and bus shelters in Kingston never would. Ornery old people were right after all. You do only appreciate things when you have to do without.

"Why. . . ? You mean why does United Kingdom have a 'the' in front of it, but England doesn't?" Stuffed if I know, he thought. It wasn't the only thing he couldn't answer. He promised he would come back the next day with a real lesson, as well as unlocking the great missing 'the' puzzle.

As he left, they all stood, five and 14-year-olds jumbled together, and politely thanked him for his lesson. It lodged in his heart somewhere, that hutful of manners deep in hostile territory. He really saw how his father had fallen in love with the Karen and had wanted to be more than just a bookkeeper.

He sat for some while drinking tea with a lady almost totally blind. She didn't have a language she could share with him. Just tea. She had beckoned him in, not knowing who he was. She sat him down, poured his drink from a permanently boiling billy, and returned to her work.

He looked at her as she sewed from memory. Her fingers deftly found the bullet holes in the freshly scrubbed fatigues, and darned them away. He didn't feel discomfort at being there. He finished his tea, refused a second cup, and left with a smile she couldn't see but knew was there.

What next. . . ? He walked across to the enormous MASH tent and stood in front of it. The red cross on the roof had been covered with green paint. The Karen had learned dearly what a good target a red cross could be.

Bamboo extensions of various shapes and sizes snaked east and west from the main tent like clumsy afterthoughts. These wards weren't occupied now. The rains had given soldiers time to heal or die from their wounds. For a month, no new battle victims had arrived. So only those with long-term infections or jungle-born diseases were hospitalized, and they were all under canvass.

John walked to the peeled-aside flaps and pushed his nose against the grey mosquito netting that blocked the entrance. It took some time for his eyes to adjust to the shadows.

Shirley, for want of a nurse, had finished divvying out the pills and capsules into the 11 seedpods she used as containers. She lifted the tray and turned to begin her rounds.

There was nothing, she had believed, that could shock her. She was puzzled by the way the world functioned, but none of the headlines she read or the cruelties she witnessed caused any physical, biological reaction in her. But when the ghost stood in the entrance to her tent that morning, her fossilized heart began to pump fit to burst. The nerves in her fingers shook away the tray and all its pills, and her legs turned to water. She fainted for the only time in her life.

31

"I always have that effect on women," John said as Shirley's eyes flickered open. She coughed from the fumes of the smelling salts. She was lying on one of the vacant bedrolls on the ground. Her patients and John were gathered around her like wounded surgeons.

"What happened?" she asked, although even as she spoke she recalled exactly what she'd seen. Without his gauze shroud and halo of bright sunlight, the man looked a lot less like a ghost. But there was an amazing similarity.

"I really didn't mean to frighten you," he added.

The crowd recoiled as the doctor sat up. She snapped at the patients in Karen and they hobbled and limped back to their own spots on the ground like the living dead returning to their graves. She climbed shakily to her feet and chose not to tell the stranger what he'd done to her.

"That really doesn't happen so often, thank goodness," she said. "Lack of sleep I guess."

She caught him staring at her, and looked away. She was used to it. Beautiful women expected such, but Shirley was never flattered by the attention. It was an annoying distraction. She honestly wished she could be plain, or downright ugly, and step back from centre stage into the chorus line.

But when she glanced back into this man's eyes, she saw again her ghost, and lingered longer than she would normally in her stare.

John had no way of interpreting the look, but it rustled his insides just enough to throw him. "I . . . er." And he couldn't think what the 'er' was destined to become.

Shirley too was uncomfortable. "What are you doing here?"

Her brusqueness brought him back to reality. "I was wondering whether there was anything I could do to help."

"Are you a doctor?"

"No."

"A nurse?"

"Actually I'm a policeman."

She laughed. "Oh. Good. Perhaps I could get you to frisk these patients for illegal weapons."

Her ghost smiled at her. "I'm here on business for a day or two. There isn't very much I can do until my friend comes back. I wanted to be useful. I picked up a couple of hours at the school, but they've already exposed my limitations. I was wondering if there was something I could do here."

Very much against her better judgement she said, "Well, you can start by rescuing those pills you made me drop. We don't have that many we can leave them buried here in the dirt."

-o-

He helped out for the rest of the day. It wasn't exactly his commitment to medicine and the plight of the sick that kept him there. Dr. Shirley was enchanting him. He knew only too well that women weren't particularly interested in him. He'd long given up grooming himself in any attempt to entice the opposite sex. He was the type who could rob a bank happily knowing the witnesses wouldn't be able to describe him. They couldn't even say he was overweight anymore, just nondescript.

But, to his surprise, he found this attractive doctor staring at him on a number of occasions. Even though it was a look of query rather than pent-up passion, it wasn't an altogether unpleasant experience. It unsettled him enough to make him say stupid things for most of the afternoon. He didn't dazzle her once with his wit or intelligence. In fact, by the time the soldier came to invite him for dinner with the elders, he was certain he'd rendered himself ineligible as either a mate or a cerebrally functioning human being.

But it had been so stimulating to feel the activity inside his chest. He wasn't dead after all.

When he'd finally left, Shirley breathed a sigh of relief. His being there had been so infuriating. He hadn't told her the truth about why he was there or who he was with. He'd given her no clues as to his background, but she knew. Her ghost had returned to her somehow, and she was determined to discover how it was possible. She wouldn't let him get away again.

John whistled his way to the general's house. The general was never there, but they called it the general's house anyway. This new, improved John was welcomed warmly by the old men he'd met the previous evening. The group was light one or two who had probably gone off with Norbert to collect data on Jim's final mission. The meal was tasty and the atmosphere cordial. John waited for a discrete juncture at which to inquire about the doctor. He didn't have to wait long.

"I hear you were helping out at the clinic today," said one.

"I don't think I saved any lives."

"There probably weren't any men in there sick enough to die. It's funny how many mystery illnesses we've had since Dr. Shirley arrived."

"What. . . ? Oh, you mean. . . .Yes. I see." He had a long forgotten ache of jealousy. Perhaps sobriety turned men into emotional wrecks. This woman was already making a mess of him. "Perhaps she's just a good doctor."

The men laughed at his unintentional joke.

"Right. Good to look at."

"Nice little figure."

"Good enough to eat."

If they hadn't been so old, he would have punched them. How dare they talk about her like that? It occurred to him what risks there would be for an unattached woman out here in the jungle. At least he assumed she was. . . .

"Does she have a husband? Boyfriend?"

"No, son. She's all yours. She's as free as a bird."

"And hard as a rock," said another.

"Hard?"

"She lives alone, eats alone, sleeps alone. Doesn't mix."

"She does her job and that's it. If you aren't sick, she has nothing to do with you." He dished out and passed around a course of unidentifiable stew mixed with instant noodles. It didn't taste nearly as bad as it looked. "She isn't here to make friends, I know that."

"The brigadier here has a . . . what do they call it. . . ? A conspiracy theory."

The white-haired brigadier's spoon hovered in front of his mouth like a hummingbird Stew dripped onto his lap. "I don't trust her. That's all. I happen to know. . . ." He lowered his voice: "That she asks questions to the patients about SLORC placements and troop movements. She wanted to know about one of their majors last week. What business is that for a doctor? And she asks them when they're drugged and drowsy so they won't remember her asking. But they do."

"You see, Jim," said the man to John's right. "Every group of eternal optimists has its pessimist to keep things balanced."

"Every Seven Dwarfs has its Grumpy," laughed another.

As there were exactly seven of the old soldiers, that was particularly hilarious. It took some while for the choking to stop and decorum to be maintained. The brigadier still hadn't docked his spoon.

"You won't be laughing when they find out she's a SLORC informer."

"Naturally she must be a SLORC spy. She doesn't talk to anyone here, and the only questions she asks are about the enemy."

"I must confess, that has confused me. Perhaps she's a spy for us."

This caused more laughter, washed down with lumpy, grey rice whisky. John gratefully passed up the offer of a taste.

All through the meal and the evening of deliberations that followed, John's mind was firmly tuned to Dr. Shirley. Without a generator and with the rationing of candles, bedtime at Encampment 8 was at 6:45. Of course, you could stay up and find faces in the moon, or join up the stars to make an animal, but most people went to sleep, particularly on cloudy nights such as this.

In Chiang Mai, Norbert had lent him a hurricane lamp as a night companion. Without it, he knew the darkness would grow over him like a vine and strangle him. But here he was again, alone with the blackness, a tadpole in ink. He couldn't see his own feet. But these evenings, with his father's courage, he was learning to appreciate the beauty of night. He had time to think. Something was coming to him out of the dark; some message. But it wasn't yet plain enough to read. He knew he had to be open to it, and enjoying the darkness was part of that openness.

He put his palms behind his head and indulged in a fantasy. It wasn't a particularly clean one, but he was able to introduce a surprisingly romantic undercurrent. He liked the image so much that he played it again and again until his insomnia got bored with trying to haunt him and allowed him to sleep. . . .

In his dream, their—his and Shirley's—wood-panelled bungalow was being bombarded with mortars and machine-gun fire. She leaned across to him in their bed. Her hand was heavy on his chest. Her voice was deep and gravelly. "Jim Junior. We have to leave now."

-o-

"Jim Junior. We have to leave now. . . .

"The hand shook him awake, and he was startled to see —or rather, feel—the black shape looming over him. The voice came from somewhere inside it. "Pack everything you brought with you. Everything. Every paper, every map, every stitch of clothing. Don't leave a thing. We're pulling out."

The weapon fire was crisp in the blackness, and close. Physically and mentally confused, John fumbled around in the darkness to collect his and Norbert's few possessions. The warning, 'this is not a drill' kept sounding in his head. This was real and frightening.

He couldn't tell whether the owner of the voice was still with him. He offered an "Okay" into the darkness.

"This way."

He followed the reply into the ink. At the top of the ladder, the blackness was spoilt from time to time by flashes of fire from beyond the trees. Explosions rocked the hut as he lowered himself to the ground. Silent shapes scurried past him with surprising assurance and a lack of fear.

The brigadier's calm face was lit by the flashes, light that came from very close now. At his feet were two huge bundles.

"Can you take one of these?" The bangs were all around them.

"Of course." John hoisted it over one shoulder, then the other. It weighed a ton, and had been packed hurriedly. It jabbed painfully into his back. He tested his balance with a few steps. Then it came. It was too fast to see whether his name was on it. A warm spit of fire creased the air by his head.

Nine years in the police force and he'd never used or carried a gun. He'd never been fired at. If he'd been an inch taller, or had better posture, he would now have been dead. That thought stayed with him.

"Stay always no more than two yards behind me," the brigadier yelled above the din. "Come."

The man's pack was larger and bulkier than John's, but he carried it as if his legs grew out of it. He set off at a trot. John was so intent on keeping the black mass ahead within sight that his feet stumbled clumsily over roots and mounds. Twice he fell to his knees. A light rain was falling and the ground was slimy.

From where they'd come, there were cries of pain; final screams preceding death. John thought about the school and the kids, the clinic and Shirley. And here he was running for his life. What was he to do for them? He was helpless himself; blind, panicked. How was he to help anyone? On they went. Deeper into nowhere. . . .

Then, without words, the old man stopped, and they stood silently. The bursts of fire made a threat of every tree, every shadow. Just as suddenly, they'd be plunged back into blindness. Still the old man stood motionless.

The torchlight came from behind John, and highlighted the white hair on his companion's head. The brigadier turned in an instant. He pushed John to one side, and lifted an automatic weapon John hadn't noticed him holding. He fired at the source of the light and to either side of it. The beam slowly swept to the sky and was gone.

"Come," said the brigadier, and continued on his way as if this were no more than a pause for a piss. John, amazed, stumbled on after him.

Long tongues of fire licked at the sky, and the smell of cordite overtook them. The camp had been razed. There was sporadic gunfire as the invaders and the incumbents battled. There was no way to tell which had been victorious.

John's ears strained to catch footsteps behind them. The further they went, all the natural sounds of the place seemed to have been erased. There was just the huff of their breaths, their own stamping feet, the whisper of branches clawing at their clothes and their skin.

The trot settled into a march, then a hike, then a realization that they would probably survive. Exhaustion was replaced by a mechanical rhythm. Just as thought can be replaced by the recitation of tables, so John recited his legs away from death. . . .

"One. Left, right. Two. Left, right."

-o-

How they reached the rendezvous point, or how many hours it had taken them, John couldn't begin to guess. Neither could he fathom how others had got there before them: children, pregnant women, the old blind sewing lady. They were all there. Some were sleeping, some being treated.

The sun, still below the horizon, was beginning to beat a mauve bruise into the sky. A bird began to sing irreverently, ignorant of the tragedy behind them. Nature went on as if nothing had happened.

The brigadier lowered his pack to the ground and smiled. John did the same. They hadn't spoken at all on the journey. John walked over to the old man and stood empty before him. He held out a weak hand and the man grasped it warmly in both of his.

"Welcome to the humdrum world of the Karen," he said.

"Thank you for my life," John replied.

"You're welcome."

"I hope everyone made it out. I don't see anyone from the hospital."

"They were all evacuated to a closer meeting point. I saw them leave. I'm sure they're safe. By the way, do you intend to wear your hair that way permanently?"

John followed the old man's gaze with his hand. The hair on his head was caked with blood. "Jesus. I thought they'd missed."

The man poured water from his canteen onto the wound and searched through the hair. There was no pain until the brigadier sloshed the wound with a strong antiseptic.

"It must be hair blood. There's barely a scratch on your scalp."

"You'd better check for holes. It could have gone in one side and out the other."

They laughed a kind of delirious, exhausted laugh, collapsed to the damp grassy ground, and leaned against their packs. John looked at the wiry old soldier opposite. His duty done, his work finished, he had changed out of his stealth and power and back into his frailty like a jungle Superman.

"The torch light?" John asked. "How could you have been so sure it wasn't one of your own people?"

The brigadier laughed. "We're Karen, Jim Junior. We aren't so foolish as to light ourselves up while we're under attack. Only an arrogant SLORC would do something like that. And now, no more questions. My old body needs rest." He slid down the bundle to a green mattress of leaves and weeds, and was snoring before John could wish him pleasant dreams.

John found a soft patch and settled down, also. The last thing he remembered was the arrival of the first milky strand of sunlight. It passed like a spear between the branches above his head. It was like a memo from God, reminding him of how narrowly the bullet had spared him. He said thank you, and slept.

32

Bruce stormed out of the tutor's office as he had many times before. He forgot to slam the door, so he went back and did it. The man was a fool. How could you learn from someone too opinionated to open their eyes to alternatives? But, that was the point of formal education wasn't it. If you wanted a sham qualification like a Ph.D. you had to play the sham rules set by sham people. The skill wasn't in knowing. It was in knowing what they wanted. It was in sacrificing pride for long enough to get that shammed-up bit of paper that made everyone suddenly take notice of your alternative opinions.

'Dr. Bruce believes that. . . .'

You have to be royalty to overthrow the kings.

He dragged his overripe and bruised intellect out to the car park and unchained his luminous yellow mountain bike from the *"No Bicycles"* sign.

The University of Reading campus at Whiteknights had rustically ignored the suburban mess that was already becoming dilapidated. around it. He sped out of one of the back gates into traffic and raised a finger at the Saab that almost smacked into him.

The frantic cycle into town cooled his temper. By the time he rounded the corner into the cul-de-sac behind the old biscuit factory, he was almost charming. He was renting a place in a terrace of houses so narrow it resembled a shelf of encyclopedias. He lived in D to G. There was a pile of circulars on the doormat. Nothing was of interest apart from the postcard.

It had a printed logo and letterhead from Kingston upon Thames Police Station. In neat handwriting, there was a request to contact Inspector Patel as soon as possible in reference to his brother-in-law. Bruce's heart thumped. It could only mean one thing. First their mother, now John. He dialed the number on the card. It was a mobile.

"Yes?"

"Inspector Patel please."

"Ah, yes. Speaking." It was a cultured but unplaceable accent. From the name, Bruce assumed it had Indian origins. He introduced himself.

"Ah, Mr. Fossel. I'm afraid I have some very bad news for you."

"John?"

"I'm sorry to say he has become the latest victim of this maniac. He died this afternoon, horribly."

"Oh Shit. I thought he was overseas."

There was silence for a few seconds.

"Yes. He just got back. He flew in this morning. Do you happen to know where he'd been?"

"Thailand I believe."

"Really? How fascinating. Er . . . we've been trying to contact his sister to inform her. But it appears she's gone away. I was wondering how we could get in touch with her."

Bruce's mind was racing. "With Susan. . . ? Right. That isn't easy."

"Do you have a number for her, or an address?"

"No. But she'll be calling me tomorrow evening. I can tell her."

"Is she in the country? I'm afraid, as the last blood relative, she'll have to identify the body."

"Well, Inspector, I'm sure you realize what danger she's in. She's much safer where she is."

"That's just it, Mr. Fossel. I'm not sure she is. The retired police superintendent who arranged her . . . departure, has also sadly joined the list of victims."

"Jesus."

"There's only one more step to finding her. Believe me, she'd be much better off under police custody. We have a system in place to look after her, and her son, and you too for that matter."

"No. I'm a bit nuts me. You couldn't lock me up. I'd save him the trouble and top myself." And he wasn't exactly sure why he added, ". . . and my French is shithouse." Les Sables was a distraction they'd come up with to confuse outsiders. There was another pause.

"Well. When she calls you tomorrow, I'd be grateful if you could tell her about her brother, and also about the offer of police protection. You may be irresponsible about your own life, but you have a family to consider. Don't gamble with their lives, Mr. Fossel. You know how to reach me. I'm away from the station most of the time, but you can reach me at this number 24 hours. I am so sorry to be a bearer of bad tidings. Good day to you."

A lot of things about the call disturbed Bruce. He went into the one-elbow-room kitchenette and made a pot of tea so he could think. When it was properly stewed, he eased himself into the living room furniture, a black PVC beanbag, and blew across the surface of the Earl Grey.

Inspector Patel, with his lovely BBC-Foreign-Service English. He was indeed a bearer of bad tidings. But he was also one bloody smart detective. How did he find him, this Sherlock of the subcontinent? Nobody had Bruce's address. He got all his mail sent to the uni PO Box. And how did Patel know that Aunt Maud was helping them? They kept that a secret even from Emma.

He sipped at the tea, put down the mug, and prodded the numbers on his cellphone. He wasn't the mobile type, but John had bought it for him to keep in touch with Susan when he went away. He'd already lost it twice. Just the day before, he'd misplaced it in the library. The librarian had found it buzzing on a shelf. It lately seemed to be losing a number of its functions in his company. He had that effect on all things regimented.

"Call me an old cynic, but you should never trust brilliance in unlikely places," he said to himself as directory enquiries answered.

"Oh, hi. Could you give me the number for Kingston upon Thames Police Station please. . . ."

He wrote it down on the linoleum.

He may have been throwing away his valuable student grant on mobile phone bills, but . . . . "Hello? Kingston Police Station? Could I speak to Inspector Patel please. . . . What. . . .? Oh. When will he be back. . . ? I see. No thanks. I'll call back later."

Well then. That was that.

33

John slept the sleep of a man passed away. Waking should have been like rising from the dead. Except he couldn't exactly rise. He was Gulliver and the Lilliputians had tied his body to the ground with twine.

"I really need to get into better shape," he told himself. After the unprecedented exertions of the previous night, his body was undergoing a muscle-boycott. Nothing he could do would elevate him from the ground. He crunched his neck to the left and right. He was alone. His colleague and their packs were gone. It was overcast late afternoon or early evening. His sky was a dome of leaves. He was surprised to hear a familiar voice at his feet.

"Well, ain't you a sorry sight."

John used his hand to raise his head.

Norbert, propped up against a tree, was smoking something natural. "Excuse me if I don't get up."

"I leave you alone for a day and look at the mess you get yourself into."

"You told me the SLORC don't attack in the rainy season." He rolled painfully on to his stomach like a beetle righting itself, and rose into a crouch. From there he was able to creak to a standing position.

Norbert thought this was hilarious. "Boy, I'd like to see you in combat. Two-week campaigns. No sleep."

"I'd adapt." He staggered over to his friend, who handed him some fruit from his pack.

"What happened, Norbert?"

"Nobody understands it. It was totally unexpected. That's why security was so lax. They'd never have got so close so fast in the dry season. It was a crack unit, not your regular teenaged draftees. They didn't open fire until they were spotted, so the theory is they were aiming to get in, do some damage, and get out again without starting a battle."

158

"So why did we run?"

"Oh, there was plenty of 'em. Once they was spotted, they wasn't about to leave a thank-you note and go home."

"What do you think they wanted to do?"

"They could have been an assassination or a kidnap unit."

"Who do you think they were after?"

"We thought for a while it was you."

"Me?"

"Sure. They didn't know who you are. If one of their spies spotted you, they would have assumed you was a foreign advisor. Good politics to capture a foreigner helping the enemy. It would embarrass the hell out of your government."

"Oops." He leant back against the tree, unpeeled the mystery fruit, and bit into it. "Aaahh! Shit!"

"Watch the stones."

"Now you tell me. Okay. But you're not convinced it was me they were after."

"You ain't completely out of the reckoning. But someone heard something during the skirmish. One of their officers called out for the men not to shoot any women."

"So?"

"Not good cricket, what, old boy. . . ? John your boys might not kill women and children, but the Burmese didn't learn them rules. They slaughter anyone outside a SLORC uniform. So it was weird they should spare the women."

"Rape?"

"It was too far to come for sex slaves; too risky."

"So, was there a woman important enough to stage a raid for?"

"The Karen have been chewing that one over. There weren't any decision-makers out here. No wives of high-ranking officials. You figure it."

John thought about Shirley. But she was just a young doctor. Why would they be after her? The smoke from

Norbert's weed wafted up into John's face. It had a sweet, sickly smell.

"Is that an illicit substance?"

"Not in this precinct. Want one. . . ? He opened his pack to reveal several more neatly rolled leaves. He handed one to John and threw his Bic into the air. John's reflexes weren't up to it. It dropped back into Norbert's hand.

"What about your trip? Did you get anything apart from fruit and dope?"

"You bet. I managed to piece together your pa's last mission. I met the guide who took him to Te Pao."

"Good stuff. What did he go there for?"

"That, he didn't know. But we do have a candidate for your nutter."

John sat beside Norbert. "Tell me."

"His name's General Bohmu Din. '*Bohmu*' actually means 'major,' but as he earned his reputation when he was a major, I guess the title stuck as a nickname. He was the regional SLORC field commander for the Taungoo area when the Karen were still active up there. He was real scary stuff. Even his own men were afraid of him. He was into everything; no scruples, no morals, no rules. He climbed the ranks from a vigilante unit that terrorized the villages. They tortured suspected KNU sympathizers and their relatives, raped girls, burned crops. You name it."

"The kind of guy who'd be very pissed off if you got the better of him."

"Right."

"But we have no idea why dad went there?"

"None at all. But we *are* sure the soldiers that delivered Jim's pieces to the Thai border were from Bohmu Din's old unit."

"Bingo. So we have a suspect."

"Well, we don't actually got him."

"Why not?"

"He left the region ten years ago."

"Out or up?"

"Up. The loved him. Or, at least they loved his record. He got recalled to Rangoon. They pinned some shiny frying pans on his chest and drafted him into the machine."

"So, he's in Rangoon?"

"Could be. That's as far as the trail took me. Next part is up to you."

"Me?"

"There's a list of persona no go at the airport in Rangoon. The names on it are so hot, the smiley lady at Immigration would pull out her old .44 and blow off the head of anyone on it. My name's at the top. But nobody knows you there. We're heading back to Chiang Mai in the morning. You can rest up there and fly direct."

"Into the valley of death."

They puffed on their weeds.

"That was probably like a famous English quotation, right?"

"Something like that."

"You Limeys are so cultured." They both laughed until tears rolled down their cheeks.

"It's good shit, ain't it."

"Rather."

34

At 7:00 p.m., Susan phoned Bruce from the regular call box on the main road.

"Hi, lover."

"Hello, Mrs. Bruce. How's 'Cognito?"

"Glorious. How's 'Cademia?"

"Excruciating. But one more month of this tutorial hell and I can ensconce myself away with you and Eddo. How's the unborn?"

"She's kicking, Bruce. I think she wants to get out of there. Eddo's having conversations with her already."

"He okay?"

"Are you okay, our son?"

Eddo took the phone. Hello, Bruce."

"Wotcha cock. How's the palace?"

"It isn't a palace. It's a staply home." Susan corrected him. "A stately home. When you coming, Bruce? I've got some great worms."

"I'm envious."

"What's envious?"

"It's like jealous but greener."

"Ow. There's a fire truck. Can you hear it? Gotta go. Bye, Bruce.

"Bye, Ed—"

"Well, there he goes chasing the fire truck."

"He'll probably catch it. . . . Sue, love. Something peculiar happened yesterday."

"Anything bad?"

"It could have been a lot worse. I got a phone call from a police officer called Patel. I have no idea how he found me. He told me some things I didn't want to hear."

"Oh God, Bruce. What?"

"Don't panic. I'll tell you later. The important thing was, I got bad vibes from the dude, so I phoned the station. There really is an Inspector Patel, so I figured it was legitimate. Normally, I would have left it there. But this Pao thing's been spooking me. Some serious paranoia was cast upon me."

"Bruce, get to the bloody point."

"Sorry. So I called back later, and this Patel bloke was there this time. And get this, it wasn't the same guy."

"What?"

"No. The one that phoned me sounded like a BBC newsreader from the sixties. The real Patel has a thick Brummie accent. He's not even on the Te Pao case."

"Damn."

"Exactly. Like, so I tell him the story and he's on to the Yard, and an hour later I've got a house full of real detectives detecting all over the bloody place, drinking my tea, sitting on my chair—"

"Did they get him?"

"No. They called the mobile number on the card, but there was no signal. That was weird too, because he was expecting a call from me. The Old Bill reckon he must have been watching me. So, you won't believe this. They've only put me up at the Hyatt, haven't they. Slept in a real bed last night. It's stimulating in an 'edge of tragedy' kind of way. I guess you don't want to know all the bull he told me to tell you."

"Too right I don't." Eddo was back from chasing fire engines. "Do you want to say anything else to Bruce. . . ? No. . . ? Okay. Give me five minutes. We'll stop off at Big C on the way back and get some Cadbury's eggs. Bruce?"

"Yup."

Listen, lover, I know you're an independent, stubborn son of a pig, but do me . . . do *us* a favour. I can sleep much better if I know you're safe. He's found you once. He can find you again. Stay out of his way. Don't go flashing yourself around Reading like some slice-me-up advert."

Bruce thought it best not to mention he'd spent the day at the library. Or that he rode his bike there. Or that the police were really pissed off that they'd lost him.

"I want my brains tested," she went on. "But I love you I guess. I want to grow old and hairy with you. Promise me?"

"Well, there are only limited supplies in the fridge in the room. . . ."

"Bruce."

"I promise."

"Thanks. I was planning to call Maud after this, but Eddo's getting frisky so I'll hold off till tomorrow."

"Shit." Bruce was hoping not to have to say anything about that. The detectives had followed up on the news about CSI Maudling, and the local police officer had dropped by to find him still hanging from the verandah door. The birds hadn't left much of him.

"Susan."

"Yes, honey? What? What is it?"

"Aunt Maud copped it."

She felt sick to her stomach.

"Mother. That's six minutes," he heard his son say. There was no reply. Bruce waited.

"Sue?"

"I gotta go. I love you. I'll call Thursday." And she hung up.

Bruce dropped the phone into his shirt pocket and slumped onto the bed. He wasn't being much help. Susan was the strongest, the ballsiest woman he'd ever known, but this all had to be getting to her. He decided to stuff the tutorials. When she called back, he'd find out where she was, and go and be with them. It was time to be a husband and a father.

Meanwhile, the room that had been cool the day before was starting to get claustrophobic. It had everything—cable TV, posture friendly mattress, hair-drier—and was all paid for out of the national taxes he'd somehow never got around to contributing to. But it was confinement. The cop downstairs in reception was the lock.

He turned on the TV and took another beer from the tiny fridge that seemed to produce an endless supply. But after ten minutes of *Touched by an Angel*, he was climbing the curtains: strangled by gratuitous luxury and tasteless entertainment.

He ignored the lift and took the back stairs. The fire door opened onto a lane. He wasn't breaking the promise exactly. It was night. Nobody would see him.

It felt good to be outside. The streets were dark and the occasional lamps struggled to change matters. In fact, they just wound the darkness into different shades of grey. The paving stones were uneven. Reading always reminded Bruce of a city where council workers came to practice before doing it properly somewhere else.

He crossed a main street and walked around the perimeter of a park where by day, cricketers in grass-stained whites wasted valuable hours, and by night, homosexuals enticed one-another by flashing cigarette lighters. He passed the window of a pub where red-nosed men sat with the dogs they were pretending to walk.

It was on the return journey that the feeling came over him. Streets he had previously shared, were now ominously empty. It felt like some portent of a storm had dropped on Reading and he'd only just noticed it.

There was one short alleyway before the bright shop fronts of the main street. It had narrowed and darkened and eeried up a good deal since he'd first walked through it. He was angry at himself for inventing all this. He focussed his mind on the far end of the alley where cars and buses passed oblivious to the paranoia he'd manufactured for himself. He took a breath and headed for them.

Most of the shadows on either side of him allowed him to pass in peace. Only one was there to kill him. Bruce knew and felt nothing of it. Before his heightened senses could react to the movement, his throat was slit and his life was gone.

It wasn't so much the life Bohmu Din was there for, as the mobile phone in Bruce's pocket. He took it and walked casually back to the rented car as if nothing untoward had happened. He climbed into the back seat of the Nissan that had been his home for a week.

He supposed he could merely have stolen the phone once again, but failure didn't perch happily on the gnarled branches of Bohmu Din's mind. All the gawky hippie had to do was phone him back as he'd told him to. Nobody had asked him to use his head. So that head was now half on, half off: a state he had brought upon himself. The Burman derived no great pleasure in killing such people, but neither did he feel remorse. He no longer had a stomach for watching his victims suffer. He dispatched them swiftly and with purpose. They were just sentries guarding Heaven.

He took out the photograph. It was soft now, like cotton, from the years of handling. The images of the white angel and her brother were smudged beyond recognition from the countless times he had caressed their innocent faces with his callused fingers. But he could see them in his mind as clearly as that first day.

In the background, the mother leaned forward and produced a glorious but imitation smile. The children were on the sand in front of her. The boy grinned. His red hair stood up like squirrel tufts, his eyes big and blue, his left ear gnarled.

The girl was so lovely. Her hair was blond like jasmine hearts, and her smile natural and inviting. So inviting.

"I'm close now, my princess. Let's see just how close."

From the toolbox under the seat, he removed a screwdriver and unscrewed the back of the phone. The recording device sat where he'd installed it the previous day. The hippie wasn't careful with his possessions. In his work, Bohmu Din had access to so many of these toys of high technology. He removed the disc and put it into the player. When he'd listened to its secret conversations, he was pleased with himself. He had more than enough information to close in on the target. He ran his thumb over the featureless faces that had once smiled on a beach at the feet of a woman in movie-star sunglasses.

"I'm coming."

35

Kruamart and the housemaid looked through the many temple photographs and wondered why the date on the bottom was the same on all of them. Norbert somehow convinced them that the device on the camera was stuck. John doubted Kruamart believed him, but she was certainly pleased to have him back.

It would have been incredible, John thought, to have someone miss him so much that her instinct told her he was on the road home. To have someone love him so much that her eyes filled with tears when she saw his face through the windscreen. To hold him so tightly he had to beg for breath. Norbert had all this and John didn't.

The couple had a very early night and left John alone on the balcony with a mosquito coil and his thoughts. He thought of Encampment G, of his near death and near love experiences. He listened to the water and the frogs and the dreams of the housedogs. When the full moon's puffy face peered through the clouds, the stream held up a mirror to it like a doting lover, and carried its image beyond the house. The clouds would get jealous of this affair and re-claim their moon, plunging John into a blackness that no longer terrified him.

Did he really use to sleep with the bunny-rabbit night-light on, tough old police inspector Jessel? Had he really needed those nightcaps to coax him into sleep?

"Man, she's insatiable." Norbert, in black silk fisherman's trousers, walked bow-legged through the house swinging a hurricane lamp. It was as if the whole house were swinging with him. "You couldn't come take over for a couple of hours could you?"

"Don't tempt me, Norbert. I could use a little TLC right now."

"Oh ho. I feel a Celine Deon moment coming on." He pulled up a rocker, lowered the lamp wick, and sat staring at the same shadows. "You missing some little honey in Inglaterra?" (n)

"No, mate." Honey was definitely not flowing in the old country. "I was starting to think they'd taken out my heart instead of my appendix."

"Until. . . ?"

"Why does there have to be an 'until'?"

"Boy, you been as bright as a brush fire since Camp G. Now, I know you survived getting shot in the brain and all that, but it don't explain the jingly-jangly in your eye."

"I've got a jingly-jangly in my eye?"

"You sure do, boy. And I know where that jingly-jangly came from, too."

"Oh, you do?"

"Yes, sir. And it starts with a 'doc' and ends with a 'ter.'"

"Rubbish."

"Oh yeah? So why was you asking everyone at the rendezvous site if they'd seen her? And why was you so happy when they told you she probably went off to some other site where all the hospital patients was taken?"

"My concern for the medical profession."

"Right. And why was you so pissed at me when I told you we wouldn't be passing that site on our way back? You got a jingly-jangly sure as I'm sitting here."

"Okay. For argument sake, just suppose I did have a jingly-jangly, and I'm not saying I do. But if I did, what good would that do me?"

"Well, it might just have something good to do with you if she was asking everyone about you after your day of 'volunteering' at the hospital."

"*She was?*"

"Oh ho. There he is. That big old jingly-jangly."

"Was she really, Norbert? Serious?"

"She sure was, boy. She asked half a dozen people she'd never spoke to before. And I tell you another thing. You two got something else in common."

"What's that?"

"She's only ever asked about one other man before, and his name is Bohmu Goddamn Din."

"No. . . ? But, why?"

Norbert turned up the wick of his lamp and stood.

"I'll leave you with that question . . . 'cause, right now, you know exactly everything I know, and I got no answers. Now, if you'll excuse me, I got a mad wife to please while I still got some wick left. You look after that jingly-jangly now, boy."

And, with that, Norbert, the light, and any chance of sleep disappeared.

36

What John had heard about Dr. Shirley was false. Not that she had been asking about him. That much was true. She asked everyone until she got the answer she was looking for.

It could have been that they were protecting his feelings, or they may really not have known, but she wasn't safe. She didn't get away from the camp with the invalids. The Burmese raid had not been a failure. The target had been identified, separated from the others, and transported to the battalion headquarters in Pa'an.

There, she was treated politely, but not allowed answers to her questions. She had been alert to the sounds around her through the thick wool hood. The raiding party had handed her over to guards, one of whom was a woman. They marched her along concrete corridors where the footsteps bounced up against tin roofing, which told her they were in a relatively permanent one-storey structure. She acted as timid and pathetic as she was able, and only one guard had a light hold on her arm as they walked.

They removed the hood in a small, sparsely furnished room. She cried and asked the guards what she had done wrong, and why they had brought her there, even though she knew. They ignored her and the men left. The woman apologized before giving her a thorough body search. As Shirley had anticipated, it wasn't quite thorough enough.

When the guard left, she looked around the room. She had to know it well. A good general always reconnoiters the field of battle. There was a portable commode, a field cot, a card table, and one chair. The walls were bare, and there was one small barred window high up one wall. She had traveled all day. It was evening.

She was ready. Calm. Now, all she needed was for him to come. She'd known she would be too focussed at this late stage to be nervous. She had read of warriors who could keep nothing down for days before an engagement, suddenly enjoying a huge meal just hours before the attack. This was the peace before war. When the scuffle of feet announced visitors at the door, she looked at her hands and they were as solid as the Madonna's. The time had come.

But neither of the men who entered her room was him. Her heart deflated slightly. Of course he would send in others first, she told herself. He would come later, more than likely alone. That would be even better. One step at a time.

The men before her were uniformed senior officers. One of them carried a bill of documents she recognized immediately, but ignored.

"Stand up," one of them barked at her in Burmese, and gestured for her to move over to the wall.

She whimpered and immediately did as she was told. Rather comically, she thought, the two soldiers took her place on the cot. It moaned under their weight. She clasped her hands behind her back and lowered her head in deference to the men.

One officer pushed his glasses firmly up to the bridge of his nose, and held out the papers so she could see them.

"You recognize these?"

She squinted as if she hadn't noticed her letter to the daughter of No Ay Me. Then she pulled an expression of shock across her face. "But. How did you get that?" she asked.

"That isn't important," the second man answered. "What you have written here, is it . . . factual?"

Shirley feigned embarrassment but managed a slight nod of her head.

"These are serious accusations, girl," said glasses.

"Very serious," added the other for effect.

"I . . . I had no intention of making the story public, sir. It was just a letter to a lady I knew. Will Major Bohmu Din punish me for this?"

"The general is in . . . he isn't in Myanmar at present."

Outwardly, Shirley showed no change of emotion. Inside she collapsed like an old building. Not in Myanmar? Then make him come back. This is the most important thing in his life. It must be. She was certain he would be there. All her planning for the last decade had been structured around his being there to meet her. How could he not be there?

She was devastated, and the tears she cried now in front of the two men, were real. They were not tears of exposure, but of hopes dropping to the ground like shot birds. This was all useless now. There was no reason for her being there; no reason to play-act to these overweight, over-decorated fools.

They interpreted her tears as humiliation. They were uncomfortable at being the mirror of her embarrassment, and they shifted nervously on the bed. They had both read her account, and knew how she must be feeling, what she must be thinking of them as witnesses to her shame. When it was clear the crying would not stop, they mumbled together behind their hands. Together, they stood.

"We will give you a little time to . . . compose yourself," said one. "But when we return, I'm sure you understand, there are many questions we will need answers to."

They walked to the door and called to the guard, who opened it for them. Glasses turned back to her. Although his voice said nothing, his expression told her he was sorry for their intrusion into her life, and for many things he had no obligation to apologize for. He hadn't been responsible for what happened to her, but he knew it should never have gone unpunished. His expression said all this, but his mouth kept shut. He left and the door slammed.

Shirley leaned back against the wall and berated herself for her weakness and her defeatist thoughts. This wasn't failure. It was a setback, but it wasn't the end. She had to keep that focus.

The idea of escape had never been in her mind. She knew, once her mission was complete, they would not have given her that option. But now it was imperative. She was not about to let these stuffed uniforms prod and poke at her life. She certainly would not let them interrogate or torture her.

She had deliberately dropped enough hints into her letter for the military to be nervous as to just how much classified material she had had access to. She knew the letter would be diverted. It may not have even made it out of Chiang Mai Post Office. SLORC spies were all over the city. She knew the junta would get hold of it, and all the questions it would raise.

In truth, the documents she'd seen as a child had been boring. There were more interesting things to read. She remembered nothing at all. But that wouldn't stop them chiseling at her memory.

She lifted the chair onto the table, climbed up, and looked through the little window. It afforded her a good view of the surroundings, and helped formulate a plan in her mind. It involved a death, perhaps two, but it would give her one chance to escape. She had been so passive when they brought her in, they wouldn't be expecting anything violent now. This was the perfect time. She sat on the dirty commode and passed the small plastic capsule that contained her weapon.

37

Susan and Eddo were well equipped for solitude. Susan had her sketchpads and acres of beauty to mess up with either charcoal or pastel. Eddo saw those same acres as battlefields and prehistoric lands and alien planets.

They left together after breakfast every day, rain or shine —but mainly rain—and headed off in a new direction across the grounds of the estate. They would agree on a site, set boundaries, and spend the day within them. They took a military groundsheet, which usually ended up as a tent, and there they would have tea parties, and banquets, and teddy-bear picnics.

Susan's drawing, while Eddo was off fighting wood monsters, gave her a little too much time to think. John going off to Thailand on some mission he didn't have time to tell her about, was a wrench to her peace of mind. She had become hopelessly dependent on her calls to him. Their love for one-another was her stability in the whole ugly drama. She could play, like Eddo, at it all being an adventure, but it wasn't. John, like everyone else involved in the case, was risking everything to protect her and her son. So many lives had been lost, and yet here they were safe and enjoying the type of life all mothers would love to give their children. She had time only for Eddo and the girl.

The phones weren't connected at the cottage, and they were too isolated to use a mobile themselves, so their lifeline was the phone kiosk beyond the village. They walked there across the fields and returned via Big C supermarket. There, they stocked up on anything healthy they could find—Eddo was staunchly against junk food—and returned to the cottage with their big plastic bags.

There were three security guards watching over the stately home, who took shifts at the gate. In the day, the workers came to renovate the main house, and the gardeners manicured the gardens. Susan and her son were officially royals, so they were afforded a polite distance. Nobody knew their names or why they were there. Their privacy was guaranteed.

Although the men knew nothing true about the houseguests, Susan and Eddo knew a lot about them and their life stories. Eddo was an insatiable interviewer. During tea breaks and at lunch, he entertained the workers with his impersonations and discovered who had girlfriends and wives and children. He was constantly trying to work out what 'normal' families were like. It intrigued him that there were mothers and fathers who actually lived together.

Ironically, John's leaving had brought Susan closer to Bruce. They had always been friends, always drunk from the other's brilliance. But they'd never lived together on a regular basis, even after the marriage. Eddo knew Bruce was his dad, and loved him, but the apartness seemed to suit all three of them. Susan and Bruce loved the state of wedlock and parenthood, but valued freedom above them. It was the happiest broken marriage in history.

Without John, Susan found herself relying on Bruce's voice as an anchor to the inside world they'd left. She wanted everything to be all right. She hadn't wanted to hear about Aunt Maud, but she appreciated Bruce's frankness. She knew, if anything happened to John, he would tell her. But with Maud dead and John away, there really was nobody on the inside that knew where they were. They were astronauts drifting away from the space station without a lifeline. Only the evening walk to the phone could re-attach the umbilical cord.

She knew he would hate the idea, and they would both get irritable. But for Eddo and sanity's sake, when she phoned Bruce the next day, she would tell him where they were, and ask him to come and stay. Just for a bit. Just for a show of family unity and love. Oh yes, and sex.

38

The piano music at the Strand Lounge in Rangoon was subdued Richard Clayderman, apparently played with one finger missing. The pianist wore a bright nylon shirt open to the navel, to draw attention from his playing.

John sat at the bar smiling at everyone and sipping slowly on a Virgin Mary. This expensive creation was advertised as a non-alcoholic relative of the Bloody Mary, and tasted, not surprisingly, like tomato soup. He was in the middle of Plan B. Plan A had failed miserably that afternoon.

The SPDC press office at the Information Ministry had the word "*INFORMATION* " on the door. The word "*NO*" must have dropped off.

"Why should we tell you something like that?" the woman had asked in beautiful but nasty English.

"I'm writing a book,'" John had lied. "Major Bohmu Din was a legend in the north. He'll be the main character."

"What other books have you written?"

"My biography of Colin Powell is on its second print run. And there was my very popular in-depth look at Churchill. That was nominated for the Booker Prize."

"The Booker Prize is for fiction."

"Right. It was written through the eyes of Churchill's fictional gay lover."

She pursed her lips. "Your name is not familiar to me, and besides that, the information you want is not in the public domain."

"Is there any way I can find out?"

"No."

"Just what information do you give out here exactly?"

She ignored the question and left him floating there like a fart. Plan A had seemed so straightforward, it was the only plan he'd brought with him.

It was the know-all bellboy at his hotel who furnished him with a Plan B. "They go there all the time," he'd said. "All the fat generals."

So there he was: in the piano lounge of the Strand.

But John was beginning to look towards a Plan C. Three Virgins and two hours and he hadn't seen so much as a postman. He'd told the barman he wanted to meet a real soldier. The barman looked at him as if he were deranged, but promised to point one out if he saw one. At last, the door opened and the barman gestured towards the men entering.

One was snappily dressed: silk shirt, dyed hair, and contacts that made his eyes red. He'd been celebrating elsewhere, and staggered through the door on the arm of an aide. When the hostesses caught sight of him, he pushed off the aide and posed for them like a muscle man. They considered this hilarious, so he was obviously a big tipper. They escorted him to a stool at the bar and helped him settle upon it.

Over the next few hours, it wasn't extracting information that was the problem for John. It was interpreting and filtering it. The general was proud of his English, but unaware of its incomprehensibility. It was he who struck up the conversation, he who got around to skirmishes at the front, and he who first mentioned the name of Bohmu Din. He had warmed to John immediately, and was only too delighted to share personal and state secrets with him.

He was obviously not used to people listening to him, and launched into private philosophy on . . . well, on everything. His account of Major— now General—Din was long and involved. Once John had learned what he needed to know, he excused himself to go to the bathroom, and fled without paying his bill.

-o-

At Norbert's on the balcony, John impersonated the Burmese general and his constant sliding from the stool like a pigeon on an icy telegraph pole. His hosts enjoyed the rendition so much, they ordered a repeat. Kruamart laughed with delight. John relished the chance to be with his friends that evening even more, knowing he'd be leaving the next day and crossing back to the dark side.

Kruamart returned to her deft weaving of fine slivers of rattan into the shape of a purse. She seemed to have so many talents John was sure she would be a fascinating person to talk to. He wished they could speak without Norbert's crude interpretations.

He and Norbert huddled over the table and put together their collective thoughts. They mapped them onto a sheet of paper.

"So, this is how it goes," John began. "It appears he climbed through the ranks more on his reputation than personality. The plum prize for these remnants of battle was a diplomatic post with all its uncontrolled importing and exporting of contraband. He'd already served as military attaché to consulates in this region before his present post."

"You telling me Burma's got an embassy in South Africa?"

"Yeah. I could hardly believe it myself. But I looked it up on the net. It's true."

"Shit. What the hell they need one there for?"

"I imagine there's a lot of mutual benefit in bartering."

"Drugs for diamonds?"

"You're such a pessimist. I didn't say that. Perhaps there's the exchange of Zulu war shields for silk skirts."

"Right. Didn't think of that. How long's he been stationed there?"

"About eight months."

"That would be about right."

"It all fits. The cheapest flights are Ethiopian, via Nairobi. He had plenty of opportunities to stop off there on his way through, and sidetrack to England. I can check that out when I get back. I figure, now we're at the diplomatic level, the Secret Service lads can officially get involved again. Don't you?"

"You got any real evidence?"

"If we can get a photo from South Africa, we can get a positive ID from the kids in Mombassa."

"You understand there are a thousand reasons why this could come to a dead end, John boy: diplomatic immunity, unreliability of witnesses, no extradition agreements. . . ."

"I know. I know. But at last I've got something. Up till now he's been a cloud. There was nothing to grab at. If I can confirm just one thing, it means I have the drop on him. I'll be in control for the first time since this nightmare started."

"Well, I wish you luck, little buddy. If there's anything I can do from this end, you know my number."

"You've already done so much. I don't know how I can repay you."

"That's easy man. Bread. Give me bread."

"All right. I'll send you half a dozen loaves as soon as I get back."

Norbert complained that the only one of his father's traits John had inherited was his dumb sense of humour. They poured over the chart for some while before John got around to the question that had been gnawing at him all the way back. Norbert had been afraid it would come.

"You heard anything from inside?"

There was something uneasy in his friend's reaction. "You talking about the doctor?"

"In fact, yes."

Norbert looked over to his wife as she worked. He picked at his teeth with his tongue.

"What is it?"

"Look man. It might be false information, right?"

John leaned across the table to urge him on.

"Well. The raid on the camp. . . . Your doctor was reported missing."

"Shit."

"Only missing. There was no body. At first they thought she'd run off into the jungle and gotten lost. But they searched all over and there was no sign of her."

"So what are you saying?"

"One theory is they captured her."

"Only her? That doesn't make sense."

"No. Unless she's got something they wanted."

"She's a doctor."

"No man. They got their own doctors. Plenty of 'em."

"Then what?" He remembered when they'd discussed the kidnap theory before; the idea of them looking for a woman had come up.

"Beats me, John. But, I told you she was asking about your major. Maybe she's got a past, too. You can bet yours isn't the only life he's screwed up."

"My God. What would they do to her?"

Norbert shook his head, and John felt a heavy turbulence around where his heart was just learning to fly. She'd been his every thought since Camp G. She was as clear in his imagination as she had been at the clinic. Now she was gone. He was being unrealistic to imagine anything between them. But to be robbed of even the fantasy was cruel. This loss was personal.

Norbert recognized the emotion, and in another of the gestures John had come to love in him, he walked around the table, stood beside his friend's seat and stroked John's hair.

"You wanna come and say good-bye to your papa?"

"Eh?"

-o-

John and Norbert sat on a concrete bench down by the stream. In front of them, illuminated by the hurricane lamp, was a simple, large whitewashed stone. "*JIM 1981*" was carved out of it.

"You mean you just stole it?"

"Not 'just.' It ain't easy walking out of a morgue with 180 pounds of friend."

"And they let you go?"

"Nobody stopped me. And I was wearing a doctor's coat and driving an ambulance. Hell, he woulda haunted me to death if I'd let them cremate him and put him in a drawer somewhere."

"You're a good man."

"I know it."

"A toast." He raised the joint.

Norbert stood and saluted. "To Jim Jessel, one crazy son of a bitch."

"To my dad."

-o-

Old Bruiser snored in the back of the jeep while John and Norbert hugged. The metamorphosis of his father's feelings into himself was complete. Norbert had quite happily transplanted his love for James into the son. They were one and the same person.

"You promised now, boy."

"I know. I'll be back. I'll have Bohmu Din's balls in a Tupperware container, so you'd better leave a space in the fridge. I'll move in with you forever, have a wild love affair with Kruamart, and you'll shoot me."

"I look forward to it." He pulled John's head down towards him and kissed him on the forehead as if imparting a blessing. He climbed behind the wheel and gunned the motor. "And don't get killed like your stupid old man."

"Okay."

And the jeep sped off, and John and his cricket bag were left bathing in the moist afternoon air on the car park of Chiang Mai Airport.

39

They called for First- and Business-Class passengers and anyone with small children to board the flight to Bangkok. John had cleared Immigration and was looking forward to the flight home.

He was a different passenger to the one Thai Airways had dumped there two weeks earlier. His hands were steady. His body was healthier than it had ever been, and his confidence to tackle Te Pao could not have been stronger. Only the loss of Shirley dented his new armour. Love was a horrible feeling.

"Mr. Jessel?" The ground hostess smiled a Business -Class smile, which was slightly narrower than a First-Class smile, but much brighter than Economy.

"Yes."

"This is for you. It was delivered by courier from your office."

"My office?" He took the padded envelope from the girl and thanked her. He felt a familiar grip on his insides whenever unexpected parcels reached him. Only Norbert knew his travel arrangements, and they'd just said good-bye at the airport. He hadn't been prepared for the game to be back on so soon.

For some reason, he could neither throw it into the bin or rip it open there in the queue. Instead, he carried it to his seat and placed it in the pocket in front of him. It frightened him. It peeked out, unmarked, sealed, secret.

He didn't take it out until they were airborne. He slowly unpeeled the tape that held it shut. It contained some twenty sheets photocopied from lined writing paper. The handwriting was large and neat. There was no cover letter. There was nothing to explain why he should read it, but he knew he had to. And once he was inside its story, he was numb to everything around him, deaf and dumb to the fussings of the steward and the probings of his neighbour. There was nothing but the story:

Sherri's Story,

I was too shocked to move, too stunned to scream. My mother had been cut down in front of me, and I couldn't cry. There were bodies all around me. Their blood was being soaked up by the dry earth. They were people I'd known all my young life. Some bodies still twitched around looking for their heads. I could only watch them dance. I realize now that I was in deep shock and my emotions had shut down. But for many years I wondered why I didn't scream or cry.

The young soldiers took us away. They led us through the jungle. We weren't tied or held. We just followed them obediently. We'd already seen their power. Only the young mother cried quietly for her relatives. We children walked silently, trying to make sense of everything. We tried so hard to be good. Even when we were tired or hungry, we dared not complain. We walked.

The sun was down when we reached the outpost. When we walked through the gate, the cicadas stopped singing. It was as if they knew what would happen to us. They dragged off the women to another place and led the children into the main hut. A man sat there on a mat. His uniform was unbuttoned. It seemed his stomach had spilled from it like rice out of a cupboard. He wasn't fat, but his belly was.

His face had been left pockmarked by some childhood disease, and his skin was dark and vaguely purple like a mangosteen. He was eating. He didn't look up when we entered, and he ignored us until he'd finished his meal. I'd never been so scared of the sight of a person eating. I remembered a story I'd heard of a great Burmese soldier who could kill people just by clicking his tongue.

He wiped his mouth, looked at us, pointed at me, and that was the end of it. The others were taken out and I never saw them again. I stood

185

there by myself like a vase. I just stood. He didn't speak to me. He didn't even look up at me for another hour. He read some papers, signed things, and drank water, and I stood, hungry and bursting to pee.

He got up slowly, went to the corner of the hut, and unrolled a dark green army blanket. He beckoned me to him with his fingers. I thought he was allowing me to sleep.

-o-

The men in the camp must have heard my screams that night, and every night for a week. But nobody came to help. The pain didn't stop then, but my lungs got tired of screaming. The more I cried, the more he beat me. When I stopped complaining, he started to feed me.

It was three months before we had some sort of conversation. I asked him why he was doing these things to me. Even now I can't bring myself to write down what he did. I was only six years old, so there were still many things I didn't understand about the world. It was a brave question. He'd already thrashed me on a number of occasions with his bamboo switch for less. But this time he answered: "Mind your own business."

So that was how I learned that what happened to my body was not my concern. As my body was no longer mine, I removed it from my mind. Still, twenty years later, we aren't really re-attached.

-o-

Major (Bohmu) Din was a cadre of the Burmese Military Council. In the village I'd heard them called Tatmadaw. They were always monsters in the stories the older children told us. But I'm sure you know all this.

Like you, I am a Karen. We are the most stubborn of the Tatmadaw's enemies. They could not defeat our army in hand-to-hand battle so they waged a war of terror against our non-combatants. All Karen, no matter how old or weak, were fair game for revenge. They raped our women, kidnapped our children, killed our youth, and took our elderly to be porters in the jungle. They hoped they could break the spirit of our soldiers by making their kin suffer.

But of course I knew nothing of all this. I was six. Bohmu Din wasn't a symbol of oppression. He was my owner, my violator, and my enemy. I heard him tell the guards, if they ever saw me more than three yards from the hut, I was to be shot. I was a prisoner of the camp as they moved around from place to place. I didn't ever find out where the other children from my village went to.

One woman they brought with us was your sister, the youngest daughter of your mother, No Ay Me, whom I loved very much. Everybody in the village loved your mother. She was always sad that she had lost touch with you. She told me she had a daughter that she had to leave behind in Rangoon. It has taken me so long to find you.

When she escaped from the student uprising that followed the military takeover in 1962, your mother found her way to our little village. She had taught at the university, and she told me that the soldiers were afraid of educated people. That's why they killed the students and forced the teachers to escape into the jungle. She was already quite old, and she was a real city lady. But she helped us so much. She shared the work and taught the children. I was very young but I learned to read basic Burmese and English from her because she was so patient.

She was a wonderful teacher. You would have been so proud of her. It was No Ay Me and her words that gave me the strength to fight through those years. I really believed that education was a weapon I could use against my enemy.

That is why I am writing to you. I apologize for using English but my Burmese has been long neglected.

EVIL IN THE LAND WITHOUT

I am sorry to tell you the soldiers forced your sister to be a camp sex slave. She had once been such a pretty girl. They filled her with opium so she would not know what she was doing. She soon lost me from her memory. She died before the end of the first year. She had stopped being pretty long before that. I had always wanted to be like her, until I saw what being pretty had forced upon her.

I was a sex slave also, but I was the exclusive property of Bohmu Din. The unit appeared to have some autonomy from Rangoon. They were given free reign to burn, pillage, and terrorize any Karen village as they pleased. Bohmu Din was in his element. He took pleasure from inflicting misery. I saw him kill so many times. I saw him watch impassively as his troops raped and murdered. I never once saw remorse or pity in him.

I listened to his hatred of my people. When he was away, I used his books to teach myself many things. I improved my language skills. He didn't know I could read (or think, or feel), so he left his secret documents unlocked in his desk. I read all of them. I know so much about his orders and the plans of his superiors. I know who controlled what, and which officers were taking what bribes, and troop movements. From his private mail I learned of coup plots and gossip about the leaders in Rangoon.

He had many books. My only happy times were when he was away and I was under lock and key alone with the books. They were my friends. I hid my writings so he would never find them. I was sure he would have killed me if he found out I had a mind. He was an educated man. He spoke and read several languages, and he too liked to study. He graduated from a prestigious British university with an engineering degree. It was incredible to me that someone with such a love of books could hate people so. Books obviously could not impart compassion. In this category he was not human.

I got to where I could sense the major's return, even hours before he kicked his big boots against the door post. My heart would squeeze up like a fist. He marched in without looking at me or acknowledging my presence. He knew I would be there, just as his cup and his pipe were always in the right place. Before even showering off his stink, he would use me. It was his way. He was like a starving man who finds fruit and has no time for table manners.

There were several times, were it not for the camp medic, that I should have died. I learned about medicine from this man, and from the bruises and fractures on the body that had once been mine. I asked many questions when I was in the sick bay. There were times they let me help out there when casualties were high. I appreciated the skills of the medic, but hated him for keeping me alive.

For three endless years I lived with Bohmu Din. I was his instrument. He began to talk, to ask questions, even to be civil towards the end. There were times he would bring me gifts, pilfered from the corpses of villagers. But day by day the pebbles of hatred in me had piled into a mountain that had buried Sherri the little girl. No man could ever understand what effect abuse has on a child. There will always be something missing in me that no end of searching will find. I only pray that

It ended there.

When he looked up, his eyes were wet with tears. The steward asked him if he was all right. He nodded and smiled but he couldn't speak. The story had taken hold of his throat.

He knew who Sherri was. Instinctively he knew. He knew the name of the major and what he would become. He knew that his doctor harbored more hate for Bohmu Din than he ever could. John's losses—his father, Mick, his mother—had all been second-hand, disconnected. Her contact with Din had been a personal violation. It would have been devastating.

From his training, he knew how the post trauma would have eaten at her all these years. It was a cancer, uncured and unresolved. He believed he knew why she had returned, why she'd gone inside, and even in some way, why she'd been singled out at Camp G. It made sense.

His receiving this package could mean one of two things. Either she had entrusted the package with someone to give to him, before she was abducted, or she was safe and had left it herself. Either way, it told him more than just her story. This incredible document told him they were allies. It lifted his spirits to a level they had never flown.

For some reason she trusted him with her past life. It was a feeling he'd never known. It was the oiling of a rusted soul that had lain all its life in some dusty corner. He felt alive. He wanted to tell her he understood. He wanted to see her. As the 747 bounced through the clouds, he could think of no more appropriate place to be.

"Please let her be safe."

40

Susan slammed down the receiver. It made Eddo jump.

"Mummy, you scared me."

She was scared herself. "Sorry, babe. The phone gave me an electric shock."

Eddo thought that was funny for some reason, and his laughter calmed his mother a little. But she was still very disturbed.

She'd phoned Bruce. The phone was answered with a muffled, "Hmmm?"

She assumed she'd just woken him. "You lazy bugger. Were you sleeping?"

The reply was another muffled, "Mmmm." But Susan knew it wasn't Bruce.

"Who is that?"

There was a moment of silence and then a voice said, "You want Bruce? Just a minute, I'll get him."

Why would someone else have Bruce's phone? The accent was unfamiliar, but she suddenly recalled Bruce telling her about the detective.

All sorts of thoughts chased around in her head. What if Te Pao had taken the phone? What if he were tracing the call? What if. . . ?

That's when she slammed down the phone.

Panic dropped on her and left her numb. She suddenly felt so very alone. Without John, without Maud . . . now without Bruce. The cottage in its vast grounds, the secrecy, the elaborate security . . . it had all seemed so protective until now. In the phone box with perspex all around them, she felt very exposed.

Could he be close? The signal was strong. Yes. She hadn't thought about it at the time, but the man's voice was so sharp, so loud.

Eddo was still laughing, still electrocuting himself by touching the phone cable, and the door, and his mother's bag. He hadn't picked up on her fear.

She breathed deeply and crouched down to him. "Eddo mate, we have to get back to the cottage as quickly as we can."

"Is it a race?"

"Kind of."

They were both caked in mud from the walk over the fields, and night was gathering her black skirts round them. She didn't want to go back that way. But the alternative was to walk beside the road where every passing car would display them in their headlights. She looked up to the sky for a suggestion, and the goddess of country buses must have been looking back.

Susan threw open the door of the kiosk and waved her arms frantically at the driver of the orange bus as it passed them. He smiled, put his foot on the brake, and even steered onto the grass verge to collect them. Country bus drivers get so few passengers, they have time for good manners.

The old Bedford trundled along the main road, the driver chatting about this and that. He let Eddo sound the horn, and told him about a sheep farm down the road that was so advanced the wool came off the sheep and it already had a zip.

"I don't believe you. You're fibbing," said the boy, who'd been fibbed to by some of the world's best. "Look mummy, Big C."

They passed the supermarket and the car park, and the rental car that was parked facing the road. The men inside were foreign. They were probably tourists. They didn't notice the only two passengers on the bus, and the passengers didn't notice them.

41

There was an hour delay at Bangkok's Don Muang Airport before the ongoing flight to London. After a frustrating time at the Long Distance Phone office, John went to look for a magazine. He found himself browsing through the trashy novels. He wasn't much of a reader. But something light would be all right, perhaps a comedy—a romantic comedy. Or even a romance.

He turned to the back pages of one or two and read the last chapters. It was something he'd always done. That way he wouldn't be surprised or disappointed. He didn't want anyone dying on him.

"That's cheating. Don't you like a little mystery in your life?"

He turned to see who was speaking, and found himself gaping stupidly like a banked codfish. Shirley stood behind him. She looked as if she'd been dragged to Bangkok behind a bus. Her left arm was in plaster. There was a thick pad of bandage over one eye, and the other was puffed up and black.

"Bloody hell." He was shocked but very happy to see her. He stared for a moment, confused. "You need a doctor. What happened?"

"Can I tell you later?"

"Well, yes, but I'm flying in half an hour."

"I know. Me, too."

"Where are you—"

"We're on the same flight."

His British demeanor was knocked down like a skittle. "Wow! That's . . . I mean that's a . . . well, it's a coincidence."

"You know it isn't. I've been following you since Chiang Mai. I left the copy at the airport. Wanted to give you time to read it."

There was a long silence, during which he was suddenly aware that he was holding a book with the title, *Be Still My Bangkok Heart*.

"Are you going to buy that?"

"Er, no. I er . . . know the author."

"Right."

42

Bohmu Din had his boots on the Elizabethan table. He had removed the protective plastic and was allowing the mud to drip from his soles and soak into the wood. In one hand he held the mobile phone, in the other a barber's blade some eight inches long. It was clean but not showing off its usual glint there in the dark.

He was angry but composed. He couldn't have missed them by more than a couple of minutes. The guard said they'd just left.

Finding the location had been a simple enough matter once he'd put together the three clues from the phone recording: a stately home, a Big C supermarket, and a fire brigade call at 5:30 in the evening. With the right resources it wasn't so difficult to arrive where he now was. And he had ample resources.

The bemused clerical staff at the London embassy had been following up on a good deal of Bohmu Din's strange requests of late. Although he was officially based at the South African Consulate, he was a senior diplomat, and he carried papers which afforded him any co-operation he requested.

The junior staff there were scared to death of him. Even those who hadn't heard of his reputation trembled when he walked smiling through the back rooms of the embassy. They were sure he was insane and up to no good, but their lucrative careers depended on not rocking any boats. This particular battleship militarily outgunned the ambassador himself. So they all kept quiet and did as they were told.

He sighed now that matters were so close to reaching their climax. He was becoming aware of how much this whole thing had tired him. Once it was put to rest, he could relax and the headaches would stop. Nothing else in his life was more pressing than ridding the world of the angels.

This girl he would make understand first. He would explain that by watching her die, he was actually allowing himself to live. She would need to understand that this campaign was not a mindless exercise for revenge. She was a tumor that had grown inside him over the years. With her gone, he could breath again. He would explain this, and then take her life slowly.

"Oh darling, I know you weren't to blame. It was him. Your interfering father took something from me you see, something precious, and all he left me was a picture of you. Then, after robbing me of my treasure, he robbed me of the opportunity for revenge. What possible chance was there for me to find peace? How could I go to heaven while this passion still bubbled inside me?"

For 18 years Bohmu Din had searched. His rage built year by year from the frustration of failure. The rage turned inward upon his sanity. His mind would give him no rest. Every decision he made, every post he took up, was with one intention. The angels in the photograph were his tormentors. He had to find them.

He had no names for them and no address. He didn't know what they had grown into, and he didn't care. Because in his mind they would always be the two angels in the picture their father had shown him that night at his camp.

"The boy's a bit of a terror. See his ear? A dog took it," he had said to Bohmu Din. "He'll either end up a criminal or a policeman. The girl's an angel by comparison. Well, they're both angels really."

Why didn't he ask more questions about them? Why didn't his instincts warn him that he would be flying after the angels for 18 years? Public records: two children about six and nine in 1981; father an IIC employee fluent in Burmese, southern—perhaps London—accent; mother, Hungarian; both parents deceased. Scratch. Scratch.

It was a hapless task that had occupied and frustrated many of his ex-officers and nibbled at his vast fortune. He tried to be there with them. He applied for the prime posting in London. He interviewed for it but failed. So all his research had been done in transit, from a distance, or by his people stationed in the UK. He could have resigned his posting of course and dedicated his retirement to the search. He was wealthy enough. But it was only by being inside the SPDC machine that he could use it. He needed the mechanism and the power.

Then the mother came back to life. His soldiers in England found first her history, then her present. They sent a photograph to Bohmu Din to confirm. After 16 awful years, he finally had his mother angel and the game could begin. There was no hurry now. First he would introduce himself.

The boy, the one who could have been a policeman or a criminal, had made the wrong choice. And to make the game more fun, he was working in child protection. What a sweet irony.

Bohmu Din hadn't lost his taste for young girls, although his appetite was finicky and he was never fulfilled from what he got. The Internet had proven a great new ally to him and others like him.

Through contacts he'd made at the underground African brothels that specialized in pre-adolescents, he had earned access to a number of closed organizations. It surprised him how many men shared his desires and how moderate he was compared to some. They boasted of their conquests on member-only websites.

The unity, the commonness made all of them artificially strong, and convinced them that they were the normal ones. If so many men needed sex with immature children, how could it be wrong? The Internet had elevated a perversion into a cult. It's members had grown from timid lone mice into mighty cat prides. As they grew in confidence and arrogance, it was the police and the child protection workers who became the perverts.

On one of the sites, they had set up a warning board. On it they told of places where "sicko NGOs" were active, or countries where the courts wouldn't take bribes, or where the police were harassing their members.

It was onto this site that Bohmu Din posted a warning: *"Beware. Beware. Southern England. Spread the word. The Surrey CPU are active undercover. Watch out for a red-headed man with one ear. Information contact this number."*

It was worth a shot. As the Surrey CPU was unlisted, this was one way to locate them and perhaps pick up his angel at the same time.

He got a result almost instantly. It came from a member of an English paedophile ring whose code name was "Dong." He said that a man answering the description had attended his group's last meeting. He was annoyed and asked whether he should inform the other members of the club. Bohmu Din convinced him to wait.

"I think it would be more fun to prepare a little surprise for the detective. Don't you?"

Dong agreed. As it turned out, Dong would contribute to the fun to an extent even the major hadn't considered.

They arranged to meet. When they did, Dong foolishly introduced himself by his actual name: Marcus Aldy. He was what Bohmu Din considered the idle British aristocracy. He lived from a substantial inheritance, and had never performed a day's work in his meaningless life. He had unlimited time for pursuing and expanding upon his perversions.

He kept three homes: a country place in Sussex, an apartment in unfashionable Colliers Wood, and a summer home in Sri Lanka. He also spent time in Kenya, and it was here that he had agreed to meet Bohmu Din.

Aldy was unlikable, the type who had filled in the gaps in his personality with cash. He drank too much and became obnoxious rather quickly when he did. But Bohmu Din seduced him with kindness and politeness and stories of the boys in his country. They drank together in the rented Mombassa house on their first night together.

Aldy was a weak-willed man with no passion for life. He was constantly hunting for excitement. So it was that the Burmese was able to implant the idea that murder was the ultimate erotica. The children were meaningless and without worth in this country that produced millions and refused to look after them. Their deaths would distress nobody. But by writing their deaths into a beautiful aria of sexual pleasure, that would give them some purpose. They would have made the ultimate sacrifice for a man's pleasure.

So the stage was set, and the opera sung. The tenor, engorged with the stimulation of death, carried the reviews to England. He endured the brief humiliation of arrest at the BLOUK raid, and escaped back to Nairobi with the ease that Bohmu Din had predicted. He had felt the ultimate power over his victims, and he lusted for more.

But his job was done. Bohmu Din was pleased. He was sent to join the cast, dust to dust.

Bohmu Din received another photograph from his men in England. They had followed the cars after the raid. Certainly the detective in the picture was overweight and unkempt. But there was no mistake. The likeness was incredible. To his delight, Bohmu Din had found the first angel. He would play with him for a while before traveling to England.

It had all been so much fun at first, but now the game had begun to bore him. It was time to end it. In the dark of the cottage he imagined his new angel-free existence. And, like a prelude to this liberty, the sound of footsteps crunched on the gravel path. He stood, stretched his aging muscles, and wrapped himself into the shadows.

43

Shirley had been able to upgrade to the seat beside John in Business, but he would have gladly gone back to sit on the floor beside her in Economy if she hadn't. He liked the way the stewardess assumed they were a couple. He liked being beside her in the nice seats. He almost accepted a glass of champagne.

". . . I mean no. Thank you."

"You don't drink?" Shirley asked, sipping at her glass.

"I suppose the answer now is 'no,' But it'll probably take another six years before the stuff's completely cleared out of my bloodstream."

"What made you stop?"

"Bohmu Din. I need to be in the ring with him in an equal weight class. I'm so afraid of losing to him through not being alert. I decided to stop beating myself."

As they flew over Burma and Bangladesh, he told her about his war with the bottle and his guilt at having endangered Susan and Eddo. He told her everything about the case. He told her about the Kenya connection, and the murders of Mick and Coletta. Shirley sat attentive the whole time with her unbroken hand on his sleeve, like a child listening to a fairy story.

Over dinner, he told her about his relationship with his sister and growing up in their mother's coven. He told her of their fantasies about what their father did, and the rare times that he came home. He found himself calling her Sherri ,and she made no objection. She seemed to like it. He wanted to tell her everything, and he was just about to divulge state secrets he had sworn to keep to himself, when she dropped a bomb that blew up his fantasy.

"You know? You're very much like your father."

He turned to look at her in disbelief.

"You met him? But when? How?"

"He saved my life . . . or actually my *lives*. He saved my physical life first, and then my psychological life."

John squirmed uncomfortably in his seat. "But you couldn't have been more than—"

"I was almost nine."

"You met him in Burma?"

"Didn't you wonder how my story ended? I was in Te Pao."

He felt a peculiar mix of disappointment and anger.

Shirley noticed his change of mood. "What's wrong?"

He shook his head and let out a sigh so deep it flapped the napkin on his tray. He couldn't force himself to look at her. "Carry on. I'm listening." But he was listening from a considerable distance.

She was aware of it but continued: "I'd seen Jim in the camp once before. He was the first Western man I'd ever seen."

"The camp. . . ? Wait. This is a Burmese military camp?"

"Yes."

"What the hell was he doing there?" There was accusation in his question.

"The first time, he was walking across the yard with an armed soldier behind him. He was carrying a pack. The second time, he was a guest. He came to eat with Bohmu Din. My reading of English was going well even then, but I hadn't had any opportunity to hear it spoken. I heard the BBC from a distance at times. I didn't get a lot of their conversation, but they appeared to be on good terms."

She wanted eye contact with John, but he stared at the seat in front of him the whole time. He was dealing with the doubts that she stirred carelessly into his disappointment.

"Go on."

"I knelt in the corner as always, and ran to bring things when Bohmu Din ordered. I remember Jim tried to talk to me, but the major told him something about me being an ignorant jungle girl. Those weren't the words, but that was the idea. I noticed your father looking at the bruises on my arms. He tried to look into my eyes, but I kept my head down.

"He looked across often to where I was sitting. Bohmu Din noticed and was getting restless. I believe at one stage Jim asked again about me. As I say, my ear wasn't quick enough to pick everything up. I did hear Bohmu Din say something about me being 'good sex.' Jim laughed and punched the major on the arm, playfully like boys joking. I suppose I was a bit disappointed, but I assumed all men had the same urges. I shouldn't have been surprised.

"I was surprised though when Jim openly made an offer for me. I quite clearly heard him say, 'How much for the girl?' The major looked angry at first, then smiled and told him I wasn't for sale. 'She makes good gruel,' he told him. 'It's hard to find a girl who makes gruel the way I like it.' I'd never made him gruel.

"Jim looked at me and made another offer. I remember it was a good price. I was proud that my body was worth so much. But Bohmu Din stood, said something I didn't catch, and the meal and the evening were apparently over. Although they shook hands in the doorway, the air seemed to be a lot heavier.

I suffered badly that night. He accused me of 'flirting,' although I didn't understand the meaning of the word. He had never been so cruel or so violent. I tried so hard to keep my cries inside, because I knew how much they angered him. But I had no choice. He pushed and pushed me towards the edge. I prayed he'd give me that final push that would send me falling into the death I'd longed for.

But when he finished, something in me was still alive. He didn't call the medic this time, just left me to swoon in and out of consciousness on the bare earth.

"It was in one of those moments of dreamlike waking that I imagined a blanket being wrapped around me, and my body being hoisted into the air. I thought the angels had come for me. I believed there were explosions and fire around, and I bounced and bounced back into unconsciousness.

"I was told it was two days later when I came to. The first thing I remember was Jim looking down at me and smiling. He had red hair and a beard, and the sun shined at me over his shoulder. He said, 'Welcome back.' And because I recognized it as English, and felt obliged to say something back, I replied, 'Two and sixpence please.' It was a phrase I'd learned from one of Bohmu Din's old books. Your father laughed so warmly I had to smile too.

"He asked me if I could speak English, and I told him I could, a little. I was delighted with the words coming out of my mouth. I asked him where we were, and he looked around pretending he was completely lost. Then he smiled and told me not to worry. He seemed so relaxed in everything he said and did that I relaxed, too.

"He had a compass he looked at often. I continued my convalescence under cover during the days, and we traveled at night. Before I was able to walk, he would carry me. He was so polite. I was expecting him to take me as Bohmu Din always did, but he told me how wrong that was. He told me a lot of things. We always spoke in whispers. It was like a secret language. He helped me with my English while we walked, and told me stories.

"We always kept 12 kilometers from the main roads, because that was the area controlled by the *Tatmadaw*. He told me eventually we'd run into a Karen patrol, and that's exactly what happened. They recognized Jim and took us to a camp.

"Your father stayed with me one more day, then told us he had to go back to Te Pao for something. I never learned what had happened at there that night, or why he had to return. Although I didn't recognize the emotion at the time, in the few days I'd known Jim, I'd come to love him very much."

John felt a sliver of ice cross his heart.

"It wasn't until much later, when I studied counseling at med school, that I realized what Jim had been able to do in those few days. He increased my value. He made me believe I was somebody. Everything he said to me—how strong I was, how pretty, how brave, how clever, how he couldn't have survived what I had, how he respected and admired me —it was all to build up my self-confidence.

"He convinced me that I wasn't responsible for what had happened to me. I had been a victim and I'd survived. I had to be proud of myself for that. In those few days he helped me to take the hate out of myself.

"But it had to go somewhere. I put all that hate I had for myself into Bohmu Din. That helped. Before that time with your father, all I wanted was the relief of death. He made me want to make the most of life instead.

"He told me he had a daughter my age, and a son. He showed me your pictures. You looked so happy, I wanted to be in the photo with you both. I imagined I was another sister.

"You see, John, it was your father who made me strong enough to survive on my own. The Karen took me to a camp on the Thai border, and by some magic Jim had arranged, I was adopted and shipped off to the States. I lived in a nice house and went to school. It was the perfect fairytale ending—except it hadn't ended. It couldn't end as long as the major was still doing what he did. Revenge isn't a healthy emotion. I tried, really tried to let it go, but there's no forgiveness in my heart for him.

"When I was still in the camp, I'd heard what had happened to Jim. I didn't mourn for him then because my emotions had been filed down to bare stubs. But I felt his ghost would always be there. His words stayed with me when I had doubts. They pushed me on. I still believe he's here. When I saw you at the camp, I was sure Jim's ghost had come back for me."

John was slumped in his seat looking at his lap . . . a victim of mistaken identity, a big sulky boy. This woman who had followed him from Chiang Mai—who had hung on his arm and listened to his stories, who had filled him with love—she thought she was with his father. Like Norbert, she was just renewing an old friendship with a dead man. She had no interest in John at all.

He was ashamed of himself. With all he'd learned about her since Chiang Mai, it was incredible that his primary feelings now were about and for himself. After what Shirley and his father had been through, what right did he have to be heartbroken? How could he be jealous of a man who had died twenty years ago?

With all his will, he tried to be unselfish, and transfer his emotions into her account. But the ache was too great. "I suppose I was half hoping you liked *me*," he said, still looking down.

She didn't reply.

"I'm afraid I've joined the legions of men who are in love with you, and I'm feeling a really peculiar jealousy for my dad."

Again with no answer, he looked to his left.

Shirley, purged of her story, slept silently.

Eventually, John slept too. His dream was complicated and vivid. His mother as a pretty young woman was there, and a man he didn't know. He saw their faces in the shadows. They were laughing at him and he was angry.

When he woke, Shirley was eating the top breakfast of a pile of two. His attitude had benefited from the sleep, and he had a firmer grip on real life. He was more prepared to be a surrogate.

"Ah, you're awake. That's bad luck. I was planning to eat your breakfast and tell you they hadn't brought any."

He smiled and accepted his tray. He ate in silence while she chatted about comparatively unimportant things. He wasn't good at trivia first thing in the morning.

"Who broke your arm?"

The bread roll stopped its flight to her mouth, and he thought he saw some guilt in her eyes. "That's not really a breakfast question. Who bit your ear off?"

He laughed. "And that *is* a breakfast question. . . ? I'll tell you mine if you tell me yours."

"Okay."

"Well, Mike Tyson came into the station one day and—"

"I'm serious."

"Tell the truth, I don't really know. Or I can't remember. They tell me it was this stupid little lapdog that used to follow Coletta around everywhere and piss on the floor. I was about five. It just went berserk one day and went for my ear. They had it put down. You think I'd remember something like, that wouldn't you, but I don't."

"Strange."

He thought about just how strange it was. The vicious little bastard had made a couple of appearances, all snarly and drooly, in some of these dreams he'd been having lately. He hadn't thought about it for years. The mind was a funny old thing.

"Your turn." She hesitated, put down her coffee, and leaned very close to John. In a whisper she told him, "They were holding me in a prison in Pa'an, and I decided to escape. The only way I knew was to use the element of surprise. They saw me as a weak woman, and I hoped that would be to my advantage.

"I called the guard—the woman who'd searched me earlier—and told her I was bleeding internally. I pointed to the commode and she went to take a look. I had a weapon that I'd learned to use from old Karen fighters in the States. It was a fish wire adapted to kill. I knew the techniques, but there's more than technique to overpowering someone. All my medical training had been to keep people alive. I had no killer instinct.

"She was stronger than me and was able to fight me off. We waltzed around and wrestled and we both knew one of us had to die. Then we fell onto the card table. It gave way beneath our weight and her head cracked against the concrete floor. She was dead.

"It was a terrible feeling to know I had caused that. I had to stop thinking of her as a person. I looked at her uniform and saw her instead as the enemy, as my trainers had taught me. I took off the uniform and put it on myself.

"There was one more guard at the gate. It wasn't a prison. It was just an admin building with an interrogation room. There was little need for security. They didn't see me as dangerous. He was asleep on his seat. It took me some time to get into the frame of mind, but again I looked at his uniform and forgot that he was just a man doing a job he probably didn't like. . . . I could do with some more coffee."

She called the stewardess and ordered for both of them.

John was stunned. Then she went on in the same unemotional tone: "I'd learned from the attack on the woman. The wire sliced through his throat and he bled to death without a fight. He died in confusion really. He woke to find himself dying. I just unlocked the gate with his key and walked out.

My eyes were swollen from the fight with the woman, and I'd cut my head. I was a bit dizzy. Somehow I had to get back to the border. Pa'an is a busy city. You'd never know there was a war raging less than twenty kilometers away. It's on a major trucking route south. I went to the checkpoint and ordered a truck driver to take me along. He looked at the uniform and told me to get in.

"I guess I fell asleep. After a few hours, I woke up and his hand was up my skirt and his disgusting breath was on my mouth. He'd pulled off the main road. I fought him, poked my fingers in his eyes, and threw myself out the door. It was a hell of a drop. Snapped my forearm.

"Luckily he didn't come after me, 'cause I was swooning from the pain and it was all I could do to stay conscious. I managed to set the arm with bamboo, then passed out in the jungle somewhere. When I came around, it was daylight and I was only a few kilometers from the border. The driver had kindly brought me all the way to Myawadi before he tried to have his way.

"Just across the river was Mae Sot and Thailand. I stole a shirt and a sarong and walked over the bridge. In Mae Sot I went to the refugee committee, got fixed up, borrowed some money, and took a bus to Chiang Mai. I got some money wired from the States, checked the passenger manifesto at Thai Airways, and found your name. And here I am. . . . I really have to go to the bathroom."

When she stood up and walked along the aisle to the toilet, John was still stunned. She had confessed to two murders, albeit in a kind of battle. She didn't appear overly distressed or remorseful. She had told it like a movie plot.

But then he compared her with himself. Most things that disturbed him, disturbed him deep inside. But he kept them there. They were nobody else's business. He understood then that the turmoil she obviously felt, she was dealing with herself. If she wanted him to share her feelings, she would let him know.

-o-

When Shirley finally got to the end of the snail-paced Immigration queue of unfortunates not born in the EC, John was deep in conversation on the pay phone. He'd tried to call Maud, Bruce, and Emma from the in-flight phone, but none of them had picked up. The night sergeant at Kingston told him to call back when the team arrived in the morning.

She held back and waited. She could tell from his expression that something awful had happened. She was sure that Bohmu Din had been active while he was away. He snapped down the receiver, looked around for Shirley, and ran over to her.

"Quick," he said. "We have to go somewhere right now. Sorry, there's no time to drop you off anywhere."

"I'd be pissed if you did."

He hurried her to the long-stay parking bay where he found his Peugeot and swore at the ignition before it would turn over the engine. She waited patiently until he was ready to tell her what he'd learned. As they emerged from the tunnel under the main runway, he seemed to have ordered things in his mind.

"The night before last, they found the body of Susan's husband, Bruce."

"Oh, God. I'm sorry."

"He was under police protection . . . which doesn't say much for police protection. He'd been on to Scotland Yard to tell them that someone posing as a detective had contacted him and was trying to get Susan's address. They supposed it was Te Pao. A few days earlier, my old boss Maudling was done in, probably by the same perpetrator, although the MO was different."

As he spoke, Shirley noticed how John was talking about people he had been close to as if they were John Does. He showed no sadness.

"That means two things. Firstly, your major pal is a lot more resourceful than we gave him credit for, and that scares the life out of me when I wonder just how close he was able to get. Secondly, it means Sue doesn't have any contact at all with the outside world. She might have got desperate and breached security. Either way, we have to get over there and move her and Eddo out."

"John."

"Yeah?"

"It won't help either of them if you and I are killed in a motor accident."

He lightened his foot on the accelerator.

-o-

At the entrance to Mendleton House, a large country constable blocked the way. The sight of him sent a wave of panic through John that Shirley sensed. She put her hand on his on the wheel.

"And where would you be going . . . sir?" the constable yelled through the closed driver's window.

John wound it down. "What's happened here?"

"No, I asked the first question, and you haven't answered that yet."

John was fumbling for his ID and getting agitated. He finally got the card from his wallet. "Just let us in and cut the crap."

The uniform took it and read it more carefully than he needed to.

"See the rank on there? If you don't open the fucking gate in ten seconds, I'll drive through it anyway, then reverse back over you. Understand?"

The constable raised his eyebrows, walked slowly to the gate, and swung it open. "Delighted you're having a nice day . . . sir," he mumbled as the car sped past him.

There were two plain-clothes men in front of the cottage filling out forms. They looked up as the car skidded along the gravel drive and stopped a few centimetres from their shins. They didn't flinch.

John threw open his door and ran around to them. "What is it? What happened here?"

"And you would be. . . ?" one of them said.

John still had his ID in his hand. He gave it to one of the detectives, who looked at it with the same country patience as had the uniformed man.

"Look. It's not my case. My sister and her boy are staying here."

"Well, they aren't here now, and it would appear they've been burgled."

"Oh, thank God. That's all?"

The two men looked at each other. "What else were you hoping for?"

"Have you been through inside?"

"We have that."

"And there's no sign of a fight? No blood?"

"You're a cheerful soul, aren't you. . . . No, there was a lot of mud from the back window to the sofa, but I didn't see any blood. Did you, Ernie?"

John had a feeling they were mocking him.

"Can't say I did, Jim."

But he was mightily pleased at the news. "Well, it's marvelous that you fellows have done such a thorough job."

Shirley got out of the car to join them. The plain-clothes men looked at her with fascination but didn't say anything.

"What have you got so far?" John asked.

"Eh?"

"About the break in."

"Ah. The gardener noticed that someone had trampled down his azaleas and broken the back window at about 6:30 when he started work. So either your sister left very early, or she didn't come home last night."

"Why the uniform at the gate?"

"It appears the security guard's done a runner. The fellow was supposed to be on duty till ten, but the workers turned up this morning and they had to climb over the gate. No sign of the guard."

"So he's our most likely suspect," said Jim. He was only doing the job casual like, so he may have seen an opportunity for a little bit of extra income."

"Have you contacted the earlier guard to see whether his relief came on duty at all?" John asked.

"It's on the list, mate. It's on the list."

When the two went off to take care of the things on the list, John and Shirley went into the cottage. If Susan and Eddo had gone out early, they hadn't taken much with them. The tarpaulin and the lunch basket were there, as were Susan's sketchpad and pastels. The beds were made, and cold beneath the blankets. The cooking pots and heater hadn't been used that morning. It was more likely they hadn't been back at all.

They talked to the gardeners. They'd seen Eddo playing the afternoon before. Then, just before 5:00 p.m., Susan and Eddo had set off across the fields as they often did. The gardeners and workers all went off shift at 5:00. The guard let them out and locked the gate. Susan and Eddo had just vanished.

"Are we going for a walk?" Shirley asked. She figured they'd have to look in the fields. It wasn't something she wanted John to have to think about, but the empty paddocks would have been a perfect spot for a murder. John knew that too, but he was curious about the break-in.

"I think, first we'll drive down to the phone box and see if anyone saw them yesterday evening. That would save us a search. Susan wouldn't have walked back over the fields in the dark."

"Perhaps they've made friends with a neighbour. You said she was cut off from the outside world."

"Possible. Thanks for thinking positive."

"I've had a lot of practice. Whatever makes you think Bohmu Din could have found this place? It's in the middle of nowhere."

"He found me, didn't he? He's persistent, and we don't know what he might have got out of Bruce or Maud before. . . ."

They got into the car and drove across to the paved driveway. Once the crunching of the deep gravel stopped, they were able to hear the shouts from behind them. John slammed his foot down on the brake. Shirley banged her cast on the dashboard.

"Sorry."

They got out and went back to where the gardener stood shouting and waving his arms. They looked across to the pond to the spot he was pointing at. There, amongst the lily pads, a tomb of air in a bright-orange waterproof jacket held up a body. It floated face down, its blond hair spidering out in all directions on the water's surface. The second body they found later at the bottom, weighted down with rocks.

44

The dull light that found its way into his bedroom through the thick curtains was only able to leave a light veneer on dark shapes. John had long given up any attempt at sleep. From his place on the peach couch, he could see through the doorway and into the shadows where Shirley slept in his bed. He could make out the slight rise and fall of her chest under the covers, and he imagined he could hear the soft whisper of her breathing. It had been a physically and emotionally draining day, but he was too busy pining for a love he couldn't have, to be able to sleep.

They had returned late that evening after a dreadful day at the temporary Murder Inquiry Centre they'd set up at the village hall at Mendleton. The team leader—a cocky, good-looking, fast-track deputy-super called Lawless, of all things —was extremely pissed off that John had taken off on holiday in the middle of a murder case. He was even more annoyed when he insisted his 'girlfriend' stay.

Lawless knew all about John's little drinking problem. The scab that parted his hair, and the bruises on his woman, just confirmed his belief that Jessel had no place in the force. If it weren't for his personal involvement in case, he wouldn't let the drunk anywhere near a murder inquiry. He also knew also that Jessel was holding something back.

John was frustrated to distraction that he couldn't say anything. They still called it 'The Paw' inquiry, and corrected him when he pronounced it wrongly. Naturally there were no leads as to whom The Paw was, and they had no witnesses that had seen him. John had tried repeatedly to get through to Woods via the Foreign Office after listening to the phone ring unanswered at the IIC.

The pedants at the FO were insistent there was no Commander Woods, or Commander Doyle.

"Look. I know there's no such person. Just leave him a message that John Jessel needs to contact him urg— Well, just in case one starts there this afternoon. Please, just—"

It was the only way. If they could get a photo of Bohmu Din, and a confirmation from Mombassa, he would happily give credit for solving the case to Colonel Muthoga and the efficient Kenyan police force. But Woods didn't get back to him.

Neither could he find Emma. She'd suddenly taken leave in the middle of cases, and left Somersbee in charge until she got back, which could be any time. It was totally out of character. She didn't answer her mobile or her home phone. He felt short of allies.

It wasn't just the excitement of having a flatmate that kept him awake. Every sound from the street below, every creak from the old building he lived in sent a warning to his instincts. Before Burma, he'd been single-mindedly irresponsible about advertising himself to Bohmu Din. The bastard surely knew he was back in England, and probably who it was sleeping here just yards from him.

'First the boys. Then the girls. You will be last, as you are the easiest.'

"Is it time for me yet, Bohmu Din? I promise I won't make it too easy for you."

-o-

At 5:00 a.m. when the world and John's flat were at their most silent, the phone rang. It jumped him.

He picked it up quickly so as not to wake Shirley.

"Jessel."

The silence at the other end made him anxious until . . . "John. It's Emma."

"Em. Where have you—"

215

"Listen. I want you to drive out towards Raynes Park. Follow the 131 bus route, and watch out for me. Make sure you aren't followed."

"Em, what—" But she hung up.

"What is it?" Shirley was awake and standing in the doorway.

"Looks like we're going for a drive."

"Oh. Nice."

45

They didn't get anywhere near Raynes Park. As they were passing the roundabout at New Malden, a car in the car park of the Fountain pub flashed its lights at them. John did a U-turn and went back to the car park. Emma's Mazda was just pulling out. They had no choice but to follow.

She led them on a chase through half-lit suburban back streets and leafy lanes. After ten minutes she pulled up beside a factory, but didn't get out of her car. She beckoned for them to join her.

John locked his car, and he and Shirley climbed into the Mazda.

Emma seemed disturbed. "Who's this?" she asked as she pulled away from the kerb.

"It's a long story, but Shirley is probably the only person in England who can identify Bohmu Din."

"Who?"

"Sorry. I mean Te Pao. Emma . . . Dr. Shirley Heigh; Shirley . . . Emma Yardly, my boss."

They shook hands.

"Now, what the bloody hell is this all about?"

"You'll see." She drove three blocks from John's car, then pulled off the narrow street and into an even narrower alleyway. At the end of it was a big metal gate.

"Get that, John."

He leapt out and slid back the gate on its rollers. Emma pulled into a tiny yard that was barely bigger than the car. When the gate was shut, she led them inside an old, single-storey brick house. It was cluttered with unmatching furniture and ugly souvenirs. It reminded John of an Oxfam shop. The only colour co-ordination was a layer of dust that covered everything.

"It was my sister's place," Emma told them. "She died last year and left it to me. Ugly bloody thing."

John was impatient. "Em. What are we doing here?"

"Like it or not, and I don't, I've become personally involved in this."

"Has he been in touch with you?"

"Not yet. But I get a feeling it won't be long."

"Why not?" Shirley asked.

"I think I have something he wants. Come with me. I'll show you. Keep very quiet."

She led them along the wallpapered hallway to a door at the back. She turned the handle carefully, but couldn't stop the hinges from creaking slightly. The light from the hallway washed across a single bed. On it, Eddo slept soundly in Susan's arms.

All he could manage was a brief smile. Emma pushed the door to, and they went back to the living room.

"Em, we've been searching for those two all day. Where the hell did you find them?"

Shirley was moved. Emma saw beads of tears in her eyes.

She took Emma's hand. "You wouldn't know it to look at him, but he's really very appreciative and happy."

"I know, love. I've worked with him long enough. I've never seen him this ecstatic."

"Come on, you witches. You know I'm relieved. Now answer the question before I thump you."

Emma spread newspapers on the dusty chairs so they could sit.

"They found *me*. Susan had your number at work. She didn't know where to go or who to tell. She'd phoned her husband, and some stranger answered. Her instinct told her to stay on the bus and not to go back to the cottage."

"Alleluia for the Jessel instincts. He was there, Emma. He knocked off two security guards while he was waiting for Sue and Eddo to come back.

"Shit."

"He weighted their bodies and chucked them in an ornamental pool. One wouldn't stay down. He was just some unfortunate student earning a bit of money in the vacation. Long blond hair. I saw the hair and I was sure it was Susan in there. Frightened the daylights out of me. The inquiry team launched a full-out search of the district. All the villagers were out in lines scouring the fields. I expected to hear the whistles any minute.

"Well, the two in the back room are absolutely knackered. They'd been wandering around all night waiting for the station to open. They got the first train down this morning. Susan called me and I drove up town to get them. I figured this place would be perfect for them. Nobody knows about it, and it's secluded."

"Excuse me for asking, but why didn't you make this an official case?"

"I make it official and the press knows. The press knows, and Te Pao knows. It was my professional opinion that the fewer people who knew about it, the better. I hadn't realized you were back, or I would've contacted you sooner. The call this morning was just on spec."

John leaned over and kissed Emma on the cheek. She looked shocked. "Em, you're the best. And if you're able to rustle us up a hot drink from the kitchen, I'm going to sit you two gals down and tell you one or two government secrets that I shall probably be shot for. But stuff 'em."

"The coffee's in the kitchen. I'm not your maid."

Shirley laughed, and all three of them went to make it.

"John, why didn't you tell me from the beginning that Eddo was your nephew's nickname? I could have helped. You didn't have to do this alone."

"I know, Em. I'm sorry."

46

It was 8:30. Emma had brought enough food for a very long siege. She was preparing breakfast. Shirley was taking apart Emma's mobile phone to check for bugs. It was one of the precautions they'd decided on during their coffee talk. John was dusting. Eddo woke up first.

"*Uunncle Johhhhn*. Penguin *crash*." He stuck out his belly and John stuck out his, and they ran into each other. They bounced back and fell to the ground with their legs and wings in the air. It was a routine Eddo never tired of. Shirley laughed at the two boys flapping their wings.

Susan, woken by her son's shout, came into the living room drowsy with sleep. She saw John, ran across the room, and threw herself on top of him. They lay there, locked in each other's arms, unmoving apart from the barely noticeable heave of Susan's sobs. Eddo, ever jealous, climbed onto Susan's back and pretended to sleep.

Shirley was overwhelmed by the closeness of the family. She had never cared enough for another human to imagine missing anyone this deeply. A lump came to her throat. Emma walked quietly over to her, took her arm, and led her into the kitchen. This was Jessel time.

John and Susan's heads were together and they whispered through the mat of her hair that fell around their faces. It was like their secret conversations under the blankets.

"I've missed you so much, big brother," Susan was eventually able to say. "I was sure you were a goner."

"I'm not going anywhere, love."

"He took Bruce."

"I know."

"I felt so alone. My strength's all gone. I really need you now."

"Stop whispling. It's rude," Eddo said loudly.

"Edward, little soldier, come up here to the talking end. I've got a super story to tell you."

Eddo crawled up to their heads and giggled as he buried his face in Susan's hair. His sweet, milky smell filled their nostrils.

"Ready."

"This is a story about a great man," he began. "But nobody knew he was a great man because he pretended to everyone that he was just an insurance assessor."

"John?"

He squeezed Susan tighter.

"What's an assy sir?"

"It's a really really boring job that nobody wants, Ed. But secretly, this man, and we'll call him James—"

"No. Edward. Call him Edward."

"Let's listen to the story, pal," Susan grunted.

"Okay. Edward-James was a secret soldier for the queen. He went off to foreign lands to fight in the queen's name. He was a great hero, and he helped a lot of people."

"Oh, John."

"But one day he went to a castle owned by a cruel wizard in a strange land where tiny brown and yellow people lived. He'd heard that the wick—"

"I've heard this one."

"*Eddo.*"

". . . that the wicked wizard had captured a beautiful princess and was making her do his washing up and ironing all day in his bedroom. Edward-James broke in with his XP-55Z flame-thrower and rescued the beautiful princess, and on the way out, he took the wizard's TV and VCR.

"The wizard was so angry—because he hadn't finished watching his recordings of 'Coronation Street'—that he traveled the land in search of Edward-James. He found him sleeping under a tree and he chopped him up into little pieces."

"Ooh."

"But Edward-James had two children back home called Jobaba and Sumama. They heard what happened and they chased after the wicked wizard and they chopped him into even smaller pieces and fed them to the pigs."

"Nice one, Uncle John. I have to pee."

"Thanks, mate."

Eddo always had to pee after John's bloodthirsty stories. Once he'd gone, Susan swept back her hair and looked into her brother's eyes.

"John. . . ?"

"True as I lay here getting number and number. He was Secret Service. That lovely but battered girl in the kitchen is the princess."

"But it's great."

"Isn't it."

She rolled off and lay beside him.

"I feel so . . . proud."

"Me, too. He was some piece of work, our dad. I listened to some old soldiers in the jungle talk about him as if he were Rambo or something."

"Far-bloody-out. And the wizard?"

"Our man himself."

"Do you think we knew? When we were making up our stories about dad, do you think we really knew he was something special?"

"No. I think we wished so hard, we made it happen."

She kissed him on the cheek. "I can't tell you how much better I feel. It was a lovely story. Thank you."

"Su, in case I forget to tell you sometimes, I really do love you." And it wasn't just talk. It was real. He could feel it —a big, chunky old love inside him.

47

This time the Foreign Office was more accommodating. The receptionist had been expecting his call. "Hold on sir, I'll put you through."

"Jessel."

"Commander."

"Are you on a secure line?"

"I'm on a mobile nobody's expecting me to be using."

"Good. Where are you?"

"Can't tell you. England somewhere."

"Can you get to the South African Embassy up town? There's a package waiting for you."

"What is it? Not the photos?"

"I expect so."

"But I haven't even told you about it yet."

"I've been in contact with our friend in Chiang Mai."

"That's fantastic."

"We have a very close relationship with the Foreign Service people in Johannesburg. They've also sent copies to your Muthoga chap in Kenya. They're looking for the boys in Mombassa now. But that could take a while. If they get a positive identification, they'll send the photos on to the investigating team here. We've come up with a story that sounds quite convincing."

"That's great. You blokes are good."

"We're the government. I believe . . . I believe they still haven't found your sister and her boy."

John considered whether there were advantages to telling him. There weren't. "Not yet."

"I'm so sorry. I'm sure they'll turn up. She sounds like a resourceful lass. They're probably hiding out somewhere. Please take down this number. It's my cellphone. You can get me any time on it. I believe we've been put onto the case officially." He gave the number and said good-bye.

John had been sitting out in Emma's car for a better signal. He walked back into the house.

"Em. Is this your own phone?"

"No. It was one of the department's."

"So, it couldn't be traced to you or this house?"

"No. Only to the department."

"Then, would you mind going back to work?"

"What?"

"No one knows you're connected to us or Te Pao. The only way anyone would get suspicious is if you mysteriously disappeared from work for the first time in forty years, without giving a reason."

She glared at him but knew what he'd said was true. "You're right, but—"

"Susan and Eddo will be safe here, and Shirley and I can keep an eye on them. Once I've worked out where to go with all this, I'll let you know."

"John, there's a team."

"They're operating blind. They don't know anything important, and I can't tell them. We're the team." He started to put on his coat.

"You going somewhere?"

"Into town. I have to pick something up."

"John. Teamwork begins here."

"Yeah. You're right. They have photos of Bohmu Din from the South African Service people. I'm going to pick them up from the embassy. They're hoping to get an ID from Mombassa, but I'm afraid the kids there aren't going to be queuing up to talk to us."

"That's better. Good boy."

48

The largest of the three photos of Bohmu Din was staring up at John from his lap. The train to Kingston was almost empty, so the other two were on the seat beside him. Since he'd opened the package, he'd been racking his brain to recall why the face of the Burmese seemed so familiar to him. He knew he'd seen it before.

These were telephoto shots, the type most secret services take of staff at dubious embassies. The man had cropped white hair, and bad skin as Tiger had described, but he looked nothing like the artist's impression. That he put down more to the artist's inability to sketch than to the boy's ability to describe.

"I know you, you bastard. Why do I know you? Where have I seen you before?"

Just by sitting in the train with Bohmu Din and looking into his eyes, John was slowly able to put together a plan. It was a ridiculous plan, and one that would lose him his job. But better to lose a job than a life.

At Kingston, his car was parked several blocks from the station. He walked away from it at first, then doubled back. Before getting in, he checked the locks to see whether they'd been tampered with, then he slid underneath and looked for electrical devices that didn't belong there. Satisfied, he got in and drove off.

But John had underestimated the lengths Bohmu Din was prepared to go to. When he'd learned from Bruce that John was away in Thailand, an incredible anger steamed inside him. Of course, he knew it was no coincidence. He'd checked the airlines and found Jessel's name all the way to Chiang Mai. The angel boy had gone too far. Whatever he'd discovered was more than he should have. He wasn't supposed to know anything.

An intensive search for John's car had uncovered it at the special bay at Heathrow. It had been an uncomplicated process to remove the number plate and attach a simple but highly effective homing device. It was in there and functioning when John and Shirley returned from Bangkok. It was in there when he drove to Mendleton House, and back to his flat. It was in there when he followed Emma the night before and parked three blocks from her sister's house, and it was in there still.

-o-

John, Susan and Shirley sat at the kitchen table looking at the photographs. Eddo was in the living room using the remote as a ray gun to zap anyone on TV who said rude things.

Susan looked into Shirley's eyes. "Do you mind me asking? How does it make you feel . . . seeing his face again after all this time?" The two women had been together all day. Shirley had re-told her story. They had developed a strong liking for one another.

"I don't know. I guess I don't feel anything. It's just a picture. It's like when I wrote my story down and tried to re-read it. It wasn't me. The words and the picture aren't what happened. That's inside me. I see his face always. I feel the story always."

John thought for a moment. "Would you be satisfied if justice took its course; if he were convicted and imprisoned?"

She didn't have to think about her answer. "No."

"I'm a copper. That's what I'm sworn to do. I have to believe the law can serve as public vengeance."

"Then I'll have to do it without you."

"Emma's home," Eddo shouted from the other room.

The conspirators in the kitchen were silent when she walked in. She was carrying a large paper grocery bag.

"Dinner?" John asked.

She poured the contents onto the table.

They looked at the pile of phones and beepers. "Hmmm. Looks delicious. How do you cook these again?"

"I brought us one each. The beepers are small enough to hide, and powerful enough to use anywhere."

"I want one," Eddo yelled out.

"Didn't your mum teach you the 'p' word?"

"Yes. But I don't want to pee. I want a beeper."

They laughed, but he had no idea why. Adults were the strangest things.

Emma bent down to him. "Yes, little spy. I got one for you, too. Here, I'll show you how to use it." She took him into the living room. Susan rocked back on the kitchen chair in a way that would have given her mother heart failure.

"We're going to have to draw him out somehow, aren't we."

"I think there's a way to find him," John answered.

"What? Without offering him our necks?"

Eddo ran into the kitchen breathless. He was so excited he couldn't pull the words out of himself.

"Eddo. What is it? What's wrong?" Susan ran to him and rubbed his back. "Calm down and breath slowly. . . . Good. Now, what happened?"

"Uncle John is on . . . on telly."

"What?" Shirley looked at John who just smiled before they all ran into the living room.

Emma sat stunned in the armchair. "Jessel. Tell me that isn't you giving a press conference."

"Man, you look official in there."

"The scar makes him look very Celtic warrior, don't you think?" Susan put her arms around him and watched over his shoulder.

The TV John Jessel, surrounded by microphones and cameras, was staring back into the living room full of stunned people.

". . . and we've just received this sketch from Kenya. The local police are searching for him in relation to murders committed there, which are very closely related to the murders we are investigating here."

"Clumsy sentence."

"I was nervous."

"*Sshhh.*"

". . . reason to believe that this man is currently in England. If anyone has information that could help police find and question him, please call the following number." John turned over his mobile phone on camera and read the number. "0121548655." It also appeared on screen.

"Surely you could have memorized the number, Johno."

"Ssshhh."

". . . picture will be distributed to newspapers and police stations. We caution you that this man is extremely dangerous and should not be approached under any circumstances."

Emma's mobile started to ring on the kitchen table. Susan and Shirley squealed with delight.

"Go, John."

Back at the studio, the newscaster spoke briefly before a full-screen version of the sketch of Bohmu Din appeared with the mobile number beneath it. The next item appeared and Susan clicked the mute.

Emma stormed into the kitchen, grabbed her phone, and turned it off. "Talk," she spat when she got back.

John sat down on the sofa, Susan and Shirley either side of him, giggling.

"We want to hear this, too."

"I don't see this as being very funny," Emma lectured at them. "You just saw a man abuse his authority, act irresponsibly, and lose his job. If I'm not mistaken, that performance may even get the fool put inside from three to five.

"Lawless was on the phone to me today, already asking where the hell you were and telling me he'd lodged an official complaint about your conduct. I assume you didn't have his permission to give a statement to the press on his behalf."

"I didn't tell anyone it was an official statement. I just phoned around and said I was on the inquiry squad and I had something to tell them. I hadn't expected quite so many to turn up."

"The whole bloody country was there," Shirley said in a bad English accent, still with a big smile on her face. Eddo crawled onto her lap with a magic marker and started to draw on her cast. She pulled back the sling for him.

"Holy Moly. There's no evidence against him. There are no witnesses," Emma ranted on. "There's nothing to connect Bohmu Din with the murders here. He can sue our arses off."

"That would certainly draw him out of the shadows," said Susan. "Either way, he no longer has the freedom to stalk that he used to have. I think it's brilliant."

"I do, too," Shirley agreed.

"Right. And what do I know? I'm just a dumb bimbo police superintendent with thirty years experience on the force. Jesus! When they find out I'm involved in this, they'll have my badge as well." Her eyes were beginning to moisten.

John went across to her and knelt beside her chair. "Em. I didn't do anything that would get you in shit. You can go into the office tomorrow and make a statement like the rest of them saying I'm mentally unstable and a drunk. I don't mind. They never need to know you were involved. But we'll get something out of this. I know we will.

"I thought about the beachboys in Mombassa. They hate the police so much, I can't imagine for a second they'll agree to act as witnesses. It could be weeks before the cops can bully one into giving evidence, and by then we'll all be dead. I really didn't see any choice. I stopped off at one of those 'instant portrait' places and got a sketch made up from the photo. The boy did a great job.

"This is a war, Em. It's more important than my job or anyone's reputation. I just want the ones I love to stay alive. We can't do that by hiding and waiting for him to make his next move. We've already proved that doesn't work. I'm going on the attack, Em, and this is how I fight."

She gave out an exasperated grunt, threw her head back, and looked at the ugly paint on the ceiling. The room was quiet apart from Eddo humming as he drew. Slowly, Emma lowered her head and looked one by one at their soldiers. At last she said, "We take the phone calls away from this place. I don't know how advanced tracing has got on mobiles. And you answer. I don't want anyone recognizing my voice."

There was a round of applause. She shook it away like flies at a picnic.

"Em, do you have a tape recorder?" John asked.

"I've got two interview hand recorders in the car. We'll need to pick up batteries. I've got some blank tapes in my bag."

They continued planning as they walked into the kitchen. Susan, Shirley, and Eddo remained on the couch. . . .

"It's a bird, right?"

"Nooo."

"Airplane?"

"No, it's a pectoractile."

"Pterodactyl, mate."

"Pterodactyl."

"Good boy. It's one of your best. Let's cut her arm off and sell it to a gallery."

"Susan."

"Uh huh?"

"Your brother. . . ."

"The one on TV?"

"Yeah, that one. He's nuts."

"Completely."

49

John and Shirley had been awake until 3:00 a.m. receiving calls. They were in the bedroom of his mother's still lonely apartment. Emma, to her increasing annoyance, had been voted off the telephone detail. It was agreed that someone had to stay at the house with Susan and Eddo that night. She would also have to go to work the next morning as if nothing had happened, so she was the only candidate.

Most of the calls were from nutcases claiming to be The Paw. Some were just glad for the opportunity to tell the police which objects they should insert in their recta.

Lawless managed to get through at one stage and burn John at the stake. John responded politely, apologized twenty times, and promised to bring the sketch and disclose its source at his office the next morning, first thing. It was an experience not unlike his many audiences with head teachers at school. Bow your head, never get into a dialogue, sing a song to yourself in your mind.

There was no doubt he was about to be kicked off the force. Lawless said as much. Bohmu Din had turned everything upside down. John loved his job. He was good at it. But he accepted he had given the chief no choice. He just prayed that it wouldn't be in vain.

Two other calls were possible sightings. One was in Scotland and unlikely. The other was at an address in South London. John phoned the details through to the commander. He thought the whole press conference thing had been a jolly good idea, but he wasn't a policeman and admitted he wouldn't have got away with such a stunt at MI6.

An hour later he called back.

"Chinese restaurant. The owner was from Hong Kong. He did have white hair and blotchy skin, but he was about sixty kilos heavier than your chap. Probably some dissatisfied customer getting revenge for bad service."

There was only one other likely sighting that night. Someone thought they'd seen him at a service station in Epsom, only nine miles from Kingston and John's flat. He phoned the sighting through, but there wasn't much that could be done. The station manager had confronted the man —exactly as he'd been told not to do—and he drove off without filling his tank.

The phone had been ringing non-stop and there were still the odd calls from drunks and lonely people. Even though they had taken it in turns to patiently listen to and record all the crap, John and Shirley were exhausted.

"Should we turn it off?" she asked. "There won't be many normal people phoning between now and the morning."

"We could I suppose. It'll be busy when the newspapers come out. Lawless wouldn't have had time to stop the first editions even though he'd threatened to. We do need sleep."

They were side-by-side on Coletta's bed, propped up with pillows and cushions.

"I get the sofa tonight, right?" she said.

Inside his head he suggested they both sleep on the bed, just for company. It sounded so pathetic and desperate, he didn't bother. "No, I prefer the couch."

She looked at him sideways.

"Serious. Mother always insisted on sleeping on porridge. The softer the better. I like my beds concrete hard with the odd spring sticking through. He switched off the phone and plugged it in to the charger.

"I suppose that shouldn't surprise me."

"G'night," he said. Without turning back, he walked out of the bedroom and into the living room. He didn't bother to turn on the light there, just walked to the couch, and lay down. From the bedroom he heard a distant "Good-night," and the click of a light switch that dropped the whole apartment into blackness.

Shirley lay back and sank deep into the feathers. He was right. The old lady must have had terrible posture. She let all the events of the week play out in her mind as she drifted. She felt grateful to have an ally like John. She liked him. She liked him as an ally. She couldn't have imagined what grief she was causing in him, or even that he had given her a thought beyond their mission. Had images of retribution not been so concentrated in her head, it may have crossed her mind. But there was nothing there beyond Bohmu Din.

John slept badly and in patches. At times he was fighting off Coletta's snarling lap mongrel. The couch he was on had been its palace, its mountain retreat. Its spirit was probably still there haunting it. He still had no idea why the little runt had made a comeback after all these years.

At times he was awake, listening for movement from the bedroom, imagining that he could hear her tiny breaths and smell the scent of her skin.

At times he would see the face of Bohmu Din. In his disturbed dreams, the major was younger, smiling; a more familiar Bohmu Din to John than the man at the South African Embassy. This one had friends. They drank together. They were. . . .

"Damn." He hadn't quite left the dream, but his body shot forward on the couch. "Damn." He moved as quickly to the bedroom as a drowsy person could, and flicked on the light switch as he passed it without thinking.

Shirley was immediately sitting up in the bed. Her reflexes were sharp, too. She was holding a steak knife, and wearing a very small, loose tank top.

John wasn't sure which unnerved him most, the tank top or the knife. "Where in blazes did you get that?"

"Kitchen World."

"Jesus. Remind me not to creep up on you in the dark." He went to the side of the bed, dropped to his hands and knees, and pulled back the skirting sheet.

"What is it, John?"

"I tell you, if it isn't here this time, it'll really give me the willies."

"What?"

"Mother's suitcase. I put it back here after they checked it for . . . ah ha. Here."

"I take it you've had another Jessel thought."

"It's been nagging at me all day since I saw Bohmu Din's pictures. I was absolutely sure I'd seen him before." He clicked at the hasps and rifled through the papers and photos. "I just wasn't able to make a connection for some reason. Now I know why."

"Why?"

"Lateral thinking. Always look where you least expect to find the answer."

"In your mom's suitcase?"

He had the photos and was shuffling through them. When he had seen them first, he'd focussed on the sour faces of his parents. He'd barely noticed the people in the background. But one of them had obviously stuck.

There had been two or three pictures taken at a reception. People were standing around. One of the photos, close-ups of two or three people, he was sure contained a character very similar to Bohmu Din.

But after a complete sweep through the case, he could find only one of them. It was a long shot of everyone at the party, like a school photo with the guests lined up in rows. He went through the case again, more carefully this time.

"Why would Bohmu Din be in a photograph in your mom's case?"

"I've no bloody idea. But I'd stake my life on it being him, or his twin brother. The other one's a much better shot, but take a look at this one. See if you can spot him."

Shirley squinted at the print. It did seem to be a reception. About thirty people in fine, light clothes were lined up in two rows. Most of them were holding glasses with tissue flack-jackets. Someone must have shouted "smile" because they were all smiling.

"You got a magnifying glass?"

"Mother's reading glasses should be beside the rocker in the lounge."

She jumped out from under the covers. If the top weren't bad enough, the bottom made her look like an erotic underwear ad. He looked up briefly then turned his eyes back to the case. "The photos, John," he reminded himself.

Even after a careful search, he was sure the other photos weren't there. Perhaps that's what had seemed different when he went through the case last time. From the other room he heard, "Darn it, John, if you aren't right."

She came back, crawled on the bed, and sat back under the sheet "Look."

He took the picture and the glasses from her. In the back row, the smiling face of Bohmu Din was some thirty years younger. His hair was short, but black. In the front row, standing next to each other but not touching, were his young parents.

"Christ!"

"John, I don't understand. This can't be a coincidence."

He turned and sat on the floor with his back against the bed to catch the light better. He studied the faces through Coletta's spectacles. He went from person to person looking at clothes, jewelry, bags. In the background there was a blurred figure in the shadows.

" Shirley. See this guy. . . ?"

She leaned down across his shoulder. He felt her breath as her mouth passed his ear. He trembled slightly.

"Yeah. He's in uniform." She took the glasses from John.

"Do you recognize it?"

"It's dress uniform; the type they use for formal occasions. Not a regular fatigue."

"But. . . ?"

"But it could be Burmese."

"We need a computer."

"What for?"

"Look. There are bottles on the table. I can't make out the labels with these things.

"But we could scan them and blow them up. Good idea."

"What time is it?"

"Half five." He stood up. "Two hours enough beauty sleep?"

"I didn't even get that much. Let's go."

50

The only person John knew who had a computer and the equipment they needed was—had been—Bruce. John had a spare key for Susan's place in his bunch. Nobody had been back to the house since they'd whisked her away to Aunt Maud's. He hoped they hadn't been victims of Britain's burglary frenzy.

Susan lived in Worcester Park, no more than five minute's from where Emma was now hiding her. The drive south out of Greater London was uncluttered and fast at that time of day. Only the traffic lights slowed them down. The phone was back on, and Shirley received their first call:

"You the police?"

"Yes."

"And you're a woman?"

"Yes. Gotta get up early to catch you out, eh."

"You want to come and suck my dick?"

"Thanks. My dentist told me I should keep small dirty objects away from my cavities. Good morning." She switched off. "Good start."

John laughed. The phone rang again.

"Good morning."

"Mr. John Jessel please."

Shirley froze. John sensed her shock. The colour drained from her face. She could neither speak nor release the phone. John had to prize it out of her grasp.

"Jessel."

"Ah, Inspector, good morning. I assume you found your small cabaret yesterday amusing?"

"Not amusing, General Din. But perhaps the only way I could get to talk to you." He pulled the car over to the side of the dual carriageway and parked. Tears were rolling silently down Shirley's face like rain dripping down a window-pane. She looked straight ahead. Bohmu Din seemed disturbed that John knew his name.

"My, you do know a lot about me. And what would you like to discuss, Inspector? My surrender? A showdown? The 'take me but don't hurt my sister' scenario? We have so little to talk about. You are both going back to heaven, you know."

"Well then, before I go, perhaps you could clear up one or two little details . . . about Burma, about what my father, Jim Jessel, did to you in Te Pao." John knew this wasn't the reason for Bohmu Din's call. It wasn't what he expected at all. He felt an enormous rage welling up in the Burmese.

"That is none of your business, brat."

"Oh, but you see, Bohmu Din, it is my business. I know all about it. I know how my father—"

"I have no more—"

". . . made a fool of you and took something—"

"Good-bye Jessel."

". . . something very special from you."

The phone went dead. So did John. He was drained by the short but intense bout.

"Well, I think that went well, don't you?" His hand was shaking. He looked at Shirley and noticed her tears for the first time. "What is it?"

"I'm . . . I'm so sorry, John. I was useless. All this time I thought I'd be strong, but just hearing his voice made me. . . ." The sobs filled her throat. He pulled her to him and put his arm around her. They sat silent for a long time, clasping one another like survivors of a disaster.

51

Susan let the shower water thud against her back and shoulders. It was so hot, she thought her blood bubbled in her veins. Her skin was red and blotchy from the heat. It was skin that Bruce would never caress, never run his soft beard over again.

When she was alone like this, she thought about their intimacies and their secrets. She ached to talk to him one last time. She couldn't recall whether she'd remembered to tell him she loved him that last phone call. She really wanted him to have that love with him wherever he'd gone. Knowing Bruce, he was probably complaining about the archangels' wingspans, his bicycle chained to the Pearly Gates.

She ran both hands over her stomach. It had proudly rounded out to make room for the new recruit. But this one wouldn't be able to say thank you to the funny man that made her.

"Bruce, Bruce, Bruce. I do wish she could have seen you, touched you before. . . ."

She turned off the water and dived into the toweling robe before the unheated house could turn the water on her body to ice. She wrapped a towel around her hair and looked at her plain self in the misted mirror.

"Hello, Salman," she said to her reflection. "Coletta was right. I could do with a very serious makeover."

She would have stayed longer in the shower. She would have looked at herself longer in the mirror, and done some preening and plucking, but when you have a four-year-old, you can add five disasters for every extra minute you're away. Emma had left for work at 8:00, so the two fugitives were alone again.

Eddo always promised to be good while mummy was in the bathroom. But he had a very broad concept of 'good.'

'Helping with the housework' was good, as in when he made the shampoo sandwiches. 'Being kind to animals' was good, like when he taught the ants how to get to the fridge by leaving them a trail of honey. How could you punish a child who was so good?

She opened the bathroom door and yelled, "Eddo, my son. Watcha doing?"

There was no answer.

"Edward Bruce Fossel."

"I'm busy, Mummy," she heard him call from the lounge.

"Good."

He continued a conversation with himself. She hoped he'd grow out of that by the time he was say, forty. She was on her way to the bedroom to get dressed, but thought better of it and detoured via the kitchen to get herself a drink.

"What are you busy doing?" she called.

She heard him say, "Just a minute," then came running into the kitchen.

"Mother?"

"Yes, small genius?"

He climbed up and knelt on a chair at the table. "You and Uncle John says—"

"Say."

". . . say I mustn't talk to strangers."

"Quite right, too."

"Well, how about policemen? Are policemen strangers?"

"Hmmm. That's a good one. You want some juice?"

"Yes please."

"Right then. If a policeman's in uniform doing his job, or he shows you his—"

"Or her."

"Good. His or *her* badge, then that's a good stranger. So if a policeman you don't know asks you questions, it's okay to answer."

"I thought so." She gave him a juice.

"Thank you. Please may I have one more?"

"What for, love?"

"For the policeman in the lounge." He leaned close to Susan's ear and whispered. "He's got holes in his face, like the moon."

52

John waited for the scanned photo to appear on the screen. Bruce's equipment was in a basement that looked more like NATO headquarters than a converted coal cellar. It was papered with charts and maps, and the system itself would have flummoxed anyone without two Ph.Ds. That's why Bruce had notebooks containing step-by-step instructions on how to plug things in and turn things on. They were for Susan. She was an artist. She even got lost with the toaster settings.

The house seemed secure. Nothing on the ground floor had been disturbed, although there was a musty, airless smell. Shirley had opened a window on their way down to the basement.

The photo, scanned at ten times its original size, appeared in front of them. John zoomed in on the bottles. With a little adjustment, the labels were just about recognizable.

"Mandalay Beer. So mother and father *were* in Burma together." He printed out the enlargement. "The next question is 'when'?"

They looked at the complete picture again and used Bruce's Photoshop to enhance the detail. John seemed to think the fashions were early seventies, and Jim was a much slimmer version than the one in the early pictures with the kids.

They assumed that some of the darker-skinned Asian men in the group were Burmese. They had short hair and wore gaudy silk shirts. One or two sported cravats.

"Okay." Shirley leaned back in her chair. "Here's my guess. Judging from the mixture—Indians, Westerners, Africans, mostly couples—I'd say it's a reception for diplomats hosted by the *Tatmadaw*."

"Could be UN people, or aid agencies."

"Could be. But there weren't too many agencies offering help to a junta in those days. And these folks have a look about them, like they're too important to be there. Wait. . . ." She got closer to the screen. "Can you zoom in on this guy?"

"The one looking down?"

"Yeah. That's good. . . . Well, hot enchiladas. Look who we have here."

"Who?"

"It's U Gyi. He was a key figure in the independence movement, and held a ministerial position in the military government in the sixties. But, like most Burmese with a mind of their own, he upset Ne Win, the big general, and found himself in jail. As soon as they let him out, he fled to the Thai border and took a role in the National League for Democracy. If he was at a reception like this it would have been before 1970."

"Jim didn't marry Coletta until 1970. If it were earlier than that. . . ."

"They were in Burma together before they married."

"That's crazy. They met in Hungary when Dad was there on business. He helped her get out. England was her first time overseas."

"That's the story."

"Oh brother. This family gets more complicated with every stone we turn over." He scrolled along the back row and zoomed in so the face of Bohmu Din filled the monitor. "And how do you fit into this mystery, you nasty bastard. I've got a bad feeling about all this, Shirley." He gathered together all the print-outs and took the original photograph from the scanner. "The people who probably have the answers to this puzzle are back where we just came from. I'm going to see Woods."

"And I'm not?"

"They'd leave you sitting outside with a cup of tea."

"Then I think I'd be more use back at Emma's."

"Good. That's what I thought. But before you go, take this." He wrote something down.

"What is it?"

"It's my log-in number for the police network. I doubt Lawless would think of canceling my code. While we're all switched on here, could you get through to the murder squad notice board and see if anything's been posted on there as a result of the press conference?"

"Ooh. I get to go into the police system? Isn't that illegal or something?"

"Absolutely."

"Cool."

"Okay. I'm off. Don't forget we've all got mobiles. Don't keep anything to yourself."

"How do I get to Emma's?"

"Ah. Didn't think of that." He scratched down an address and gave it to her. This is the factory we usually park behind. Can you get a taxi?"

"Money."

"Damn. Do I have to do everything for you?" He dredged through his pockets and gave her a handful of change. He smiled, shrugged, and was gone up the stairs.

-o-

For twenty minutes Shirley went through messages the public had left on the open channel, as well as comments and follow-up from the internal police messages. A few people had claimed to have seen the man in the sketch in the Kingston-Epsom area after the broadcast. One even had the sense to jot down the number of his car. But there seemed to be an order out to ignore reports based on Jessel's conference. She noted down the few credible leads and was largely unimpressed with the squad's progress. In fact, there hadn't been any.

She logged off and looked at Bruce's room. In her place in the States, if she left a room like this untouched for several months, there'd be a layer of dust everywhere. But all the equipment looked store-new. It must have been its location in the cellar, or the English weather.

She turned off the light and walked up into the house proper. Susan kept an interesting home. It was full of bizarre artwork and curious furniture that all magically blended together to reflect her personality. Eddo must have loved this house. The only thing it was missing was a bathroom. It would have to be on the top floor.

Shirley had long believed that empty houses enjoy playing tricks on people. They could mess with your mind and plant ideas that you would never have thought to put there yourself. The feeling of walking around an empty house can be an eerie one if your mind tells you it is. This was the first time she'd been alone since Bangkok. She had become used to John being around.

She climbed the stairs slowly. Each step had its own squeak, like an instrument you play with your feet. Even before she reached the top landing, her instinct told her that something wasn't quite right up there. She stopped on the top step and held her breath, listening for sounds from the three upstairs rooms. All she heard were the steps unsqueaking behind her and the tap dripping water into a bowl in the kitchen. Upstairs was deadly silent.

She was angry with herself for creating something that wasn't there. She willed herself to go on. The first door, ajar, led to the bathroom, but she'd lost the urge. She peeked in through the crack between the hinges. There was nowhere for anyone to hide in there. And why would anyone be hiding there anyway? There was an ornament beside the bath, quite heavy, thin enough at the neck to hold like a baseball bat. She reached in for it. She had a weapon now, but no free hand.

The second door was also slightly ajar. Her body was crying out to her to be careful, to go back downstairs, but she had to know what her instincts had smelt. She pushed the door with her foot, listening for sounds. It was Eddo's room. There was a wardrobe. She walked to it along the far wall so she could see under his bed.

To open the wardrobe door and keep hold of the weapon at the same time, she had to use the ends of her fingers that poked from the cast. They had become numb and useless. "One . . . two . . . three," she counted in her head. "Open."

Toys.

Two rooms down. One to go. But her nerves let her know she'd been stalling. The vibrations had been coming from the last door, which was shut. From the process of elimination, she knew it had to be Susan and Bruce's room.

A tap dripping.

A dusted keyboard.

Someone was here.

"He'll have a knife. He'll be by the door waiting," she thought. "He'll slash at my throat when he sees me standing there." So she knelt. It would give her a fraction of a second. She breathed deeply to regain control. "It's just one man. One small, insignificant old man. The guards in Pa-an were young and strong, and because of me they're dead. I'm not afraid of one old man." She didn't believe what she was telling herself.

Her heart thumped and her lungs fought against her deep breaths. She counted again, this time in her native tongue, so all the spirits of the Karen warriors would be with her,

"Ter . . .

"Khee . . .

"Ser."

With her plastered hand she threw back the door and poised to strike. The door swung faster than she expected, with no obstruction, and crashed against the wall.

There was no Bohmu Din. Not now. But from where she knelt in the doorway she could see everything in the room, and she could hardly believe, nor begin to understand, what she was looking at there.

53

"I brought you the mobile," John said, walking into Commander Woods' office. "But your gorilla lady on the door wouldn't let me in with it."

"I'll tell her to send it over to the people following up on your calls." He picked up the phone.

"She forcibly removed my beeper and another mobile as well."

"Then she's doing her job well. Nothing remotely electrical is allowed in these offices that hasn't gone through very strict security checks."

"They're for emergency purposes."

"Anything that gets as far as us is already an emergency. Rules are rules." He spoke to the receptionist about the phone and ordered two cups of tea. He then turned back to John. "I must say you're looking a lot better than you were last time I saw you."

"Thanks. And if you tell me I'm the image of Jim, I'll put a chair through your window."

"Then I won't tell you. I take it from what I heard, that your mission was a success."

"In some ways. In others, it just opened up some very big gaps in the top-secret information you gave me before I left."

"Really? I'm certain everything I told you was the truth."

John decided it would be a disaster to have Woods as a bridge partner. The man's face projected every thought that went through his mind. John couldn't believe he had ever succeeded in the field. Right now Woods projected that he'd been caught cheating. "Perhaps you could give me an example of one of these 'gaps.'"

"Well, for example, you led me to believe that Jim and Coletta met in Hungary."

"I did no such thing. I don't even recall mentioning the relationship between your parents." A slight 'you got me' smile turned up at the corner of his mouth. "And are you telling me they didn't meet in Hungary?"

"Are you telling me they did?"

Woods was rescued by the tea. It was delivered by a smaller version of the reception gorilla.

When she'd gone, Woods blew the steam from his tea and smiled again. "All right. Why don't you tell me everything you know."

"There isn't time for that. I already know everything I know. It's what I don't know that I've come here for. And, by the by, I was a little bit more sensible this time. Taking my memory away won't do you any good. I wrote out a full report of everything I learned in Burma and deposited a copy with a few people. They won't open it unless something happens to me. The report includes everything I found out about Coletta's Burma connection."

Woods was still smiling as he got to his feet. He sipped at his tea and said, "Impressive. I don't suppose you'd like to come and work for us would you? You really are jolly good."

"I want that in writing with a salary statement. But first, suppose you tell me everything you know about Burma."

"Yes. I really don't have much choice do I . . . ? Come on over to the sofa. This could take a little time."

They carried their teas to the library corner of the large office, and sat at either end of a paisley-print couch. John was impressed at how civilized espionage could be. Woods began to recount the history as if he were the official state storyteller:

"Your father was with us from his early twenties. He was recruited from university; good grades, political science, Eastern languages. He was the sort the service was looking for. By the late sixties, he was already one of the department's top field operators. Not surprisingly, with his background, and all the hell that was breaking loose in Southeast Asia, he spent most of his time there.

"One of our main concerns then, as it still is today, was the flow of drugs into the Soviet bloc. When communism was at its most rampant, it was very difficult for us to get in to curb the flow on into Britain. So we had to focus on the source, which was the north of Burma. As long as the Americans were in Vietnam, there was a very lucrative regional heroin market. But we were afraid that once Nixon pulled out, the market would shift to us.

"We got Jim stationed at the IIC office in Rangoon. How am I doing so far. . . ?"

"That's pretty much what I've got," John lied. "Now, Coletta enters, stage left."

"Very left. She was such a pretty girl. I was stationed in the region then. I remember her well. I tell you, if John hadn't fallen for her, I would have had a crack at her myself." He suddenly turned as red as the flag. "Oh, I say. I am sorry. This is your mother we're talking about."

"No problem. I'm sure it gets worse."

"Oh, it does. She was in her mid-twenties I guess, and already a very experienced operative; what we referred to as a 'jam tart'."

A doubting smirk came to John's face.

"Yes, it's a rather crude simile, but that's what we called them then. Most of the communist bloc used them. In country, they'd pose as office workers, wait at restaurants; generally get in a position where they could flirt with foreign diplomats before getting them into bed. In the—"

"Are you telling me Coletta was a whore?"

"Well goodness me, I assumed this was the part you'd worked out already. I am sorry. But in fact they weren't really whores. They were trained agents."

"Spies who slept with diplomats?"

"Right. The overseas legations took them as junior office clerks and secretaries, and dangled them in front of ministers. It was a good source of information, and even better for blackmail."

Given everything he'd heard lately, John assumed he'd become unshockable, but this news shot his kneecaps off. The commander wasn't finished:

"Coletta was in a very difficult situation. She'd been widowed by the communists. She had her two children back in Budapest, and the government was holding them as hostages to keep her in the Service. She'd been trying to get out for a long time."

"Coletta had two kids before she met Jim?"

"Yes."

"Whew."

"You didn't know that either? What exactly do you know?"

"Keep going."

"Coletta was supposed to seduce your father to find out what he, and we, knew about Hungary's involvement in the drug trade. It was a Mexican stand-off really. We knew she was a. . . ."

"Jam tart."

"Yes . . . jam tart. It's actually the image of being red and sweet and—"

"I got it."

"We knew what she was, and they knew about Jim. So nobody was really fooling anyone. Except Coletta had decided to use Jim to get herself out of the work, and her children out of Hungary. She was prepared to share and steal secrets for us in return."

"And she sucked Dad into falling for her."

"She was very lovely. And to be honest, although it's hard to tell with women like . . . like that . . . I do believe she had feelings for him. Jim had been a very unattached person before Coletta, even though he was a good-looking chap. He was certainly head-over-heels about her. Who knows? They could really have been in love."

"So?"

"So, through Coletta, Jim got introductions to all the *Tatmadaw* involved in drugs. Most of them dealt illegally with producers in the top end of the Golden Triangle. She was able to convince them that John would be a good ally. He put contacts their way."

"He helped them sell?"

"It was necessary to establish trust."

John chewed over the facts so far. One horrific thought came to him. "You don't suppose Coletta and Bohmu Din were. . . ?"

"Oh, I doubt that very much. He was a very small fish when she was there. Barely worth baiting the hook. But he was certainly involved, and he was a messenger to the Hungarian Embassy, so they must have known each other. He didn't start to make serious drug money until the eighties when the Eastern European cartels became more powerful than their governments."

"So you did know about him?"

"We only made the connection after you got his real name. We knew of General Din, but we had no way of knowing he was Te Pao."

"But you knew Jim was going inside Burma to meet his drug contacts."

"Yes."

"Thanks for telling me all this. What happened to Coletta?"

"Something of a tragedy I'm afraid. We kept up our end of the bargain. The information she got us was very useful. We located her children and planned to smuggle them out at the same time as Jim and Coletta returned to England. Jim seemed delighted that he'd have an instant family. Coletta was over the moon that she'd be reunited with her sons.

"I saw them just before they left Rangoon. They appeared to be so content with each other. I was quite envious. I suppose that was the only time they were really happy."

"Something went wrong."

"Drastically. It should have been the simplest thing. Our Hungarian agent was to pick the kids up at their school during the day. They weren't under guard or anything. They walked to the school from the government boys' home they were staying at. He contacted them on their way home and told them to expect to be called for a medical check-up the next day. He told them they'd be going to see their mother and that this had to be a secret.

"Well, I'm afraid the youngest boy was so excited he told his best friend, and word got to the director. When the agent arrived at the school, the secret police were there waiting for him. After some horrendous punishment he told them about Coletta's escape. The Hungarian Embassy missed her at Rangoon airport by ten minutes.

"And the children?"

"A lot of women had been coerced into the same type of work in the same way. Many of them had children in state homes. I suppose the secret police wanted to make an example of Coletta's children so others wouldn't try the same thing."

"Oh, God."

"It was rumoured that their throats were cut."

"Coletta must have been devastated.

"She reacted as any mother would have. Jim offered her what support he could. He blamed us for the disaster. He even considered leaving the Service. Coletta was naturally very bitter. In order to stay in Britain she had to marry Jim, as had been stipulated in the Immigration documents. He gave her the option to live apart, but she found she needed to be close to someone at that time. Your father was the only one to have shown her any genuine kindness. We gave him an extended leave to be with her. "

"So they were close."

"At that time, yes. And you were the result of that closeness. They hoped that having other children would help her get over her loss. It was a precarious psychological decision. A lot of people argued against it, but Jim was convinced they could make a go at being a happy family. Sadly, he was wrong. She couldn't bond with you at all. She was naturally afraid that getting close to you would leave her open for more heartbreak. She was very cruel to you at times. There was—"

"Wait. Please." John was winded. He needed a rest from the punches that were giving him little time to think.

So much was becoming clear. His hatred for Coletta now had a backdrop. So much about his childhood suddenly made sense. He had blamed her for his sadness, when in fact she had been the victim. He was just the recipient of her misery—not the cause of it.

He reached, without thinking, for his gnarled ear. As he touched it, the events leading up to it flashed in front of him like the opening reel of an 8-mm home film. It was like he had always known. . . .

He is almost five. Susan is just a baby. Jim's final attempt at happiness lays neglected in her cot, just had John had done before her. But John could be her protector. Knights were protectors, so he is her knight, and knights have swords. His sword is a rusted bread knife he rescued from the rubbish and sharpened on a stone. He keeps it hidden under the carpet beneath his bed.

He is woken in the night by his mother's screams from the next room. She is being killed. Even if she is a wicked mother, she needs a knight. Still half-in and half-out of sleep, he takes his sword and goes to her room.

Coletta is being murdered by a naked man. John is afraid, but he knows that as the protector of Susan and the house, he has to kill the man. He climbs onto the bed in the dark and attacks him with his sword.

There is confusion. Coletta's screams wake her dog. The dog comes to her aid and attacks the attacker. . . .

Woods was still sitting patiently with him, waiting for the end of John's day-nightmare; his daymare.

He looked at the Commander with disbelief on his face. "I . . . I just remembered. It's unbelievable. I could see the scene as if it had just happened. My bloody ear. I had no idea what happened to it."

Woods edged towards him. "You were very brave, lad. At that age, it's unlikely you were acting out of malice. It was a game that got out of control. If I recall the doctor's report, you made a number of holes in your mother's lover, killed the dog, and fought like blazes when she locked you in the wardrobe."

"Woody, I remember. I was in there for some time wasn't I."

"Several days before they found you."

"I remember . . . the smell."

"She locked the dog's body in there with you as a lesson."

"I was four or five years old."

"She was a very disturbed woman then, John. The second birth had dropped her into some dark pit. When Jim left for Asia, she was thrashing around . . . lost. They took her away to a home."

"No wonder I'm so fucked up."

"You could have been much worse, John Jessel . . . much worse."

-o-

Sitting in his car in the car park, he was still winded. He was shaking and smiling, and tears were in his eyes not knowing whether to be joy tears or sadness tears. Some programme in him was going back through his memory, knocking down old myths—standing up and dusting off old corpses.

As his past slowly re-arranged itself, so the present took on a whole new shape and feel. Who he was there and then was different to who he had been an hour earlier. He had gone to see Woods expecting to get a few details that would make him feel badly about his parents. What he got was a new mother and an even better father.

Anyone who had suffered as Coletta did would need time to evacuate the misery. With counseling and drugs, Coletta had mellowed out of hatred and into a more consistent sourness. But she was never to know happiness again.

When the wars in Southeast Asia had burned down to embers, Jim was called upon to renew the contacts they had made together in Burma. The old friends who remembered him and Coletta as young lovers were anxious to hear about her and his family. To protect them, the cover the Foreign Service came up with was that in giving birth late in life to Jim's third child, both mother and child had died. The truth was that most of her had died before giving birth to his first. Then Bohmu Din finished her off.

He tried to imagine how that could have happened.

She gets a call from Bohmu Din. She has no reason to associate this man from her past with the maniac pursuing her family. They talk socially on the telephone. Perhaps he reminds her of the receptions at the ministry in Rangoon. She tells him she still has photographs from one of them. He says he'd like to see them, perhaps get together?

So, because I'm in the hospital, Coletta comes to retrieve her own case. She invites Bohmu Din to her apartment. She opens the door to him and. . . .

"Coletta," John said, looking into his rear-view mirror at her ghost. "Your death was as much of a tragedy as your life. I'm sorry, old girl."

His trembling fingers bungled the job of turning on his mobile and activating the beeper. He'd almost forgotten both of them when he was leaving the building. Once it was on, the message on the beeper slapped him back: "*To Em's —Urgent.*" It was from Shirley.

He first called Shirley's, then Susan's phones, but both were switched off. He'd told them not to for any reason. Why were they off? He called Emma but she was in court. She'd left the phone with a clerk, who promised to give the message when she came out.

He called back into Woods' office to tell him what had happened, and gave him the address. Something had to be wrong. He didn't want to call the police and have the address broadcast to cars in the area, just in case Bohmu Din was listening in. There was no choice but to drive down to Emma's place. He prayed that whatever had been so urgent was a false alarm.

The adrenaline helped him take control of the wheel and drive out into King Charles Street. He turned left and headed past the mews where the prime minister was taking afternoon tea. Two Asian tourists had come to watch from a distance. They hurriedly put down their cameras, ran to their car, and drove off after John's old Peugeot. They had finally received the order they'd been expecting: "Eliminate Angel One."

54

Susan slowly came around, the fumes from the chloroform were still burning and heavy in her nostrils. Her first thought had been to take Eddo out of the house through the front door, but Bohmu Din was standing in the hall behind the kitchen door. She saw the briefest flash of cloth, felt a strong hand on her neck, and heard Eddo shout for her. That's all.

Now her eyes were wet and puffy, and she was shivering from the cold. She squinted to see where she was. She recognized the back bedroom at Emma's where she and Eddo slept. She was on the cold floor and slowly noticed through her dizziness, that her bathrobe was wide open, revealing her nakedness. She looked at her belly, moved her legs slightly, but saw and felt no evidence of rape. She immediately pulled the robe shut, and clumsily tied the belt.

She pulled up her knees to a fetal position, but her right ankle tugged against something metallic. She was joined to the long-abandoned metal radiator with leg irons—the type they put on convicts in Asian gaols.

She breathed deeply to clear her nausea, and looked slowly around the blurred room. Two small legs poked out from beneath a large overcoat on the bed.

"*Eddo*! Eddo wake up. It's mummy." But there was no movement.

"I'm afraid I've killed him. I'm terribly sorry." The man's voice came from a point outside the doorway.

Susan took some time to understand.

"*No*! Oh, God. No. It's not true. *Eddo*!" She tried to stand, to walk, but the chain. . . . She couldn't catch her breath. She kicked and kicked against the leg iron until the skin on her ankle split, and blood covered the chain. Crying deeply, she fell to the floor. "Eddo. Please wake up." From where she lay, she could just see beyond the doorway.

The man from the photographs, Bohmu Din, had pulled the lounge armchair as far as the bedroom door. It had been too wide to fit through the doorway, so he sat in the hall, frustrated.

He saw her looking up at him. "Sometimes I forget my own strength."

Susan found a second burst of energy. "No. No. *Eddo*! Mummy's here. It's all right." She crawled on her hands and knees to the radiator and, still crying, grabbed it with both hands and used all her strength to try to wrench it from the wall.

Bohmu Din grew impatient with the chair. Even by leaning forward, he couldn't see the show Angel Two was putting on. In a huff, he stood and walked into the bedroom. Susan, her strength flagging, pulled weakly at the metal pipe she was connected to.

"That's quality workmanship," he said. His words were blotted out by her scream. It was shrill and annoying.

He had to shout to be heard. "Screaming won't help you. All the houses around here are slated for demolition. This is the only one with life. For the time being."

But she didn't stop; neither screaming nor clawing at the radiator. Her histrionics were causing him to desend rapidly into one of his slumps. He was not totally responsible for his actions when he was down there. They'd given him pills for it, but he'd started to enjoy the purple moods far more than the bright yellow ones.

"Why?" she shouted, her voice breaking. "Why my son? He hasn't done anything to you, you sick bastard."

"Oh dear," he said, fighting to haul himself out of the slump. Trying hard to stay lucid enough to explain. He sat down on the bed and caressed the naked foot with the back of his hand.

"Don't you touch him, you freak."

"Why do you both make it so personal?"

"Personal?" She gave an ironic laugh. "Killing my family's not personal? How much more. . . ." The tears overcame her.

"You see what ranting does? I think you should calm down and listen to what I have to say, so we can get this over with. I want to be sure you've heard."

"And I'm next?"

"If things have gone according to plan, you will be last. Your angel brother will be waiting for you in heaven."

Susan crumpled to the floor beneath the combined weight of grief upon grief. It suffocated her. She put her face in her hands and breathed deeply into them.

"That's much better." He got down on the floor and sat cross-legged in front of her. The knife stood proudly out of the breast pocket of his shirt, its blade always close to his cheek. He seemed unaware of the danger of it.

He looked up to the wall as he tried to remember the script he had written for her. He was dipping in and out of his slump like a trawler in a high sea. It was important to him to stay in control long enough to do it right.

"I was surprised you are still producing. I took a peek while you were sleeping. Hope you don't. . . ." His head pounded. The pain deafened him to his own words. "Hope you don't mind. This way is even better. I get one bonus angel, you see? It's like a reward. I didn't touch you down there, of course."

He put his hand into the knife pocket. He didn't notice the slash the sharp blade made across his palm, just calmly pulled out the well-mauled photograph. He held it towards her.

"This is the way I prefer you. I often imagine having you like this. Oh do look. I'd hate to think I was wasting my last speech." He waited for the ringing to pass from just behind his eyes. "*Look*!"

Susan looked up from her palms. He was happy to see the anger in her eyes. She looked at the square of paper he was holding up to her face. She could barely make out a picture. A woman in a chair could have been her mother. If that were so, the two children at her feet were herself and John. But their faces were gone. The paper there was so worn through, she could see the light from the window behind where they should have been.

His hand bled onto the photograph and blood spread across the picture like a theatre curtain closing a last act. Susan made the decision then that she would not merely fade away like her image.

"You knew my father."

Something tightened in his head. "You don't have to speak. Just—"

"What was he like?"

"Like. . . ? He was like nothing. He was a fool, a coward, a liar, and a thief. Is that enough? He was a mindless bag man for some drug dealer." He put his blooded hand to his forehead to squeeze out the pain. "He was a child abuser."

"He was all those things, yet he was still able to make a fool of you. How pathetic you must be." She looked him in the face and laughed at him.

And she saw it as she looked at that face. When he took his hand from his jaundiced eyes, she saw a tempest build in them. She had sent him swirling backward to a time that gave birth to his hatred. And she saw him cross over into insanity like a man crossing from the bright side of the street to the shady side.

Very slowly he said, "Why did I think I could speak to you?"

She knew that she had just talked herself to death.

He took the knife from his pocket and held it in his unsplit hand.

Then the sound came. It was barely audible. Someone like Bohmu Din would never have recognized it. But to a mother, the sound of a child's breath is a fanfare. It filled her with hope, and will, and strength. Before he could draw back his arm, she was on him, punching, and scratching. The second blow cracked his nose. The knife fell from his hand and he was stunned.

But his instincts hit back. He tore into her with his fists. She knew then she was going to lose. He beat her until she was unconscious, but even then he didn't stop. It wasn't until his rage was overtaken by his pain that he jerked back and looked down on the body like an innocent witness.

He saw her face, a map of blood and misplaced features. She hadn't used her hands to protect herself. They were cased around her belly, stiff like gauntlets protecting her daughter.

It sickened him to think of a love so deep, one would sacrifice one's own life to save another's. And it had all been a waste of time. He fumbled around him, half blinded by the ache inside his mind and the blood in his eyes. He held the knife tightly in his bloody hand and peeled back Susan's robe. Before cutting, he ran his palm across the mound of flesh.

"It's a miracle isn't it?"

He hadn't heard Shirley come in to the room. He would not . . . *he would not* tolerate an interruption at this stage. It was the boy angel's girlfriend. He had seen her from a distance. *Remove her.* The searing, shooting flashes of lightning scythed through his brain. *Stand. . . . Kill.*

With amazing agility he was up and upon her in a fraction of a second. She didn't flinch. She didn't run from him or beg or fall. She stood and smiled. And her smile was a weapon more powerful than any he had met in battle.

"*Who* are you?" He stood in front of her. His blade was drawn back to strike.

In the Karen dialect they had used together, she replied, "Don't you remember your little girl, Major Din?"

He looked at her closely, and in the same dialect he asked again, "Who are you?"

"I am Sherri Ya Hei . . . your girl."

He leaned forward even closer and stared so hard into her face that he peeled away the wrinkles and the bruises and the bandages. He stared so hard, he tore away the days and months and years. Until in front of him was Sherri as she had remained in his mind for 18 years.

He dropped to his knees like a worshipper before an altar. There was no doubt then in Shirley's mind what it was Jim had stolen from him all those years ago, what it was that had wrung the sanity from him.

"Sherri. . . . You came back. I knew you would."

"Yes."

"Have you come forever?"

"Tell me why I should."

"But you know."

"If you don't tell me, I'll go again."

He could not bring himself to look up at her for fear he'd be turned to rock by her magic.

"I am not. . . . I do not have the words." He saw her feet turn to leave. "*No*! Wait! I . . . you were . . . you are the only love I have ever known in my life. You are the only living being to enter my heart. My love for you was so great. . . ." The turmoil inside his head was interfering with his speech.

". . . so great that I was miserable when I was away from you. Always. My heart was emp . . . empty without you. I ate for you. I slept for you. I breathed every breath for you. I lived for you and killed for you. So . . . so many of my kills were sacrifices to you."

"And when you came home?"

"When I came home to you, it was as if you didn't care how much suffering I had been through for you. I had to be strong for you. I had to show . . . to show you that I could protect you." He rocked back and forth as he spoke.

"So you beat me."

"I had to. You know I had to. It was the only way to show you my love. The more I hurt you. The more I loved you. You always stayed so calm throughout. Your calmness and sweetness. *Aaaaghhh. . . .*" The pressure was squeezing the last sense from his mind. . . .

"I tried and tried and tried and tried and tried to let you know. I loved you. I needed you. And *he he he* came. He insulted me with talk of money for you. *Ogled* at you like you were some common whore. You were mine. Was he blind?"

As he ranted, Shirley reached inside her shirt and pulled out a coil of fishing wire with small metal grips at each end. It was a weapon the boys in the camps had introduced her to. It was a weapon she took with her to the States, and learned from old soldiers how to use well. And here it was, the weapon that would avenge her abuse and rid her of anger.

He was before her. His head bowed. It wouldn't be difficult. But she wanted to hear him out. She wanted to understand how evil feathered its nest. He spoke loudly, saliva dripped from his mouth to the floor like from some untrained animal.

"He started a fire at the munitions tent. I knew it must have been him. I went . . . I went to see, just briefly. When I came back, you . . . you . . . you my sweet, sweet love had been taken, stolen from me. *You were mine*!

"I knew. I knew you didn't want to leave me . . . ever. I knew he had kidnapped you for his own disgusting purposes. He would have your body. *The body that belonged to me*!" Bohmu Din's hands were beating rhythmically on the floor in time to the heartbeat of some growing monster. His nose began to bleed, but still he spoke and rocked.

"I searched . . . all my men searched. If it hadn't been for my superiors, I would have used the whole battalion to search until they died of starvation. For five days I was out looking for you. I didn't sleep." His voice gradually became quieter, as if he'd forgotten Shirley was there and he was telling himself. . . .

"If you weren't there beside me, how could I rest? And you know he came back. He came back to the edge of the camp . . . right under our noses. And he waited for me to grow tired enough to sleep. Just patiently he sat in a tree waiting. And eventually, exhaustion climbed on top of me and wrestled me down." He seemed to laugh, but it was so soft Shirley had to strain her ears to hear. . . .

"My men caught him. There was no skill involved. One of the battalion drunks was going for a piss and saw him slip into my barracks. I was two seconds from death. It took five men to overpower him.

"I hated him, and he was coming to kill me because I loved you. That's ironic isn't it. '*For what you've done to the child*' he said. Why ever would he go to so much trouble to kill me for loving you? He was quite mad.

"But before I could touch him, before I could cut your whereabouts from his throat, he bit on the poison and left me with nothing; no information, no revenge, and no love."

She heard him begin to cry.

"And all he left me were his two angel children to fly over me all these years. *But he . . . had . . . stolen my love!*"

Shirley looped the wire, leaned forward, and dropped the noose over Bohmu Din's neck. She saw her own tears drip into his white hair.

"I was six years old," she whispered. "I didn't deserve your kind of love."

55 - Chiang Mai

"Okay, all I'm missing now is the ending." Norbert sat on the recliner with the last of a very cold beer in his hand, and his feet on the balcony rail. "Man, I love these true-life dramas."

John had an eye on Eddo, up to his knees in the stream, spearing imaginary sharks. "Eddo. If you drown I'm going to be very, very angry."

"Yes, Uncle Johhhn," he shouted back.

John sipped at his soda. "Okay, so I arrive at Em's place —"

"With the Burmese guys in the back seat of your car?"

"With the Burmese guys in the back seat of my car, at about the same time as Woods' chap. He'd already been inside. He said the front door was wide open when he got there. There was nobody inside, but there was blood and all kinds of shit on the floor of the back bedroom. Of course, I assumed the worst. I was furious with myself for not calling for back-up when I first got the message."

"Oh, this is so exciting. Wait. . . ." He chugged back the last dregs of his beer and ran off to get another one.

John walked over to the balustrade and waved at his nephew. He wondered how long it would be before he appreciated how lucky he was to be alive.

Eddo waved back. "I killed a whale," he said, rolling a huge boulder over to the bank.

"I'll tell Greenpeace."

Beyond Eddo, the small, whitewashed stone that marked Jim Jessel's grave was picked out by the sun. John raised his soda to his dad, glad to see he was enjoying the nice weather, too.

"Okay. I'm back. Don't spare me any details." Norbert fell into his chair and popped his can.

"Well, I tried all the mobiles again and got nothing, so the Secret Service chap and I decided it was time to call in reinforcements. I phone Lawless' mobile number expecting another war. He wasn't ever in a great mood, so I wasn't surprised when he shouted, 'Jessel, you irresponsible piece of shit, where the fuck are you?' I told him, but I was surprised when he said, 'Our lot should be there any second, but I don't want you waiting for them. You get your arse over here to Kingston Hospital, now.'

"I was in a right mess. I had no idea what to expect. So I motored over to the hospital like a madman."

"With the Burmese guys still in the back seat."

"Right."

Norbert chuckled. "Hot dog, I love these stories."

"They probably thought they were being punished. I almost crashed a dozen times, the way I was driving."

"He's not telling this bloody story again?"

"Yes ma'am, he is, and I'm loving it." Norbert stood politely to welcome Susan, her face completely bandaged except for her eyes and mouth. He offered his chair to her.

"So nice to see there are still gentlemen in the world." She sat down and noticed Eddo in the stream below. "He's still down there? He'll be growing fins soon. He really loves it here."

"And he's more than welcome, ma'am."

"Tell me Norbert, where did you get that unfortunate accent?"

Norbert laughed from his belly. "Oh man. You Jessels just slay me."

"Can I finish this story or not?" John butted in.

"What version are you telling today, brother John? He makes most of this up, Norbert. He kills more baddies every time he tells it."

John laughed, walked over to her, and kissed her somewhere on the gauze.

"Darn it, John, you just moved my nose two centimetres to the left. It isn't set yet."

They all laughed.

"I can't wait to see who you'll turn out to be when the bandages come off."

"She'll be beautiful," Norbert said. "I know it. But you should have waited and got it done here in Thailand. We got the best plastic surgeons in the world you know?"

"Yes," John agreed. "But they specialize in sex-change operations so I've heard. I rather like having a sister."

"If only they could have given me a face that doesn't itch so. I really want to get in there and have a good old scratch. Oh, sorry big brother. I'm ready. Go on with the story."

John looked at Norbert. "Where was I?"

"You was just taking the Burmese guys to the hospital."

"Right. I just left them in the car park with the keys in the ignition and sprinted inside. Ran straight into Lawless in reception. I asked him what had happened. 'Calm down,' he said. 'They're both okay. Your sister and the boy. They're alive.'"

"Thank God," Susan shrieked.

"Stop interrupting. Eddo there had taken enough chloroform to knock out a horse. He was still out when I saw him, but through the worst of it, and his breathing was back to normal. But this one here. My goodness. She looked like they'd taken her head off and replaced it with spaghetti Bolognese."

"It was ravioli last time you told it."

"Spaghetti's more graphic. It really gives you the feel of all the blood and skin, and all the brain parts falling out. I almost fainted."

"My big police hero."

"That's a yellow card. One more interruption and you're off the balcony."

Norbert giggled. He was truly delighted to have them at his house. It made him feel closer to Jim. If only the old corpse could heave himself out of his hole and come see how nice they turned out.

"Now don't forget," John continued. "Lawless still had very little idea of what this was all about. So when I told him there were two Burmese in the back seat of my car who'd like to help him with his inquiries, he went bananas. He was yelling and storming up and down. He had an idea the case was solved, but didn't know how all the pieces fitted together. And suddenly there he was with two mystery Burmese."

"Solve the mystery, man."

"Well, I was speeding along the motorway on my way to Emma's when this rental car pulls alongside. My first instinct was to duck. I swerved across the road and was almost wiped out by a truck. I was sure they were going to shoot me.

"But I look across, and one of them's holding a note saying 'Hello. Please pull over.' I didn't think they'd write me a note before blowing my brains out, so I pulled over. These two get out of their car, with their hands up—"

"You had a gun?"

"No. Certainly not."

Norbert and Susan laughed.

"But they came over and told me they surrendered, and they were prepared to give evidence if we could come to some 'arrangement.' I had absolutely no idea what they were surrendering for, and I was in a hurry to get back. So I told them to get in the car and tell me on the way.

"It appears these two were ex-SLORC who'd been hired by their old commanding officer, Bohmu Din, to do detective work . . . follow people, take pictures, record conversations, that type of thing. They'd even broken into Susan's place at one stage. That's how Bohmu Din knew about Eddo.

"He'd arranged their UK visas. They'd been there for almost a year and were getting quite attached to the place.

Unbeknownst to the major, one had brought his wife over, the other was dating a local girl. They were quite settled and earning a lot more than they would in Burma.

"But eventually they came to realize that what they'd been doing wasn't just plain old political espionage. When the news of the murdered guards in Mendleton appeared in the papers, it occurred to them their spying was setting people up to get killed; normal people. It didn't take a lot of deduction to work out that their psychotic boss was the murderer, and it had nothing to do with their government.

"They were afraid that eventually he'd expect them to do the killing, or he'd get caught and drag them down, too. So they opted for a deal. As soon as Bohmu Din ordered them to do me in, they . . . what. . . ? Defected to our side. And that's why I'm still alive."

"And the world's a better place for it."

"Alleluia."

"Mummy. There's blood on my foot." Eddo limped smiling on to the balcony.

"Is it yours?"

"Yes."

"Then come over here and we'll plug up the hole."

"I'll go get the Band-Aids." Norbert walked into the house for the first-aid kit. He passed Kruamart on her way out and kissed her cheek. She was holding the newest and tiniest member of the Jessel clan.

Susan looked up. "Oh, don't tell me she's hungry again. Where does she put it all?"

Kruamart lay her gently on Susan's lap.

John watched his sister unbutton her shirt. "Sue, darling. If you had decent sized udders, she could get all she needs in one sitting."

"I know. I bet they'd have been huge if she'd arrived when she was supposed to."

The beating had brought Coletta into the world a month premature. At the hospital they were fighting to save two lives at the same time. Susan had lost a lot of blood, and was in no state to help with the birthing. But the little lass found her way out somehow and waited patiently on life-support for her mother to join her. It was a long wait.

Given the state of Susan's face, they had been forced to bring in a team of cosmetic surgeons to help put her back together. John, the only living relative, gave permission while Susan was still unconscious. He sat with her day and night at the hospital, talked her through the ordeal that had put her there, and told her about their mother. It was the decision of both of them to name the little girl who was so very small, but so very tough.

At some stage, while John was beside Susan's bed with the employment section of the newspaper spread out on her cover, Lawless received a visit from someone very important. John wasn't sure what had been said, but it resulted in a retraction of the complaint against him, a commendation for bravery, and the option of staying at a higher salary.

Despite Emma's warning that promotions like this didn't come along every day, John declined—or at least deferred. He told her that if the job were still there in a couple of years, he might very well take it. But he had something else he needed to do first; something that had been niggling at him since it became obvious that his relationship with Shirley was doomed to purity and platonic respect.

As soon as Susan and the baby were well enough to travel, John loaded them on a flight to Thailand. Norbert had phoned the hospital and insisted they come to his place. The change of scenery would do them all good. For very good reasons, Susan didn't even get a chance to go home first.

John had decided not to mention Jim's drug involvement to Norbert, especially as much of his work in the region had been in drug suppression. He may have known already of course, but there was no reason to float a storm cloud into a sunny memory.

They had arrived early that morning, but already felt that Norbert's house wanted them there. They ate dinner together. To John's amazement, Eddo and Kruamart were already exchanging Thai and English words. Susan sat at the table with the baby at her breast. Norbert perched at the head of the table overseeing the scene like some happy, beer-buzzed grandfather.

He and John had looked for opportunities to continue the story, but the mood was too good to bring down. Norbert had of course heard the general facts, but he wanted the details. It wasn't until much later that night that the opportunity presented itself.

-o-

They were in the jeep on the road into Chiang Mai. They hadn't been able to shift old Bruiser out of the front seat, so John sat in the back. At first, once Norbert had refused to let him drive, John considered the back seat safer. He'd counted more than 12 cans of Singha beer pass the Thai's lips. But in fact he seemed to drive better on beer.

"Okay, boy. We only got an hour. That has to be enough time. I been real patient."

"All right." John leaned forward between the seats and watched the road magically unwind in the jeep's headlights as he spoke.:

"I'd left Shirley alone at Susan's house. She had a feeling something was wrong there. At first her instinct told her she wasn't alone. But in fact, what she was feeling was Bohmu Din's presence. He'd been staying there all the time in Susan's room. He'd been there from the day he arrived in England.

"Shirley went up to Susan's room and I can't begin to imagine what she felt when she opened the door and looked in there. One whole wall had been turned into a kind of altar, a shrine to her."

"To Shirley?"

"Yeah. He'd saved everything of hers from the first day she arrived at his camp. He had her clothes, all the things he'd ever given her as presents, small things she'd made and hidden from him, even the utensils she used to cook. It was all there.

"He'd bought dolls, the largest ones they sell, and dressed them in her clothes and lined them up across the wall. Their faces had been melted off. There was a platform of Eastern gods and saints or whatever, turned to face the name 'Sherri' painted across the wall in big letters. It wasn't until the investigation that they found out it had been painted in blood."

"Man. Whose?"

"His own."

"Damn."

"And all of Susan's photos of her and me from her albums had been plastered across the shrine. In every picture our faces had been burnt out with a cigarette. In the tiniest letters, a thousand times on each photo, he'd written Sherri's name.

"And there were two corners—sacrificial corners—one for me, one for Susan. He'd made body outlines on the floor in the same blood, with our names. I suppose he planned to put us there after our deaths. Except the outlines were too small—like the outlines of children."

"This is one seriously disturbed mother." Bruiser yawned agreement.

"You're telling me. But Shirley realized that all of this . . . revenge . . . this blood lust, it stemmed from an obsession he had with *her*. We'd all assumed he was angry that Jim had helped her escape, but that there was something else that drove him nuts. In fact, there wasn't.

"In his sick, twisted way, he had really loved Sherri. He'd only been able to show his emotions through cruelty. It was all he knew. After she'd gone, he grieved because he hadn't been able to tell her. That grief ate away at his sanity. The man wasn't just suffering from a psychosis. There was real damage. He was dipping in and out of a clinical insanity."

The jeep pulled into a familiar car park at Chiang Mai Airport, and Norbert turned off the motor. He jumped out of his seat and joined John in the back.

"Shirley couldn't see a taxi, so she ended up running to Emma's. It was a couple of miles. When she got there, the car outside was the one reported on the police site. She knew Bohmu Din was inside. She found Susan beaten to a pulp and Bohmu Din about to cut her stomach."

"Jeez!"

"She said she was calm by then. She didn't care for her own safety. She just wanted to protect Susan and the baby. He didn't recognize Shirley as Sherri at first, and she was certain he intended to kill her. But at the last second, he realized who she was. It clicked some switch in him. He went from being chronic aggressive to chronic passive.

"He told her how Jim had returned to his camp that night to kill him. There had been no other motive than to make him suffer for what he'd done to Sherri. When Jim was alone with her, she'd quite openly told him everything as if it were normal. He was so outraged that he decided to go back and stop Bohmu Din from abusing other girls.

"Jim must have known his chances of getting out a second time were remote. But he could never have known how deeply Bohmu Din felt about Sherri, or that he wouldn't rest before wreaking revenge on us. Jim just wanted to rid Kawthoolei of one of its evils.

"Shirley had a weapon—a length of fishing wire. She looped it over Bohmu Din's head and prepared to rid herself of him. But Jim's ghost was with her. He told her he had already died administering her revenge. He had planted the seeds of insanity in Bohmu Din's troubled mind all those years ago, and they had grown, and taken root, and were gnarled and knotted. No other revenge was necessary. Bohmu Din, rocking, dribbling, crying there at her feet, was already destroyed.

"She did what she could for Susan and Eddo at the house. She told Bohmu Din they'd need to be taken to a hospital. He helped her carry them to the car, and nursed Eddo on his lap as they drove.

"When the police arrived at the hospital, she and the old man were sitting hand-in-hand on a bench. He was rocking gently to the sound of an old Karen nursery rhyme she hummed for him."

"Oh man. What happens to him now?"

"They're looking at the diplomatic immunity issue. He wasn't in the UK officially, so he could be tried as a regular citizen. But the Burmese will probably ask for him to be sent back. Either way it doesn't matter much. His mind's gone. He'll be put in some institute for the criminally insane, and be forgotten. The professional opinion is that he's no longer a danger to society."

"Wow. One hell of a story, John boy."

The flight from Bangkok boomed over their heads as it came in to land.

"And finished just in time I might say. There she comes. How's ya jingly-jangly?"

"Now, I've told you not to get excited about this, Norbert. Shirley went to the States for a while, but it wasn't where she wanted to be. She's on her way back to finish her work on the border. Get it. . . ? She's stopping off here for a week or two to get her mind back together. She's been through a lot. She's exhausted, like all of us. This trip has nothing to do with me at all. I have an unexploded jingly-jangly."

"Well, I'm mighty sorry to hear that, boy."

"That's real life, mate. No happy endings."

"She ain't the reason you're going bush, is she?"

"Africa? No. I think I'd already got my head sorted out about her before I made that decision. I don't really believe anywhere's far enough to run away from disappointment. No, this is something that started burning in me when I was there, in Kenya."

"You ain't gonna solve all their problems by yourself, you know?"

"I know it. It's all modest: a modest little organization, a modest salary, and modest objectives. But it's a pilot project. If we can make a difference with some of the beach kids in Mombassa, who knows how big it'll get?"

"Two years in Africa, man. I can see it. There's you and some leggy Masai princess trailing around a pack of black and white striped babies."

"There you go again. Why is it married people are always trying to fix up single blokes?"

"We want you to be as happy as us, boy."

They headed off towards the terminal arm in arm.

"But that reminds me." Norbert grinned. "I got a mighty pretty sister-in-law wants to meet a good-looking rich guy."

"Will I do?"

"Well, actually, she wanted an American. But I'll ask if she's willing to lower her expectations some."

"Thanks."

The End

CPSIA information can be obtained at www.ICGtesting.com
Printed in the USA
LVOW10s0002310516

490496LV00027B/710/P